Emily's Choice

HEATHER McCOUBREY

EMILY'S CHOICE

Heather McCoubrey
http://heathermccoubrey.com

Edited by Chrissy Wolfe, EFC Services, LLC

Cover Photo by Merbe

Cover Art by Carol Wise, WiseElement

Author Photo by David Buser

Acknowledgements

It's summer 1993. My family and I were living in Colorado and I was going into my senior year of high school as a 16-year-old and I knew I wanted to go to college back in my home state of Maine. My grandmother made me an offer I couldn't refuse–live with her for my last year of high school to regain residency for college tuition rates. I moved back to Maine, to a small town where my father grew up and where I was born and lived for a short time as a baby.

Other than family, I didn't know anyone and there really wasn't anywhere to meet people except school. At issue, for the most part, was my age. I was a young senior because I'd skipped a grade. I fit in with the age group of the junior class, but it was hard to really get to know them because my schedule was different than theirs. Even though I made some friends, I was still lonely, so I turned to my writing to get through the long winter and loneliness.

I started out with poems and had quite a few finished. Then one day, I was reading an article about Pocahontas and learned that her Native American name was Matoaka. I thought it was such a pretty and unusual name and I wanted to use it somewhere, somehow.

That's when I had the idea to write my first novel, with a young woman named Matoaka as the star. My grandmother used to have old issues of National Geographic magazines laying around and I loved to read them and look at all the pictures. Inside one of those magazines, I found a map of the Old West. My eyes were drawn to a barren section of New Mexico, to a specific town called Mosquero. Right away I knew that would be the perfect setting for Matoaka's home.

One afternoon, not long after that day, I sat down at the table in my grandmother's kitchen. I had a pencil and a notebook in front of me and a story brewing in my imagination. The story that began as Matoaka ends here as *Emily's Choice*.

That was the winter of 1993. Now, twenty-three years and two published novels later, I am finally ready to share the story of Emily Camancho and Jason Vaughn with you.

It's been a long journey, and without the help, support, and encouragement of many people along the way, *Emily's Choice* would never have made it to your hands and heart.

First and foremost, I must thank my husband and children. They are the light of my life and I wouldn't be here doing what I love without their love and support. We added a new little blessing to our family last year and it has been a wild and fun ride. I can't wait to see where we go from here!

More often than not, my friends and family are the ones who listen to me go on and on and on about plot points, plot twists, character development, character names, sales and marketing, book covers, and they answer my panicked calls when I'm sure I've gotten myself way over my head and need someone to help me find my way out. The fact that they listen, offer feedback, and are still speaking to me goes to show just how much they love me.

This year I did something a little different when it came to my beta readers. Instead of reaching out to writers, I put a note out on Facebook asking my friends and acquaintances if they would be interesting in beta reading. The response was overwhelming! I had an almost entirely different team and I loved it. Here were readers, the very people I needed!

Vicki, Carolyn, Heather, Niki, Kacy, Kathy, Darlene, Sam, Beth, Michelle, and Heidi . . . You all helped make *Emily's Choice* the best it could be. You helped make the story interesting, you helped me find dropped plot points, you helped me tie up loose ends and you fell in love with the characters. I can't ask for more than that. Thank you!

Stacey Wiedower helped me flesh out Emily's career choice with tips and pointers on Interior Design. Anything that doesn't ring true is on me; I took quite a bit artistic and writer license. Stacey is also an author (and the only one I used for this book!), and she's an amazing writer. I hope you'll take some time to read her books!

Carol Wise, my mother-in-law and graphic artist extraordinaire. She has been the paintbrush behind my artistic eye, giving my covers the professional look they deserve. Every one of my covers are amazing because of her hard work and attention to detail.

Chrissy Wolfe, my editor from EFC Services, LLC. I first sent this project to her right after I finished *Back to December*. I asked for a critique to see whether this book was salvageable or if I should just throw it away. After much back-and-forth and several lunch dates, we determined that *Emily's Choice* was, in fact, salvageable. Without her ideas, handholding, encouragement, and kick in the pants, I probably never would have rewritten this book.

When you have a project that spans twenty-three years, you have to know that a lot of people helped along the way. I remember back in the day, before Google searches were the thing, I spent many hours on the phone trying to get an idea of what Mosquero was like and a picture in my head of what Mosquero and New Mexico looked like.

Paul Maurer, a resident of Mosquero, was someone I called out of the blue. I looked him up in the phone book (what?!?!) and he spent about an hour on the phone with me, a complete stranger—an aspiring author—answering all kinds of questions from the weather, to what businesses were in town, to what the area looked like and what the culture was like.

Renee at City Hall provided me with a map of the town and she hand-wrote the locations of all the businesses, schools and courthouse on the map. She also answered so many of my questions regarding what it means to be the county seat to the type of cattle that is popular in the area.

My long-time friend, Sam Brady. Sam has read almost as many versions of *Emily's Choice* as I've written. He's given me plenty of advice and ideas over the years; I still have emails and notes from him from back in 1998 when I was working on Draft #6! He's also the reason Jenny is STILL sick as a dog, poor girl.

Last, but not least, Michelle Perkins Holmes. She was the first friend I made at Calais High School and she not only befriended the new girl but spent hours brainstorming plots and adventures for Matoaka with me. Those hours were so much fun and it's a time I look back on with fondness.

This final version is nothing like the original story we worked on, but I think it's a better and stronger story. I hope each of you can spare a spot in your heart for Emily & Jason.

I'm sure there are more people I've forgotten to thank. Know that I am grateful for each of you and I appreciate and love you all so much!

xoxo

~Heather

Dedication

For David.

The love of my life.

The one I would choose again and again.

Emily's Choice

Chapter One

May 2008

Emily Camancho was scared, no doubt about it. She took several deep breaths to calm her racing heart as she wiped her slick palms on her dusty jeans. Sitting in the driver's seat of her beat-up rusty red pickup truck, she rolled down the window to let a breeze blow through.

She was late. *Three weeks late* to be exact.

Yesterday, she'd finally worked up the courage to take one of those pesky tests she'd bought last week at the pharmacy. It had been hiding under the bathroom sink since she'd brought it home. Once Jason had left for class, she reached her shaking hands into the cabinet and tore open the box. She sat down on the toilet with the test stick and placed it in the stream for five seconds and then replaced the cap on the end of it. She carefully set it down on the floor and went out to wash her hands.

When she checked the stick after washing her hands, well, there had been no mistaking the results. Two dark blue lines. Positive. She'd let out a shuddering breath and collapsed against the door. What the hell was she going to do?

Catching a glimpse of herself in the truck mirror, she grimaced. Searching through her purse, she blew out a sigh when all she could find was a ponytail holder. Shrugging, she dropped her purse back on the bench seat and pulled her long, auburn hair up into a messy ponytail. It would have to do, and she was out of time anyway. Jumping from the truck, she grabbed her purse and walked slowly into the Urgent Care facility. She'd come all the way across town to lessen the chances she would bump into anyone she knew from school. For a split second, she had thought about going home to see old Doc Martin but quickly nixed that idea. It would have spread like wildfire through the town, her parents finding out the results before she did. There was no such thing as doctor-patient confidentiality in Mosquero. Hell, there wasn't any confidentiality at all.

She'd told Jason that she wasn't feeling well and was planning a visit to the doctor to see what was wrong. He'd offered to go with her, but she turned her baby blues on him and told him she would be all right. It didn't make sense for them both to miss classes today.

Emily walked into the facility and wrote her name down on the sign-in sheet. She picked up a gossip magazine to browse through while she waited but let it sit on her lap while her mind skidded all over the place. Was she really pregnant? They'd been careful every time. They both were fanatical about condom use, but she supposed one could have broken. How would she tell Jason? How would she tell her parents? What would everyone say?

They were in their last year of college, she at Santa Fe Community College for Interior Design and Jason at New Mexico State University for Animal Science and Rangeland Resources. Jason was planning to return home to Mosquero after graduation to help his father with the ranch. Emily had planned to stay in Santa Fe to work with the design company she'd been interning with while at school. It was going to be a hard adjustment for them, seeing as they'd never spent any real amount of time apart, ever. But if she was indeed pregnant, how would she balance a baby, a new city, a long-distance relationship, and a new job? Santa Fe was only two and a half hours from home but that was a long way to commute every day if she had to live at home.

Everyone would be shocked and appalled at first; she knew and accepted that. She hoped that part was quick though. She wouldn't have an abortion, and she wasn't giving the child up for adoption. Emily knew enough about herself to know that once the baby was born, she wouldn't want to let it go. Everything would be okay, and everything would work out the way it was supposed to. Emily was sure of that. She had an amazing family; they were incredibly supportive and she knew they'd help her reach her dreams regardless. Once the baby did arrive, they'd all be happier than a rooster at dawn.

By the time the nurse called her back, she'd almost gotten herself talked into a positive outlook. She calmly followed the nurse back and answered all the embarrassing questions. The nurse took a blood sample and told Emily it would be about twenty minutes for the results. Instead of waiting in the cold, sterile room, Emily opted to go outside instead. She walked around to the back of the building and was pleased to see a picnic table, a garden, and a nature path. She walked along the path, keeping an eye on the time as the nurse had cautioned her to be back on time as they had a lot of patients to see. Emily let her mind wander as she enjoyed the sights and smells of nature.

She had no idea what she'd do with a baby. Her life plan didn't include children, at least not for another several years. She and Jason had been an item for as long as Emily could remember, and their parents had always joked they'd been betrothed at birth. She and Jason had begun as playmates and friends, moved on to being a couple, and now they were lovers and practically engaged. She imagined their parents would want them to wait until after they'd settled into their jobs, but she and Jason had already talked of going to Las Vegas at Christmas to get married. She could picture all the lights, the people, and the excitement. The sounds of the slot machines, the range of emotions from the players at the tables. And their wedding ceremony. She'd always dreamed of a big, elaborate wedding, but the closer they got to Vegas, the more excited she was about just eloping and leaving the stress, cost, and craziness behind. Emily was confident she and Jason could take this next step together and come out with a stronger relationship, even if it was several years earlier than they had planned, at least in the baby department.

Checking her watch, she turned around and hurried back to the examination room. When she stepped into the room, she noticed the nurse had laid out a gown, so Emily stripped down and put it on. The doctor knocked on the door just as Emily was climbing onto the table.

"Come in," Emily said shyly.

"Hello, Emily. I'm Dr. Williams," she said kindly as she shook Emily's hand.

"Hello."

"All right, I'm sure you're on the edge of that table wondering what the results are." Dr. Williams paused as Emily nodded her head and twisted her fingers. "The test was positive. You are pregnant, Emily."

The breath she didn't realize she'd been holding came rushing out along with a strangled, "I am?"

Dr. Williams nodded, pressing the button to recline the table flat and motioning for Emily to lie down. "I'm going to order an ultrasound for you so we can pinpoint exactly how far along you are. Let me just check your tummy, and then we can talk prenatal care."

Twenty minutes later, Emily walked out to her truck in a daze. She couldn't remember one thing the doctor had told her, and if there'd been a test, she would have failed. The drive back to the apartment was a blur, and Emily was shocked when she pulled into the parking lot with no memory of the drive home. Running a hand over her face, she took a deep breath and let it out slowly. She climbed out of the truck and shuffled to the apartment. Exhausted from stress and the pregnancy, Emily collapsed onto the bed and fell asleep instantly.

"Emily? Babe?"

She reached out her hand and pulled Jason down onto the bed with her. She peeked a quick glimpse of him, sighing with pleasure. She was so lucky. At six feet tall, Jason was head and shoulders above most of the guys in school. His dark blond hair was ruffled, and she could picture him running his hands through it in frustration during classes this morning. His eyes were a deep chocolate brown that twinkled when he laughed and only looked at her with love. Working on the ranch his whole life had given him a lean and toned body. Many underestimated his strength, especially on the football field.

"How are you feeling? What did the doctor say?"

Emily's eyes snapped open and she bolted upright as the morning's stress and results came rushing back to her. She inhaled sharply, ready to tell him, but she couldn't find the words.

When he sat up with her, she turned and buried her face in his chest, taking several deep breaths to calm down. She couldn't fathom why she was panicking. Jason loved her and she loved him.

She tried her best to smile but failed miserably when tears gathered in her eyes.

He wrapped his arms around her. "What's wrong, babe? Are you okay?"

Shaking her head no, she hid her face against his shirt as the tears fell down her cheeks, hugging him hard.

"Can you tell me what's wrong?"

Sighing, Emily buried her face in his neck and nodded. "I will, I promise. I need you to hold me a little longer."

"Babe, you know I'll hold you forever, but you're scaring me. You never cry, what's going on?" He slipped a finger under her chin and raised her face so he could look into her eyes. He wiped her tears with his thumb and offered her a comforting smile.

"I don't know how to start. I thought it would be easy, but now that you're here, I'm scared." She turned her face into his neck and took a deep breath. He always smelled so good, like the outdoors mixed with sunshine.

"It can't be that bad, babe," he soothed. "Spit it out, we'll figure it out."

"I'm pregnant," Emily blurted quietly.

She felt Jason stiffen and thought for a moment he was going to push her away and flee. Instead, he tightened his hold on her. "Are you sure?" he asked quietly.

Emily nodded. "They took a blood test, and I have to call tomorrow for the results of the ultrasound. She thinks I'm about six to eight weeks along."

Tears began to flow in earnest down her face. Frustrated with them, she swiped her hand across her face. "What are we going to do, Jason?"

Smiling, he hugged her close. "Sounds like we're going to have a baby!"

Shocked at his easy acceptance, she pulled out of his arms and searched his face. She saw a broad smile gracing his lips, a sparkle in his eyes. Breathing a sigh of relief, she wrapped her arms around him and squeezed.

"You're surprised at my reaction."

"Honestly, I really wasn't sure what to expect."

"It's scary, a little exciting. But it's happened, and we can't undo it. We're almost done with school. Instead of getting married at Christmas, we'll just get married this summer after we graduate. We can still elope if you want."

"What are we going to tell our parents?"

Jason shrugged.

"We've got to tell them something!"

"Babe, we don't have to tell them anything right away. Let's get used to the idea first."

"What do you mean?"

Sighing, Jason leaned back against the pillows, taking Emily with him. Sprawled against his chest, Emily felt her heart rate pick up. Jason rolled with her and gently pushed her back against the bed. Lowering his head, he brushed a kiss against her lips. "I mean . . ." he drawled. "Let's enjoy the news, and the secret, and we'll tell them when it's right."

She put a hand against his shoulder to stop his descent. She needed a clear head, and once he started kissing her, she'd fog up and forget everything. "Jason," she pleaded.

Sighing, he lifted his head. He ran a hand up her torso and brushed a thumb over her nipple. When it hardened under his knowing hands, he grinned. "Babe, it's not a big deal. Our parents are going to freak out and wonder what we were thinking, but it's our life, Em. Don't stress. We've got each other and that's all we need," he said against her lips.

Emily moaned when his tongue slipped through her lips. The hand that was holding him off slid up his neck and tangled in his hair.

Jason was right; all they needed was each other. They could get through anything so long as they had each other.

Chapter Two

September 2008

It was almost one. The early morning was dark as pitch, the moon hidden behind the clouds. Emily paced a circuitous route in her bedroom—along her bed, passing the door and desk, ending at the window. She glanced outside during each pass. Her fiancé, Jason Vaughn, was due back from his bachelor party any minute. She could just barely make out the driveway of his house from her window. In a little over fourteen hours, she'd be walking down the aisle in her backyard to marry him. Placing a hand on her extended abdomen as she glanced outside again, she smiled. She couldn't wait.

She saw headlights and squealed quietly to herself. Grabbing her phone and her light jacket, she silently made her way down the stairs and out the back door. She crossed through the line of trees separating the Camancho and

Vaughn properties, the well-worn path a testament to the many trips made between the houses.

She was young, in love, and far from the superstitious type. Her stepmother, Grace, or Mama G, as she affectionately called her, had told her earlier in the day to stay away from Jason until she was standing next to him this afternoon. Emily had snorted and rolled her eyes. What difference could it make? They'd known each other their whole lives, had lived together for four years at college in Santa Fe, and had made a baby together. Bad luck? Please.

Emily waited in the shadows of the trees, shivering in the cool fall air, until Jason's buddies had him safely in the house and were on their way home. She watched as her brother, Tyler, waved the guys off and turned toward the trees and the house. He was staying at the ranch for the weekend for the bachelor party and her wedding. The house he shared with his wife, Sophie, was on the other side of the ranch—a good 45-minute drive since there wasn't a road through the land. Sophie had opted to stay at their house with their three boys until the wedding. No doubt Tyler was enjoying the short break away from his family. The boys were rambunctious and crazy full of energy. But they were also the sweetest, too. Sophie didn't leave the house often. With three boys under five, Emily thought she probably wouldn't go many places either.

"Tyler? How'd it go?" she asked when he was about three feet from her hiding spot in the trees.

Tyler brought his hand to his heart and swore loudly. "What the hell, Em? You just scared twenty years off my life!"

Emily giggled and hugged her brother. "I'm sorry. I thought you saw me!"

"How could I see you? It's pitch dark out here and you're mostly in black, hiding in the trees," he said against her hair, hugging her back.

"Did you guys have fun?" She felt Tyler nod and stepped back out of his embrace. "So, how drunk is he? Did you show him any mercy?"

"I tried, but the guys weren't so nice. He's hammered," he said, thumbing toward Jason's house. "I doubt he can make a coherent sentence. But he's up in his room. Jake and I deposited him there ourselves. Good luck!"

"I don't need to talk to him; I just need to snuggle with him. I miss sleeping with him every night. BUT," Emily said, pointing a finger at Tyler's chest, "he better not be a wreck for our wedding today or I will personally take it out on you later!"

Tyler held up his hands. "No way, it's not my fault. I tried to be the voice of reason, but no one wanted to listen. Anyway, I'm beat and I had my fair share of booze. I'm heading to bed. See you later." He turned and walked through the trees to their house.

Emily watched him walk up the steps to the kitchen and disappear into the house. Once he was gone, she skipped to the back door of Jason's house and quietly slipped inside.

The house was dark, but she knew where she was going. She'd spent as much time in this house as her own. Jason's father, Joe, never changed anything. It was the same as before his wife, Kelly, had died. The same carpet, the same paint, the same decorations, the same furniture, the same school pictures hanging on the wall.

The same couldn't be said about her own home. Grace had changed some things when she'd married Emily's father, but for the most part, Emily had always been the one to change things. It had started with her own room. Growing up, her bed, dresser, and desk were never in the same spot. Sharing a room with her new stepsister had made the constant moving around a little harder. With an extra bed and dresser, there had only been so many configurations she could imagine. Thankfully, Hope hadn't cared much about the ever-changing bedroom and sometimes had offered up her own ideas, which Emily was only too glad to incorporate.

She would have liked to redecorate as well, but her father and Mama G had drawn the line there. It cost nothing to rearrange furniture, but the same couldn't be said about redecorating. Emily had talked about repurposing old furniture and sheets and stuff. Sometimes she could talk her way into acquiring something new, but more often than not, she was limited to just rearranging the furniture.

It was no wonder she'd studied interior design at college, interned at a design firm in Santa Fe the entire time she was at college, and had plans to open her own firm once the wedding was over.

As she silently crept up the stairs to Jason's room, she made sure to jump lightly over the seventh stair from the bottom. No reason to alert Joe of her late-night visit. Her plan was to slip into bed with Jason and sneak home before anyone got up in the morning. She covered her yawning mouth, ready to snuggle with Jason and find sweet oblivion in sleep. After four years of sleeping together every night, this forced separation was wreaking havoc on her rest. Well, that and the pregnancy-related exhaustion.

Finally, she stood outside his door, and as she turned the handle, she thought she heard voices. She let go of the doorknob and looked behind her, scared his father had caught her. The hall was clear. Shrugging her shoulders, she opened the door and walked inside.

Tears immediately filled her eyes, and a barely stifled gasp nearly gave her presence away. Her hands slowly rose to her mouth, pressing firmly against her lips to keep the scream of horror locked inside.

Jason stood next to his bed, his arms wrapped around her cousin's naked body. Lila's hands were busy unbuttoning his shirt and Jason's lips were dancing across her face and down her neck. His hands were busy reshaping Lila's breasts, and judging by her moans, she liked the new shape.

Emily's eyes closed against the picture in front of her, bile rising fast. She cast one last glance at the love of her life and caught Lila's pale blue eyes shining with satisfaction, a smirk on her face. Emily spun on her heel and raced down the stairs not bothering to avoid the squeaky step. She ran out of the house and across the yard in tears.

Out of breath and devastated, Emily crashed into the kitchen, collapsing against the door. She covered her face with her hands, sobbing as her knees gave out and she slid to the floor.

They were supposed to get married this afternoon. How long had this been going on? Had he ever loved her? What about their baby?

Her mind spun out of control with all these thoughts. There was no way she could go through with the wedding. No way could she spend the rest of her life with him. She'd never be able to look at him again.

Anger, disgust, and a deep hurt settled in her heart. She couldn't bear to face the reaction this news would bring in the morning. The pity and righteous anger would surely be present when her family heard. It would make the whole thing more real than she could handle.

She had to get out of town before everyone woke up. Rising shakily to her feet, she stumbled up the stairs to the room she shared with Hope. Finding the room empty, she briefly wondered where Hope was as she pulled out her suitcases. Shrugging aside the thought, and more than a lot grateful for the solitude, she threw enough clothes into one suitcase to get by for a couple of weeks. She could always have the rest of her things shipped to her when she got to where she was going.

She snuck down to the bathroom and gathered up her makeup, toothbrush, and shower gear, throwing them into her toiletry bag.

"What are you doing, Em?"

Emily gasped and spun around. Hope, her stepsister by marriage but her sister by heart. They were as close as real sisters; they shared everything and were hardly ever seen without the other. It had been an awful adjustment when they'd graduated high school and gone off to college. Emily had gone with Jason to Santa Fe, and Hope had returned to her roots and traveled back East to Boston to attend Harvard University, which was her father's alma mater. She was getting a business degree while also beginning her modeling and photography career. Like Tyler, she was home for the wedding, though unlike Tyler, she had a condo in Boston rather than a house on the other side of the ranch.

Groaning at the intrusion and heart racing, she ignored her stepsister and ran back to their room.

Hope followed closely on her heels, slipping into the room before Emily could shut the door on her. She gasped at the scene in front of her. "Oh my God, Emily! Are you and Jason eloping?"

Emily burst into a fresh round of tears. Clutching the toiletry bag to her chest, she sank down onto her bed and buried her face into the bag.

"Emily?" Hope said uncertainly, placing a hand on Emily's shoulder. "What's wrong?"

"Lila. He's kissing Lila!" Emily choked out.

"Who?" Hope asked in confusion.

"Jason!" she wailed.

"What are you talking about? How could you possibly know?"

"I . . . I . . . I saw him."

"When?"

"A few minutes ago." Emily stood up and threw the toiletry bag in the closest suitcase. "Oh God, I have to get out of here!"

"She was kissing him? That bitch! When I get my hands on her. Mom's going to . . ."

"Shh!" Emily cautioned, worried Hope was going to wake the house with her yelling.

"What about the wedding?"

"Wedding?" Emily growled in disgust. "There isn't going to be a wedding," she spat out. "I'm leaving. I can't be here in the morning. Not when everyone finds out. I can't bear it."

"But where will you go?"

"I don't know, and I don't care so long as it's far away from this place."

Hope put a staying hand on Emily's arm. "Why don't you come to Boston with me? I have a huge condo, and you're welcome to stay with me as long as you want. I'm hardly ever there, and when I am, I'm so freaking lonely. It'll be nice to have a familiar face around."

"I don't know. Isn't it expensive? I won't have a job right away."

"It's okay. My trust pays for the condo."

"But that money is for you from your father," she stated flatly, keenly aware that it was the only thing Hope had left of her father, who had died of a heart attack when Hope was four.

"Whether you're living there or not, the trust is still going to pay for the condo. It's just money. I have my memories of him in here," she said, pointing to her heart. "The past four years have been amazing, getting to know his side of the family again, hearing stories, seeing pictures, and just being surrounded by them. That more than anything has brought him back to life for me." She shook her head and waved her hands in front of Emily's face. "We're getting off-topic though. This is a no-brainer, and I'm making the decision for you. You will come live with me."

"I don't know, Hope, it just seems wrong. And what about the baby?" Emily asked, wrapping her arms around her belly. "I'll have to find my own place before the baby comes."

"Why? It's a three-bedroom, Em. There's plenty of space."

"I don't want to take advantage of you."

"You aren't." Hope reached out and squeezed Emily's hand. "I'm offering. You're my sister and you need this. Please come."

"I don't know, Hope," Emily hedged.

"How about this? Come stay until you figure things out. It's far away from here, and the distance will help you sort through everything. I don't care if you stay forever, but if it makes you feel better to think of it as a temporary thing, then be my guest."

Emily scrunched up her face while she thought it over. It sounded great, exactly what she needed. She just worried about overstaying her welcome. Hope had a whole new life, and she hadn't planned on a roommate, or a baby, for that matter. But she did need someplace to go, at least temporarily. And Hope was offering that to her. She nodded slowly, coming to her decision. She'd go and she'd be grateful; she wouldn't overstay her welcome and she'd do whatever she could to be a good roommate, for however long she stayed. "Okay, yes."

Hope's face lit up. "I'll go pack."

Fifteen minutes later, the sisters were driving down the road in Hope's rental car, heading to the airport in Santa Fe. Emily had taped a note to her bedroom door telling her parents not to worry and that she'd call later that morning with an explanation. And knowing her best friend slept like the dead, she didn't hesitate to send Gina a quick text telling her the wedding was off and she'd talk to her later in the day.

Emily leaned her head against the passenger window, hands resting lightly on her belly, her pregnancy weighing heavily on her mind. She'd be alone now. A single mother. The weight of responsibility would rest solely on her shoulders. Would she be able to handle it?

*****

The earliest flight from Santa Fe to Boston wasn't until 7:52 a.m. As Emily paced the gate area waiting for their seats to be called, she second-, third-, and fourth-guessed herself. Was she doing the right thing? Was running the answer? What if it had been a mistake?

Then for the second, third, and fourth time, she reminded herself that she hadn't mistaken what she'd seen. The memory wouldn't leave her in peace, and she knew without a doubt that she needed space and time to decide what to do about it.

When their seats were called, Emily gathered up her purse and ticket and breathed a short sigh of relief. She knew she'd feel a little better once she was on the plane.

Landing in Denver, Emily settled on one of the chairs by the windows. Fingers shaking, she dialed her parents.

"Are you okay?"

Emily did her best to keep the tears at bay, but hearing the concern in her stepmother's voice was almost more than she could bear. She considered herself extremely lucky to have Grace. Emily's mother, Sara, had died when she was two. She didn't know all the details just that it had been complications from scarlet fever. She couldn't remember much about her mother but knew Sara had been well loved and respected in the community, and people were always eager to share their stories and memories. Mama G never discouraged it either. She herself had been happy to help ferret out information. When she'd married Clint, it had been something she'd been adamant about. She wouldn't let Emily forget her mother, and Mama G never sought to replace Sara. Instead, she had tried to be a friend, a mentor, a guiding influence to mold Emily into an adult her mother would have been proud of.

Her father was a man, down to the marrow of his bones. What he knew of hairstyles, fashion, and girl stuff wouldn't fill a thimble. When Emily had needed her hair done, school clothes shopped for, the first time she'd gotten into a war with Gina, the first day of her period, the first time Jason had kissed her, when she left for college, having Mama G in her life had been a godsend. And hopefully, despite the distance Emily was putting between them, she would be there for the birth of her baby, too.

Grace may not be her biological mother, but she was her mother as far as Emily was concerned. And Emily sorely needed her mother right now.

"Not really, no," Emily said through her tears. She turned her back to the gate and stared unseeing out the window. She told Mama G the sordid details.

"You're going to Hope's then?"

Emily heard her father in the background and listened as Grace explained the situation to him. It was rare for her father to swear, and Emily was a little taken aback at what she heard through the phone line.

"Are you sure of what you saw?" her father growled.

"Yes, Daddy, I'm sure." Emily said, clearing her throat. She could imagine him stomping down to his den to pick up the phone in there and Mama G rolling her eyes at his intrusion on their phone conversation.

"He's gonna wish he'd never been born," Clint threatened.

"Daddy!" Emily yelled. "Don't hurt him."

"You'll do no such thing," Grace said shrilly. "Get off the line before you upset her more."

Emily heard her father mutter, "He'll be lucky to be alive when I'm done with him," before the line clicked, indicating her father had hung up his phone. Her heart stopped for a second, before she realized she was angry and what did she care what punishment her father meted out to Jason on her behalf.

"Oh, darling girl, I'm so sorry this happened to you," Mama G soothed after Clint had hung up the phone.

Emily nodded and leaned her forehead on the cool glass. "Me, too. We had our whole lives ahead of us, Mama G. What am I going to do now?"

"You're gonna go to Boston, get your emotions straightened out, your head on right, and make a plan. You call me whenever you need me. We're all here for you, darling."

"I love you, Mama G. So much. I'm so sorry I didn't listen to you," Emily said sadly.

"What do you mean?"

"When you said it was bad luck for Jason and me to see each other before the wedding. That wasn't just an old wives' tale." Emily paused to wipe her nose. "I'd better get going. I need to use the restroom, and we'll be boarding again soon. I'll call or text when we land in Boston."

"All right, darling girl. Be safe. We love you both."

"I will. Love you."

Chapter Three

The plane ride seemed to take forever, which gave Emily plenty of time to think. Not that she wanted to, though. Her thoughts weren't of the happy variety. No happy childhood memories, no hopes for her new life in Boston, no exciting dreams for the tiny miracle in her womb. Memories of Lila's initial arrival in Mosquero and all her dirty tricks raced through her mind like an old-time newsreel. She needed a distraction, anything, from the memories swirling in her mind. Unfortunately, Hope being a frequent flyer meant she had no trouble sleeping on the plane. As soon as they'd boarded in Denver, she'd passed out. Emily wished she could be so lucky, but sleep wouldn't come to her, even though she was desperately exhausted.

No, it seemed she was destined to relive one of the most awful moments in her life. The first time her trust in Jason had been tested.

Lila had come to live with them the summer before Emily and Hope entered eleventh grade. Lila's life had been turned upside down by a stalker. He was her ex-boyfriend and apparently hadn't taken the breakup well. His name was Edward, and he was from a family as well-off as Lila's own. He called her, texted her, stopped by, and followed her around school. It got to the point where Lila was afraid to leave her house. The police's hands were tied though because he never made any threats to Lila and had never harmed her. Lila begged her family to leave town for a while, to let Edward forget about her and so Lila could feel safe again. Her mother had been all for the idea, having wanting to spend some time at their home in France and getting tired of life in Boston. Winter was coming and she did not want to spend another cold, snowy, bleak winter there. She wanted sun, warmth, and the Mediterranean.

Lila's father, on the other hand, had many business dealings in the works and couldn't get away. Besides, he'd said, Edward knows about the house in France, surely he'd be able to find you there. So a plan had been hatched for Lila to go spend some time with her aunt in Mosquero. The original plan had been for Lila to stay for six months and then go with her parents to France. The second part of the plan never happened. Instead, Lila had conned, manipulated, and cajoled her way into being able to stay for the entire school year.

Emily sighed, leaned her head back against the seat, closed her eyes, and let her mind take over. You couldn't stop a freight train and she was done trying.

Initially, Emily had been excited for Lila's arrival. She was curious about Mama G's family and wanted to meet Hope's cousin. She thought they'd be similar people, their fathers being brothers and all, but she couldn't have been more wrong. Where Hope was kind, loyal, and helpful, Lila was cold, rude, and lazy. Lila had hidden it well when she was in front of Mama G or Clint. To them she was everything she needed them to think she was. But as soon as their backs were turned, Lila's inner bitch appeared.

She made life difficult and reveled in it. The first few weeks weren't bad, and Emily chalked up Lila's odd behavior as nerves and apprehension and the change and growing pains of living with people you didn't know well (or at all). Misunderstandings and miscommunications seemed to be the norm for those first few weeks. Emily thought they'd never get their differences figured out. Not having to ever share a room before, Clint had surrendered his office temporarily so Lila could have her own space. Hope and Emily had shared a room since Mama G and Clint had gotten married. Their room was barely big enough to fit them both and putting Lila in there would have made the room burst at the seams. Tyler was due to leave for college at the end of the summer, and once he was gone, Lila would be given his room. Tyler was spending the summer packing up his room and spending as much time with friends and family as he could before he left. He was going to college in Albuquerque, so he was staying in the dorms and would only be back for breaks and holidays.

When school started, Emily and Hope showed Lila around school and introduced her to their friends. They tried to include her in much of what they did, but Lila made it difficult. She complained, shied away, and grew testy when they would stop to chat with their friends. Eventually, they left Lila out most of the time and went about their normal lives, tired of her nagging and general crappy attitude with whatever they were doing. By Halloween, Lila had made her own friends and seemed, if not happy, content. Emily hoped this meant they would start getting along, but she was wrong.

Emily and Jason had been a steady couple since the beginning of their sophomore year but had been "together" since seventh grade. Everyone knew they were an item. Everyone. And since she'd been living with them for some time, Emily just assumed Lila knew, too. So it came as a major surprise to her when Lila began spending time with Jason and flirting with him every chance she got. When Jason would come pick Emily up for a date, Lila would greet him at the door and chat and flirt with him the entire time Emily was getting ready to leave. After a month of this, Emily made sure she was ready and met Jason out on the porch.

Lila was in the same grade and had a couple of classes with Jason. After their class, she would loop her arm through his and have him walk her to her next class. Sometimes, she'd even get him to hold her books for her. She'd smile up at him and coo at whatever he was saying. Rumors started to swirl through the school that Jason was hot for the "new" girl and that his and Emily's relationship had burnt itself out. When those rumors first found Emily's ears, her face had turned pink and tears had sprung to her eyes. She'd been in the toilet stall and some girls were talking at the sinks. Emily kept herself hidden in the stall until the girls left, and then she'd slowly come out and skipped the rest of her classes that day. She'd gone home, cried betrayed tears, and then promptly gone to Jason's house and waited for him.

He'd gently taken her face in his hands, kissed her mouth ever so sweetly, and assured her that his heart only beat for Emily. He was being nice to Lila because she was her cousin, but he felt nothing for her and certainly didn't want to date her. He knew her type and he wasn't interested. End of story.

Happy and relieved, she had returned home and tried to put it to rest. Rumors continued to swirl through the school, though, and it became harder and harder for Emily to blow them off. Jason had stopped walking Lila to class and tried to avoid her at all costs. But she was tricky and found ways to insinuate herself. She would "miss" the bus and ask him for a ride home. He was too much of a gentleman to refuse. She would "forget" what their homework assignment was and need to run over to his house to get it. Stupid little excuses that began to add up to a lot of time spent in his company and more fuel for the school gossipmongers.

Two weeks before the Valentine's Ball, Hope and Emily went to Santa Fe with Clint. He had supplies to pick up, and they were in need of dresses for the ball.

They had spent a lovely afternoon in Santa Fe, enjoyed the one-on-one time with each other and then with Clint. He'd even treated them to a nice dinner, and they had felt a sweet bubble of love and happiness. That bubble popped when they got back home.

Mama G was waiting for them when they got home. She was wearing her scowl, her movements were jerky, and she had no interest in seeing their dresses. Clint, sensing trouble, hightailed it out the door and straight to the barn.

Emily and Hope tried to escape to their room with their dresses, but Mama G told them not to leave. Lila, hidden in the shadows of the living room, betrayed her excitement with the smirk she wore on her face.

"I am disappointed in both of you," Mama G began.

Emily and Hope both let their jaws drop. Disappointed? What had they done?

"Why, Mom?" Hope asked tentatively.

Lila made a small movement in the corner and Grace sent her away. She waited until Lila had disappeared up the stairs before she answered Hope.

"Lila and I had a long talk today. She has confided in me how alone and left out she's been feeling. You haven't made her feel welcome. And to top it all off, you conspired with Clint to leave her here today and went dress shopping without her!"

"That's not true!" Emily said indignantly. "We offered, but she said she had many dresses at home that she could have her mother send. She said she wouldn't be caught dead in something she could get here!"

"It's true, Mom," Hope confirmed. "We asked her again before we left, but she was adamant."

Mama G nodded. "Well, maybe it was a misunderstanding. But that still doesn't excuse the way you've let her down. She's family and she should come first!"

"What do you mean?" Emily asked.

"She's alone at school. She has no friends. No one to sit with at lunch. You don't talk to her on the bus. You don't involve her in your extra-curricular stuff. She's miserable."

Emily couldn't help it, she growled in frustration. Who was Lila trying to kid? What was she hoping to gain? Surely she knew getting them in trouble wasn't going to make the situation any better?

"Mama G, we tried," Emily said, anger barely concealed. "She sneered at our attempts. We showed her around town, around school, we introduced her to all our friends. We've invited her to parties, to our after-school stuff, to sit with us at lunch. We've tried. She doesn't like us. Everything is "backwoods," as she calls it. Nothing is good enough." Emily ran her hands through her hair in frustration and shot a look at Hope, who nodded in agreement.

"We did, Mom. She makes fun of what we do and where we go. I don't know what else we can do." Hope sat down on the couch and stared at her mother.

"Mama G?" Emily asked, glancing at her stepmother.

Grace was standing in front of them, a thoughtful look on her face. She stared off into space for a moment and then shook her head. She motioned Emily to sit down next to Hope on the couch.

"Listen, girls," she began, kneeling in front of them and taking their hands in her own. "You two have been sisters and best friends since Clint and I got married. You've been glued to each other's sides, inseparable. And that has made me so happy. I'm glad you are close to each other, and I hope you stay that way forever. I know it can be hard to loosen the bond a bit to let someone else in, but I need you to do that. No," she said, shaking her head, "let me finish." She took a deep breath and continued. "It's about perception, girls. You perceive that you've included her in everything and she perceives you've left her out. Her perception is the one that matters because *she's* the one who is hurting. Does that make sense? Her perception is one of hurt, loneliness, and a form of betrayal. You're her family, and you're letting her down. Do you understand?"

Emily and Hope nodded.

"You may have been doing your best and she may have been rebuffing your efforts. But she's here and she's not going anywhere. You have to keep trying."

"Yes, ma'am," they said in unison.

Grace leaned forward. "I know she can be difficult," she said in a hushed whisper. "She is my niece, after all, and even though I haven't seen her in years, I do know what she's like. Come to me if there's trouble, but don't ignore her. And keep trying."

"Yes, ma'am," Emily said, eyes wide in surprise.

"Go upstairs and try to make amends, please."

Both girls rose and slowly walked out of the room and up the stairs. Neither said a word, knowing Grace would most likely hear their whispered words. And who knew where Lila was hiding. Emily didn't think she was hanging out in her room, not caring about the conversation being had downstairs. The last thing they needed was for Lila to overhear and have her be even more offended than she already was.

They went straight to Lila's room and knocked on her door.

"I'm not in there," Lila said, smirking when they spun around. "Did you really think I would go to my room like a good country girl and miss the chance to see you get a dressing down?"

"So you did it on purpose?" Emily asked, glaring at Lila.

Lila laughed and opened her mouth to say something but Hope stepped between them, raising her hands for quiet.

"Em," Hope started. "Calm down. Remember what Mom said."

"Yes, Em, do what Hope says. Wouldn't want you to get into more trouble." Lila laughed. Then she turned flashing eyes on Hope. "Protective of her, aren't you?"

Hope ignored Lila's words and turned pleading eyes on Emily. Emily shook her head, angry eyes boring into Lila's.

"I know, Em," Hope soothed. "Unfair, but it is what it is."

Emily sighed and started counting. It never really worked for her, even though she tried it every time she got angry. She was still angry when she got to ten, but at least she didn't feel the need to punch Lila in the face anymore. Not that she didn't deserve it, but Hope was right. They had to make peace and keep trying. Not matter how bad Lila got under her skin.

Taking a deep, cleansing breath, Emily took a step closer to Lila. "I'm sorry for making you feel left out and alone. I will do better. Perhaps if you could tell me what you enjoy doing, we could save ourselves a lot of trouble."

Lila scoffed. "There is nothing to do here. No theater, no dance clubs, no museums, no culture. This is about the most uncultured place on the Earth. And anyways, why would I want to hang out with you, Miss Perfect? You're always shoving in my face your perfect life, and I'm sick of it. Sick of you, sick of your perfect relationship, sick of your perfect friends and your perfect grades, your perfect horses and your perfect riding. You make me sick!" Lila spat at Emily, her eyes glassy with the force of her emotions.

Emily's face turned beet red. The urge to punch Lila was back but so was the urge to cry. She'd never had anyone speak to her that way before, and she had no idea what to do with it. She turned to her stepsister. "Hope," she pleaded, though unsure what she was begging for.

"Go," Hope nodded toward their bedroom.

Emily turned and ran to their bedroom, closing the door behind her. It took every ounce of her willpower to keep from slamming the door. She didn't need Mama G back up here interfering and wondering what she'd done to provoke Lila now. How could she and Dad be so oblivious to Lila's behavior?

She could hear Hope talking to Lila and knew they were on their way to the bedroom because their voices were getting louder. Emily stood by the door and opened it a crack so she could better hear what Hope was saying to her nasty cousin.

"What is your problem, Lila?" Hope asked angrily.

"My problem?" she asked incredulously. "She's been rude and mean to me since I got here. She's always flaunting her friends and her boyfriend."

"She doesn't, Lila! She was so excited to have you here. She was excited to meet you, and she only wants to share her life with you. To make you feel welcome. And you've done nothing but make her feel like a country bumpkin by making fun of her and blowing her off all the time."

"God, listen to you!" Lila sneered. "You stick up for her without batting an eye. It's like a reflex. Someone picks on poor perfect Emily and you're right there to take up the charge." Lila jabbed a finger in Hope's shoulder. "She likes to show off and brag about herself. But she's about to find out just how imperfect her life really is!"

Lila shoved past Hope and pushed the door to their bedroom open.

"What are you talking about, Lila?" Hope asked, charging after her and almost colliding with Lila who was stopped just inside the door, face-to-face with Emily.

"Eavesdropping, perfect Emily?" Lila asked, a nasty grin on her face. "That hardly seems like a good idea. You're likely to hear something you don't like. Then again," Lila said, pulling a piece of fuzz off her shirt, "you probably don't know any better."

"Lila," Hope warned.

"Back off, cousin," Lila said, waving her hand at Hope. "She doesn't need you coming to her rescue."

"Say what you want to say, Lila, and then get out of my room," Emily snarled. Was this what Mama G meant when she said to come to her with trouble?

"Did you keep tabs on your boyfriend today?"

Emily scrunched up her face in confusion. "No. Why should I?"

Hope took two steps and stood next to Emily. She shot a grateful smile in Hope's direction and faced Lila again.

"It seems to me that you should know that he was with me all day. We had a lovely day down by the stream. We held hands, we talked, and he kissed me good-bye when he had to go do his chores."

The blood drained from Emily's face, and she grabbed hold of Hope's hand, hoping it would stop the room spinning around her. Her knees wanted to buckle, but only sheer force of will kept her from collapsing in front of Lila.

"What?" Emily choked out.

"Yes, I can see you're shocked. That's the normal reaction one feels when they realize their perfect world isn't. I'd say I'm sorry, but," she laughed, "I'm not. He's a fine catch, and it's too bad you lost him." She took a step and got in Emily's face. "So much for your perfect relationship. How does it feel to finally be on the outside?"

Hope took a step toward Lila, her hand raised. Emily tugged her back. "No, Hope," she said hoarsely, shaking her head. "Don't."

Hope turned sad eyes on Emily and wrapped an arm around her shoulders. "You can leave now, Lila. You've done enough damage for one day," Hope growled.

Lila waggled her fingers in their direction and sauntered from the room. As soon as she was out of sight, Emily sank to the floor, tears streaming down her face.

"He wouldn't, right? He couldn't," Emily said between hiccups. "We're solid. I thought we were solid? Maybe he's been unhappy. I mean, she's pretty—not inside where it counts—but she's beautiful. And sophisticated. Hope?"

Hope was shaking her head, anger flashing from her eyes. "No, Emily, you can't believe her. Go to Jason and ask. I doubt it's anything like what she described. She's a snake, you know that. And likely she's only saying this to rattle your cage."

"I don't know, Hope. I just don't know. Why would she say that though? I mean, really? Yeah, she's mean, but that's just," she paused, trying to find the right word, "horrible. It's just a horrible thing to do to someone."

Emily was startled out of her trip down memory lane by the voice of the captain over the loud speakers. "Attention, passengers, please return to your seats and secure your belongings. We're coming into some turbulence, and it's important for everyone to be safe. Again, please return to your seats and secure your belongings. I'll let you know when we are through the turbulence."

Just then, the plane dipped and Emily gripped the armrests. She closed her eyes and counted to ten, then twenty, then thirty. They were going to crash; she just knew it. Panic welled up inside her and all she wanted was to be back on the ground, safe and sound.

"Emily?" Hope asked quietly, prying Emily's hand off the armrest and holding it tightly in her own. "Emily, it's okay. It's just turbulence. We're safe, I promise."

Emily grimaced and kept her eyes closed. "How do you do this all the time? Every time the plane dips, my stomach ends up in my throat."

"I'm just used to it. It's just pockets of air that push against the plane's wings, and once we're through them, we dip back to where we're supposed to be. I promise we're safe and the plane won't crash."

Emily nodded, eyes still shut tight. "I couldn't sleep, you know. I went back to the beginning. To the start of the rumors. To the start of her taking him away."

"Why didn't you wake me up?"

"One of us needed sleep," Emily said wryly. "I went to him, time and again. Every time there was a new rumor or a new story from her. I would go to him, like he told me to, and he would promise there was nothing going on."

"I know. He was good at relieving your mind."

"He really was, wasn't he? God, I was so naive. So stupid."

"No, you loved him. And you wanted to believe in him. To believe he was the man you thought he was."

"I should have known, though. All those rumors, Hope. All the whispers. All the side glances and conversations that suddenly stopped when I walked in. I should have known he was just playing me."

"They were both playing you. I would have bet my modeling contract on those rumors not being true. I mean, it was *Lila* we were talking about, how true could they be?"

"All the way, true." Emily released the armrest and wiped a tear from her cheek. "I'm going to kill Tyler when I see him. Why didn't he warn me?"

"What do you mean?"

"I passed him outside on my way to Jason's. He told me that he'd delivered Jason to his bedroom himself. Said that Jason was hammered, and Tyler wasn't sure if Jason would even realize I was there." Emily sniffed and wiped another tear from her eye. "I just giggled and said it didn't matter. I'd just snuggle with him."

"He better hope Dad doesn't find out he was the last one to see Jason. He'll get just as much of an earful as Jason's gonna get," Hope said grimly.

"Why wouldn't he tell me, though?"

"He probably didn't see her. This is Lila we're talking about. No doubt she was hidden in the shadows or behind the door or in the closet."

Emily nodded. "The thing that really gets me, though, the part that just makes me want to vomit is that I placed my faith in him. Time and time again. Every new rumor that cropped up, we'd discuss it. He insisted that I come to him if ever I was feeling low. And I did. Often. All my trust. All my faith—I poured it into him. And now, I feel so empty. Bereft. Just plain wiped out. How idiotic was I?"

Hope shook her head and squeezed Emily's hand. "You weren't, Em. You weren't. He's the idiotic one."

"Yeah. But he's not the one running away, is he?" She squeezed Hope's hand and let go. Staring out the airplane window, she tried to turn her brain off and nap. But between the turbulence, which never let up, and the memories, sleep was elusive. Thirty minutes before they were to land, she fell into a fitful sleep, dreams of dragons and snakes terrorizing her. When Hope nudged her awake minutes later, she wasn't sure she'd be able to deplane on her own. She was bone weary, and all she wanted was to escape the pain and sleep for a week.

After collecting their luggage, Hope led her to the parking garage and her bright yellow Jeep Wrangler. Despite her exhaustion, Emily stared, wide-eyed, at the vehicle. It was not what she was expecting, considering Hope's wealth.

"Surprised," Hope laughed.

"A little," she admitted, sheepishly.

"Ha. You can take the girl out of the desert, but you can't take the desert out of the girl." She opened the trunk and stored their luggage in the back.

"I expected a BMW or something."

"Yeah, and I thought about it. But this felt right, and I love it. I don't drive often or far, so comfort isn't really a big deal for me. And it reminds me of home," she said wistfully.

Emily grinned and hopped up, albeit with some difficulty considering her girth, into the passenger seat.

With curious eyes, she stared out the window as they drove through the streets of Boston. She'd never been east of the Rockies—really hadn't been anywhere outside of New Mexico—and she was amazed at all the shades of green. There was grass and trees and flowers—everywhere it seemed. The buildings rose tall against the sky. People were bustling here and there, in a hurry to get where they needed to go. Cars crowded the streets and horns shattered the air, a testament to their drivers' frustrations. She was awestruck and intimidated by the sheer volume of activity happening around her. It was a different world compared to the shades of brown that she was used to at home.

"This is us," Hope said, pulling into the parking garage beneath her condo building.

"I think it'll be an early bedtime for both of us," Emily said, smiling as she patted her belly.

"For sure but food first." Hope parked in her spot, and they gathered their things. She led Emily to the bank of elevators. When they entered, she pressed the button for the thirtieth floor.

"Thanks, Hope," Emily said softly, emotion making her eyes water and her lower lip tremble.

"Anytime, sis." The elevator pinged and they rolled their bags out of the elevator. Hope led them down the quiet, carpeted hall and then opened the door to her condo. "Welcome home, Emily," Hope said, holding the door open so Emily could pass through first.

"Hope, it's gorgeous!" Emily breathed. She rushed to the wall of windows in the living room and looked out onto the view before her. It was amazing. Back home, when she was riding her horse and out on the ranch, she could see for miles. But that couldn't compare with what she saw now.

"How do you get anything done? I'd sit here and look out these windows all day!"

"I thought that at first, too. But as time goes on, the view is the view. It doesn't change. Much like the views at home." Hope laughed.

Reluctantly, Emily turned away from the windows. "I'm starving."

"Follow me. I'll show you your room, and then we can order some food." Hope led Emily through the condo, pointing out the obvious areas. "This is you, unless you like the room across from it better. But this one has a nicer view."

The room was larger than Emily's at home and decorated in creams and deep purples. Emily fell in love with the color scheme immediately as purple, in any shade, was her favorite color. "This is wonderful, Hope. I love it!"

"I'm glad." Hope laughed, swiping her fingers across her forehead in mock relief. "What do you feel like eating?"

"Anything."

Hope laughed. "How about pizza and a movie?"

"Sounds wonderful," Emily said and unzipped her suitcase. "I'm going to take a quick shower. I feel grimy."

"Bathroom is across the hall."

"Perfect."

Chapter Four

God, his head hurt. No, *hurt* was too tame a word for what was going on inside his head. Squinting, he searched for his clock. The glowing numbers were a tad too bright for his bloodshot eyes, and before he squeezed them closed against the brightness, he read six thirty. Groaning, he buried his face in the pillow. What the fuck? Who does this to himself? He was supposed to get married today. How could he marry the love of his life when he felt like total fucking shit? He wasn't even going to be able to keep his eyes open, the light from the sun was going to split his head in two . . . if the noise didn't do him in first. Just a groan had him clutching his head to keep it from littering blood and brains all over his bed.

If he ever felt better, which was a big *if* considering the amount he'd had to drink to feel this bad, he was going to kill his friends. Slowly and painfully. They deserved no less.

He crawled out of bed, staggered to the bathroom to relieve himself, and took two Advil. Using the wall as a crutch, he slowly made his way back to his room, and shucking his shirt and jeans, he slid under the sheets. He just needed twenty more minutes, time enough for the Advil to kick in and take the edge of this torture off.

Rolling over, he gingerly opened one eye. Bright sunshine scorched his retinas, forcing him to slam his eyelid closed. Yep, the sun was going to be the death of him today.

"I don't care how late the bastard got in last night. Go wake up that cheating, no good, selfish asshole you call a son!"

"Now hold on, Clint. I think you're overreacting. Jason loves Emily . . ."

"If you won't go get him, I will!"

Jason bolted upright at the sound of the heated argument downstairs. He flung the blankets away and fumbled with the doorknob. Three stairs from the bottom he came face-to-face with Emily's father.

"You son of a bitch," Clint greeted him, fists raised.

Jason, hands outstretched, stopped short on the stairs and looked over Clint's shoulder to his father. That was his first mistake. Clint coldcocked him in the jaw, knocking Jason back against the railing.

"What the fuck?" Jason growled, jumping up and curling his hands into fists. He didn't want to punch Emily's father, he liked and respected him, but what the fuck was going on that Clint was storming into their house and punching him in the face?

Jason's father wrapped his arms around Clint's shoulders and pulled him away from Jason. "Let's talk about this, Clint. Beating my son isn't going to solve the problem."

"What problem?" Jason asked. "What's going on?"

"Like you don't know, you little maggot."

Jason breathed through his nose, counting to ten silently. "Sir, I like and respect you immensely, but I'm not going to stand by for much longer while you call me names and punch me in my own home."

Jason watched as Clint visibly took a moment to calm down.

"Let's move this into the kitchen. There's coffee and whiskey there," Joe said. He pushed Clint toward the kitchen and looked back at his son. "Go make yourself decent, boy!"

Jason looked down and saw he was just in his boxers, his junk hanging out. Rolling his eyes, he trudged back upstairs, working the kink out of his jaw. Clint may be old, but he was still as strong as an ox. The man packed a lot into that punch, and he'd be lucky if there wasn't a bruise on his face for the wedding this afternoon.

He pulled on a pair of pants and glanced at the clock. Ten o'clock? Jesus! He must have fallen back to sleep. Last he remembered was waking at six thirty. Shit! There were less than five hours until the big deal and he had so much to do. Why the hell had his father let him sleep in so long?

He was so screwed; Emily was going to kill him. He should have picked up the cake an hour ago. He still needed to get a haircut and pick up the boutonnieres. Maybe he could sweet-talk Gina into picking them up when she picked up all the bouquets.

Hell, this was not the way he wanted to start the rest of his life.

He stopped short in the doorway of the kitchen. Clint was glaring in his direction, and his father was standing by the sink with a cup of coffee. He looked up when Jason entered the kitchen and shook his head.

"What's going on?" he asked to the room in general.

"Emily is gone," Clint announced.

"Gone? What do you mean gone? Gone where?"

"Away, as in, she left because you had a naked woman in your room last night."

Jason pulled himself up to his full height. "I most certainly did not!"

"You calling my daughter a liar?" Clint said, taking a half step in Jason's direction.

"Sir," Jason said uneasily, "I was out with my friends last night. They brought me home drunker than I've ever been in my life. They carried me to my room because there's no way I made it up there by myself. I passed out and woke at six thirty this morning, *alone*, my head pounding and feeling as low as I've ever felt in my life. I fell back to sleep until I heard you two down here arguing. There is no woman in my room—feel free to go up and check it out if you'd like."

"Just because there isn't one there now, or when you woke at six thirty, doesn't mean there wasn't one last night. Emily saw it with her own eyes."

"Why didn't she say anything?"

"What would she have said? She's devastated and gone."

"Well, where did she go? I'll go find her and explain."

"I don't know where she went. I just know there isn't going to be a wedding today, and I'm this close to murdering you, boy," Clint said, holding up his thumb and forefinger, which were centimeters apart.

"Who does know where she is?"

"Grace, but she's not telling."

"What about Hope?"

"Hope is with her," Clint said.

Jason pulled out his phone and dialed Emily. Straight to voicemail. Trying again, he raised his eyes to Clint's when it went straight to voicemail for the second time.

"Sir, I promise you I did not cheat on Emily. I don't know what she saw, I don't remember a damn thing from last night. But I know me, and I know how I feel about your daughter. I would never cheat on her. Never. I swear I will fix this."

Running up the stairs to his room, he grabbed the first shirt he saw, threw on his sneakers, all the while searching his room for clues. He didn't see any women's clothing, no condom wrappers, no evidence in the trash, nothing.

Why would Emily lie to her parents about this? Did she have cold feet? Was she nervous? Didn't she love him anymore? He had to get to the bottom of this. Their future was on the line.

Chapter Five

Several hours later, he returned home, discouraged, defeated, and in pain. His epic headache from overindulgence never went away—fear and worry replaced it. True enough, Emily was nowhere to be found. Grace wasn't giving up the location, and neither was Emily's best friend, Gina. He hadn't been able to locate Phoebe, Emily's other best friend, either.

He sat at the kitchen table, mind spinning, trying to come up with an idea of where she could have gone. He'd called the hotel they were supposed to stay at tonight in Santa Fe before they left for their honeymoon. He'd been to Gina's house, Phoebe's house, Emily's house—all to no avail. In fact, Clint had glowered from the door, and Jason had decided not to press his luck by demanding entrance. He assumed if Emily had been home, Clint would have said something then.

He'd searched all her favorite haunts and had driven to Santa Fe to do the same kind of search there. They'd spent four years there for college, and she'd racked up plenty of favorite spaces.

He hadn't been able to find her anywhere, which left only a few other options. She drove, flew, or took a bus out of town and who knows where one of those options took her. She was with Hope, which meant the world was their oyster. With Hope's trust fund, they could, and apparently had, disappeared, and no one would be the wiser until one of them wanted it. Neither Hope nor Emily was answering their phones, and Jason felt like his body was trying to escape his skin. He felt helpless and despondent and unsure what his next move should be.

Where the hell was she?

That was the question that kept rolling around in his head . . . and he imagined it would be the same question he would ask until he found her. He popped another dose of Advil and paced his room.

Looking at his watch, he noticed it was a little after eight. His heart sank. They'd be leaving the reception about now and heading into Santa Fe for their wedding night. And tomorrow morning they'd be boarding a plane for Hawaii.

He heard a knock at the door and got up to answer it. The last thing he felt like was company, but his father was already retired for the night and there was no one else to answer the door.

He opened the door and found Tyler standing on the steps. Unsure of his welcome, Jason kept the screen door in place.

"Have you heard from Emily?" Jason asked urgently.

Tyler growled. "No."

Jason could see a glint in Tyler's eyes and watched his jaw working in anger. Sighing, he popped open the screen door and motioned Tyler to enter. He knew why Tyler was here, and it wasn't to chitchat. Better to get the unpleasantness over with.

"It's probably better if you come out here," Tyler said. "I don't see this conversation ending well."

Nodding, Jason walked outside and down the steps into the dirt and gravel of the driveway.

Turning to face Tyler, Jason held up a hand. "Your father was here this morning."

"I know. After getting an earful from Grace when I woke up, he barged his way into the house and gave me a second helping." He took a step closer to Jason, who held his ground. "You know, if you didn't want to marry her, you should have been man enough to say something. This was a low-down dirty cheap shot, and you're lucky to still be alive."

Tyler grinned, though the mirth didn't reach his eyes. "Sure would love to know how you sweet-talked your way out of an ass-kicking this morning. Dad was fit to be tied."

"I noticed," Jason said, rubbing his still sore jaw. "Do I get to tell you my side of the story or are you going to just take Emily's word for it all?"

"She's the one who's gone, Jase. She left everyone behind, and you're still here."

"I swear, I didn't have sex with Lila. I was still fully clothed at six thirty when I woke up, hung over as all hell."

"That's not how Dad saw you when he came by."

"I know. I took some Advil, ditched my clothes, and went back to bed. I didn't wake up until I heard your father downstairs."

"Where was she?" Tyler demanded. "Jake and I brought you up to your room, and I didn't see her anywhere."

"I don't know. I swear," Jason said, hands raised in front of him. "I don't remember a thing from the point we left that bar in Santa Fe. We did those shots as soon as we got back in the limo and after that, nothing. I've got nothing from that moment until I woke at six thirty."

"It stinks. The whole thing stinks. There have been those rumors off and on since Lila got here. Emily has been sick over them for years. I think the only time she's been at ease has been while you guys were in Santa Fe. They started back up again once you two came back. Did you know that?"

Jason shook his head. He wasn't lying, either. He hadn't heard any new rumors, but then again, it wasn't like he'd been listening. He'd been focused on helping Emily plan the wedding and his job of house-hunting, all while doing his own duties around the ranch. Truth be told, he wasn't much of a listener of rumors anyway.

All the rumors that Em had brought to him their last two years in high school had been news to him. He went to the same school, had the same classes, but never heard one rumor until Em brought it to his attention. He'd done a lot of consoling and reassuring, but he'd never resented it. Emily was the love of his life, and he'd go through hell to prove it to her, and anyone else, who didn't believe him.

"How are you so oblivious?" Tyler roared.

Jason knew him well enough to know that Tyler was on the verge of losing his temper. "I don't know. I just don't listen, I guess. Or no one talks around me. It's not because I'm in cahoots with her, if that's what you're thinking."

"What I'm thinking is that you're a low life. A cheating bastard. I'm thinking you broke my sister's heart, and you should pay for it!" Tyler took two steps and swung his fist at Jason's face.

Knowing he deserved it, if for nothing else than not doing enough to deter Lila from her machinations, he stood still and took the punch on the jaw.

Tyler quickly followed it up with a left hook to the face and then pummeled him in the gut. Jason bent over from the force of the gut punches and Tyler laid him out on the ground with another punch to the face.

"Seriously? You're not going to fight back?" Tyler fumed, standing over Jason's prone body.

He shook his head. "Nope, figure I deserve this."

"Pathetic," Tyler spat.

"You get this one time, Ty. You come at me again, on a different day, and you'll get a different scenario."

"Well then, I guess I better take care of you once and for all," Tyler said, placing a well-aimed kick to Jason's ribs.

Clutching his ribs, Jason slowly got to his feet. He glared at Tyler. "Well, come on. Finish me off," he taunted.

Tyler shook his head and waved a hand. "You're not worth it. I'd advise you to stay away from the house for the foreseeable future. Dad was telling Grace he was leaving his shotguns by the doors and she was to use them if you showed your face on the property. He's furious, and I'm right there with him."

"I didn't cheat on her."

"Whatever man. Seems to me you're protesting too much, and the evidence is damning. Did you forget Emily was planning to come by? You need better lessons in juggling women, Jase. You don't invite the whore over the night before the wedding, especially when your pregnant fiancée is waiting by the door for your return."

Jason watched him turn on his heel and walk across the yard to the house. He waited until Tyler had passed through the trees before he turned and shuffled up the steps and into the house. He walked into the kitchen and got another beer out of the fridge and a bag of peas out of the freezer. He went into the living room, fell into the La-Z-Boy and cracked open the beer. After taking a swig, he leaned his head back against the chair and carefully set the bag of peas on his face.

What the hell? He had to find Emily. He had to explain. Hell, he had to find out what happened last night.

He tipped the bottle up to his lips and took a large gulp of beer. He didn't dare show his face anywhere Lila might be, and he couldn't ask her. She'd never tell him the truth, and if anyone saw them together, no amount of protesting, pleading, or begging would convince them of what he was doing. So if he couldn't go to the source, how was he going to find out?

All this thinking was making his head pound even harder. Where was Emily? He knew if he could just talk to her they'd be able to straighten the whole thing out. He was sure it was something simple, something easy to fix. Cold feet, nerves, something silly that was probably 99% hormones. Or stress. They'd just graduated, she was pregnant and searching for a place to open her design business. They were getting married. She was doing the heavy lifting on everything but the house-hunting. That was his job. He had several showings set up for when they returned from Hawaii, but what he really wanted to do was to build a house on the other side of his father's property, kind of like Tyler had done. Close enough so he could still work the ranch with his father but far enough away that they were alone.

All the stress along with the hormones . . . maybe it was too much and at the last minute she just snapped. Dammit, he needed to talk to her. Why wouldn't she answer her phone?

Chapter Six

A Month Later

"Emily Camancho?" a petite brunette asked.

"That's me," Emily said, struggling to her feet. Would she ever get used to her new center of gravity?

"Ms. Nickerson will see you now."

When she'd arrived for her interview with Kendra Nickerson of A Touch of Flair, she hadn't expected the interview location to be a house. She'd been shown into the living room and had sat on the most comfortable couch she'd ever sat on in her life. Ms. Nickerson was on the phone when Emily entered the dining room and she was glad. It gave her the opportunity to observe the woman she hoped to work for. She had long, red curly hair and was dressed in a dark blue pinstripe suit with a bright white shirt underneath. She was studying the paperwork on the desk in front of her, so Emily couldn't see the color of her eyes, but she could see that her skin was flawless and pale. She had freckles everywhere, as most redheads were affected.

Taking a deep breath, Emily sat in the chair opposite Ms. Nickerson and waited.

"I don't care what it takes, Ed. I want that office space by the end of the month." She hung up the phone, moved the papers to her file bin, and cast the greenest gaze on Emily's face.

"Sorry about that, Emily," she said, smiling and holding out her hand. "I'm Kendra Nickerson. Nice to meet you."

"Likewise," Emily said, returning the handshake.

"So, you're here . . ."

"Mommy, Mommy, Mommy!" A tiny redheaded girl ran into the room and straight toward Kendra. She climbed into Kendra's lap and wrapped her chubby arms around her neck. "Aiden is poking me."

"Where's . . ."

"I'm so sorry, Ms. Kendra," a plump, gray-haired woman with a Spanish accent said as she hurried into the room. "I turned my back to scold Aiden and she ran right out of the room."

Kendra turned apologetic eyes on Emily and smiled. "This is why I need that office space."

Emily grinned.

"It's okay, Juanita. I understand." Kendra pulled the little arms away from around her neck and set the toddler on the floor. "Izzy, you can't run from Ms. Juanita, and you can't bother Mommy when she's working. Ms. Juanita will take care of Aiden. Go back upstairs now." Kendra gave the little girl a hug and then playfully swatted her diaper-clad bottom. "Shoo!"

The little girl laughed and clutched the hand of her nanny. Emily watched them leave the room and rubbed her hands over her belly. Soon, very soon, she'd have her own to love.

"Never a dull moment around here." Kendra laughed. "Shall we start again?"

"Not necessary," Emily smiled.

"You're here to save me from the mountains of work I'm drowning in?"

"I hope so," Emily said as she passed Kendra a copy of her resume and letters of reference. Kendra glanced through everything quickly then looked up at Emily. "When are you due?"

Emily sighed and tried not to let her disappointment show. "December fourth. I only plan to take the six weeks and then come back to work. I know it's a pain to hire me only to lose me so soon, but I promise you won't regret it." With her heart racing and her clammy palms clenched in her lap, Emily finished her passionate plea.

"I wasn't asking so I had a reason not to hire you. I asked because I was curious," Kendra said, smiling. Emily relaxed.

"Do you have any experience with AutoCAD?"

"Yes, I interned at Santa Fe Designs for four years while I was in college. AutoCAD was my not so best friend," she answered, smiling.

Kendra laughed. "Yeah, it can be a pain, can't it?"

Emily nodded, and Kendra continued with her questions.

"What is the standard height for a kitchen countertop?"

"Thirty-six inches."

"Have you passed the NCIDQ?"

She leaned forward taking two papers out of her briefcase and passing them to Kendra. "Yes, here are my certificates. One from New Mexico and the one from Massachusetts."

Kendra quickly looked them over and then shuffled them under Emily's resume, which she was glancing at.

"It says here on your resume that you were part of the team to redesign the Governor's mansion?"

Nodding, Emily leaned back in the chair, trying to ease the pain in her lower back.

"It was a fun project. I was a junior designer; it was my second year in school. We completely redesigned the main level of the mansion. Kitchen, bathrooms, living spaces. I brought photos with me, if you're interested?" Emily motioned toward her briefcase.

"I would. Let's finish up this interview, and then we can get to the fun stuff." At Emily's nod, she continued, "What is your favorite color combination?" Kendra asked her.

"Right now it's cream and deep purple."

"What type of window treatment would you put in a living room with south-facing windows?"

"Sheer draperies layered with blackout panels."

"Why?"

"The light-blocking curtains will keep the room cool and dark during the strong light of the day. The sheer curtains will allow the user to open the room, while still having some privacy, so they don't feel claustrophobic all the time."

Kendra nodded. "What is your favorite design?"

"Simple and uncluttered."

"When can you start?"

"Wha . . . ? Um. Seriously?"

Kendra smiled and nodded.

"Right now. Tomorrow. Whenever." Emily grinned.

"I think tomorrow morning is soon enough." Kendra stood up and walked around the table. She held out a hand and helped Emily to her feet. "You'll be my right hand . . . and probably my left. Let me introduce you to Jenny, my receptionist and office manager. Next week, we'll talk about getting an intern in here to fill in for you while you're out on maternity leave."

Emily stopped mid-stride through the kitchen. "Thank you so much," she said, reaching out and awkwardly hugging Kendra.

Kendra laughed and returned the hug. "We'll see if you're still thanking me in a week when you realize how much work there is to be done."

When Emily got home, she called Gina to tell her the news.

"That's great, Em! So, I guess that means you're staying in Boston for a while?"

"At least for the foreseeable future."

"I miss you. I was hoping you'd be coming home soon."

"Is Jason still there?"

"Yeah."

"Then I can't come home. I'm not ready to see him."

"He still loves you. He's so confused, Em. He swears he didn't cheat."

"I'm sure," scoffed Emily.

"I'm serious. He cornered me at The Dustbowl the other night when Fred and I were out with some of his buddies from the station. Anyway, he was in there drinking, and he came right over when he saw me."

"And you let him speak to you? I thought you were my friend!"

Gina groaned. "Seriously, Em? He's miserable. It took everything I had to keep your secrets."

"Don't say another word to him, Gina! Have you forgotten what he did? The night before our wedding?"

"Of course not. But he was trashed. Fred said some of the guys had to carry him in the house and up to his room."

"I saw them carry him inside. And then I saw what he was doing with Lila. He didn't look drunk to me."

Gina sighed. "Maybe you should talk to him?"

"Talk to him?" Emily said quietly. "I'm the one who has to reach out? The one who has to make the effort?"

"Who else? You won't let anyone tell him where you are."

"It's not my problem."

"I just wish you could see for yourself that he's hurting."

"Oh, and I'm having the time of my life?"

Sighing deeply, Gina said, "I know you're hurting, too. I hate to see either of you this way. I just want it fixed and you both happy and together."

"He ruined it. I'm in Boston with no family except Hope. Instead of running my own business, I'm working for someone. Instead of having a husband, I'm single and about to have a baby on my own. He has everything, and I lost everything." Emily kept her eyes tear-free and her voice strong. She would not shed another tear over him.

"Em."

"Enough. Drop it. I don't want to waste any more time, or tears, on this subject. I want . . . no, I need to concentrate on my career. Concentrate on building a new life. Concentrate on being the best mother I can be. Concentrate on loving this baby. But most of all, I need to concentrate on moving on."

"Consider it dropped."

"Thank you," Emily said curtly.

"So, have you picked a name yet?"

*****

When Hope got home later that afternoon, they decided to go check out the baby shop. They found several cute outfits, and Emily couldn't leave without the soft white bunny toy.

After exhausting themselves with shopping, they decided to let someone else cook and stopped at Legal Sea Foods for dinner. After giving the server their orders, Hope turned to Emily with her serious eyes.

"I talked to Mom today."

"How is she?"

"She's good. Have you spoken to her recently?"

"Over the weekend, but not so far this week. Been too busy interviewing."

Hope nodded. "Well, you know Jason has been showing up there every day, right?"

"What?" Emily asked, sitting up straight and almost spilling her water as she set it down on the table with a loud bump.

"Okay, you didn't know."

"No, I didn't know."

"I guess he waits until Dad leaves, and then he knocks on the kitchen door. Mom lets him in, and he's been asking every day where you are and how you and the baby are doing."

"Well, at least she hasn't told him where I am. Does she tell him about the baby and me?"

"We didn't go into the specifics of what she's telling him or not. But, she did mention that he's confused. Everyone is accusing him of cheating, but he doesn't remember a thing about that night."

"Oh my gosh. Gina said the same thing today when I spoke to her."

"She's spoken to him?"

Emily nodded. "At the bar the other night. He cornered her and asked for all the details. She didn't give me up, but she said it took all she had not to."

Hope moved closer to the table. "Mom said he's hurting, a lot. She said he's beside himself with grief. He's devastated."

Emily shook her head and leaned back in her chair, crossing her arms against her chest. "I don't buy it. He has to remember, and he's just trying to talk everyone into believing him. Devastated? Please. He's devastated because he got caught, not because I'm gone."

Hope opened her mouth and then promptly closed it. She sat back in her chair and picked up her water glass. "You're probably right. I hadn't thought of it that way."

"Mama G and Dad still coming for Thanksgiving?" Emily asked, desperately trying to change the subject.

*****

It was the week before Thanksgiving and Emiy was exhausted. "I've been working twelve-hour days to get things caught up and ready before Baby Girl arrives."

"Don't wear yourself out, darling. You need to rest as much as you can before she's born."

"I know, Mama G, but it's my first real job, and I don't want them to forget how awesome I am while I'm out on maternity leave."

"Darling, no one could forget that."

Emily laughed. "You're still planning to be here Wednesday?"

"Yes."

"Fabulous. I'll do my best to get this place ready for you and Dad."

"Don't stress too much about it."

"Can't wait to see you guys!"

"Us either. Love to all three of you. Get some rest, Em."

Emily hung up the phone and glanced around the apartment. It was Sunday afternoon, and she had a lot of work to do to make their place presentable before Wednesday. Dishes, dusting, vacuuming, laundry, bathrooms. The list was never ending. Plus, the baby's room was a disaster. Everything she'd received and bought had been dumped into that room. Nothing was organized. The crib wasn't even put together.

Since she'd started at A Touch of Flair, the time had flown by. She loved the job, she loved Kendra, and she felt she was making a difference. Kendra had brought on the promised intern, Phil, to cover for Emily while she was out on maternity leave. Emily really liked him.

Lying under the covers, the lights off and her alarm set, Emily rubbed her burgeoning belly. Baby Girl was due in twelve days, and she was terrified. Of caring for this tiny human. Of juggling work and child care. Of being solely responsible for raising her to be the best woman she could be. Of all the little things and all the big things.

She wasn't supposed to be in this situation. Jason was supposed to be with her, standing next to her and helping her. She wondered what he was doing right now.

Adjusting the pillow under her head, she closed her eyes, wishing for sleep to claim her, but fear was eating away at her fragile confidence. Everyone said she'd make a wonderful mother, but how did they know? How could they be sure? Just because she'd always been able to make babies coo and little children laugh didn't mean she had what it took to raise a baby.

Frustrated at being unable to fall asleep, she sat up and reached for the baby name book. She picked up at the O names, added a couple to her short list and continued to the S names. Her eyes were immediately drawn to the name Sadie, which meant princess.

"Sadie," Emily said out loud. Smiling, she reached for her laptop and searched for feminine flower names. The tradition in her family was that all the girls, for as far back as Emily knew, had a flower middle name. Her own was Rose. She scrolled through the search results, and like a flashing beacon, she saw a name near the bottom, her favorite color and flower.

Violet.

Sadie Violet.

It was perfect. Too excited to sleep now that Baby Girl finally had a name, Emily slipped out of bed and went to the kitchen for a glass of milk. She picked up her phone to call Gina with the good news when the doorbell rang. She glanced at the clock and wondered who could be at the door at 10:00 at night.

Cautiously, she walked to the door and looked out the peephole. All the blood drained from her face. How had he found her? What was he doing here? Should she ignore him? Would he go away if she didn't answer the door?

Emily let out a squeak when he rang the bell again.

"Emily?"

Kicking herself for making a noise, she reluctantly opened the door, standing in the small space she'd opened.

"What are you doing here?"

Jason's eyebrows rose to his hairline. "That's how you greet me?"

"I don't have to greet you at all," Emily said, and started to shut the door in his face.

He put his foot in the way and pressed his hand on the door, pushing it open and walking past Emily into the condo.

"Get out!" Emily yelled. "I didn't invite you in. I don't want you here."

"That much is obvious, Em. But I'm not leaving until you tell me what's wrong."

He reached out for her hand, but she wrapped her arms around the baby. His face dropped, and for a second, Emily could see the pain and devastation Gina and Hope had spoken of. She couldn't believe he was here. He was still so handsome, so tall and strong. He still made her heart flutter and her breath catch in her throat. He was still so perfect. It pained her beyond words to see him standing in front of her and to know she couldn't walk into his arms and hear his steady heartbeat beneath her ear. To know that she didn't belong in those arms any longer.

Emily laughed harshly. "You might be able to lie to everyone else, but you can't lie to me."

Jason stared at her with wide, innocent eyes, and Emily couldn't believe he was pretending not to know. Well, two could play at this game.

"I paced my room for hours," Emily said calmly. "I waited for you to get home and when I saw the headlights, I hurried over. I hid in the trees until Tyler and Jake deposited you in your room. I saw Tyler and he told me that you were drunk, but I laughed." Emily blinked rapidly, trying to dispel the tears that sprang to her eyes. Hadn't she already promised herself she wouldn't cry over him anymore? "I laughed because I was happy. Happy you'd had a great time and happy that we weren't going to have to wait much longer. We'd be together, and I wouldn't have to sneak out to sleep with you anymore." She turned from him and walked over to the windows, glancing outside.

"But it wasn't me you were waiting for. You were very busy with Lila when I walked into your room."

"What?" Jason yelled. Two steps had him at Emily's side, and he gripped her arm, spinning her to face him. She tried to shrug him off but he held tight. "Lila? I keep telling people and no one is listening. There. Was. No. One. In. My. Room," he ground out, enunciating each word harshly.

"You were kissing her and had your hands all over her naked body," she snarled, glaring at him. She pulled her arm from his grip and quickly moved away from him when she saw his dazed expression.

She watched him stare off into space and wondered if he was trying to fabricate a lie. She wouldn't fall for it, though. Fool me once, shame on you. Fool me twice, shame on me. She'd done some heavy duty thinking since arriving in Boston, and she was going to do this on her own. She and Jason were over; their relationship was dead. Her trust in him had been irrevocably broken and there was no going back.

"Emily, I don't know what you're talking about. I woke up alone."

She snorted. "That's what you're going with? Amnesia?"

"I don't know what else to tell you. The last thing I remember is leaving some bar in Santa Fe. There were drinks in the limo, and I don't even know where we went after that. I don't remember coming home."

She shook her head. "You need to leave. I can't even look at you."

"Emily, please!" Jason implored. He strode over and gripped her arms. "I love you. Only you, I swear it. I'm going to fix this. Please, please don't give up on us. On me."

"It's over, Jason. I'm done. I can't look at you. I can't close my eyes without seeing your hands on her body. I can't trust you." The hated tears flowed down her cheeks and she angrily swiped at them. "You have to go." She walked over to the door and opened it, gesturing with her hand for him to leave.

Jason stood in the center of the living room, hands on his hips and gaze fixed on the carpet at his feet. For a moment, Emily thought he wouldn't leave, and she wondered what she'd do if that happened.

He walked over and stood in front of her. Reaching out, he lifted her chin with his finger. Staring into her eyes, he sighed. "I love you, and I will figure out a way to prove it to you. To prove to you that I'm not the man you think I am. I'm going to get to the bottom of this, and I'm going to win you back."

He leaned down and placed a gentle kiss on her lips. Then he was gone.

Emily stood in the doorway, shock written on her face as she brought her fingers to her lips. God help her, she still loved him.

Chapter Seven

The bar was busy and Jason was glad for it. He chose a corner table, hidden in the shadows. Sipping his beer, he waited for her to show. And show she would. Since Emily left town back in September, she'd been following him all over the place.

His trip to Boston had been enlightening. Emily still loved him, of that he was sure. She was angry, hurt, and distrustful—and she had every right to be. But she still loved him. All he had to do now was find a way to win her back.

First, he had to know what happened, and the only person who could tell him was Lila. He had to know how far she had taken him, how far her deception went. He had to know her plan, and then he had to shut it down. He was a one-woman man. Emily, not Lila, was the love of his life, and he would fight until his last breath to get Emily back.

He watched her walk in, watched as she sauntered up to the bar and ordered her usual glass of white wine. He watched as she slowly perused the bar, a confused look crossing her face when she couldn't find him. He watched as she asked the bartender and Ben's nod toward Jason's direction.

Lila squinted into the dark after picking up her glass of wine. She strolled over to his table and pulled out the chair across from him. Doing his best to keep calm and not leap over the table to strangle her, he casually took a sip of his beer and kept his face neutral.

"Howdy, stranger," Lila said brightly. "Haven't seen you in a few days."

Jason nodded. "Took a trip."

"Oh?" Lila asked, sipping her wine. "Where?"

The "why didn't you take me" hung in the air. It all made sense to him now. Her showing up everywhere he was. Her calls and texts. Her insistence that they spend time together. The whispers and dirty looks in town.

Oh yes, she'd been busy since that night in September spreading lies, rumors, and half-truths. It was no wonder everyone in Emily's family, save Grace, wouldn't speak to him.

"Boston."

The expression on her face didn't change, which made Jason think she either didn't know Emily was there or didn't think Jason saw Emily. No matter. She'd know soon enough.

"Boston? Whatever for? There aren't many cows in Boston," Lila smirked.

"It was enlightening," he remarked. Taking a pull from his beer, he stared into her eyes. He set the beer down on the table and sat up. Making fists, he laid them on either side of his beer.

"I missed you. I wish you would have told me you were going." Lila pouted.

"Why?"

He watched as shock entered her eyes, confusion replacing it a second later, followed closely by a coy smile. "I used to live there, you know that. I could have shown you around to all my favorite haunts. Think about how much that alone time, away from the prying eyes around here, would have taken our relationship to the next level."

"Relationship?" Jason asked. "You mean when you hid in my room, naked as the day you were born? Or when you laid in wait for me to come home from my bachelor party, drunker than a sailor? Or when you threw yourself at me, knowing I was expecting my fiancée?" He paused to sip his beer, wanting desperately to smash it over her head. "That relationship?"

"I-I-I don't know what you mean," Lila spluttered.

"Oh now, Lila, don't lie to me. Emily saw you in my room. Saw my hands," Jason held them up in front of her face, "all over your body. Saw my lips kissing yours. And she saw all of this on our wedding day!"

Shaking her head, she raised her hands in defense. "Jason, she's lying. I would never . . ."

"Bullshit!" he yelled, banging his fists down on the table and shooting to his feet. He leaned over the table and got in her face. His voice pitched low and menacing, he growled at her. "You ruined my wedding day. You made the love of my life, who is pregnant with my child, flee across the country in heartbreak. She can't even look at me and wants nothing to do with me."

Lila smiled. "Then we can be together n—"

"No," he cut her off. "There is no us, Lila. There never has been, and there never will be. I don't want you. I've never wanted you."

Lila stood and splashed her wine in his face. Jason didn't even flinch.

"Your body said otherwise that night," she sneered.

"Only because you pretended to be her and I was too drunk to know the difference."

"She'll never take you back."

Jason shrugged. "Whether she does or doesn't changes nothing between you and me. Stay away from me."

"You can't avoid me forever, Jason. Emily isn't the only one who's having your baby."

Jason stilled, sure he heard her wrong. Pregnant? Was she serious? How could he have been so stupid? Picking up his beer, he launched it across the room and watched as it shattered against the wall. A half second later, he realized what he'd done and couldn't help but notice the curious looks the other patrons were giving him. Closing his eyes, he counted quickly to ten. He had to get himself under control. He'd never get to the truth if he lost his shit every time Lila lied. He turned his icy stare on her as she continued to plead her case.

"I want you, Jason. I've wanted you since I came here six years ago. Emily doesn't appreciate you; she takes you for granted. I would never do that," Lila said quietly, standing in front of him and wrapping her arms around his waist.

"So you did this all on purpose?" Jason said, glaring down at her.

"Of course, how else would we be together?" Lila laid her cheek against his chest and tightened her hold on him. "I saw her walk in that night. I saw her face, the shock and devastation. The realization that she lost you. And I basked in it. The perfect girl was no longer perfect. Her world was shattered and you were finally mine."

Jason's stomach revolted and only sheer will kept the contents under control. "There's only one flaw in your plan, Lila," Jason said, removing her arms from around his waist and pushing her away from him.

Lila arched an eyebrow. "And what would that be?"

"I don't care if you are pregnant. It changes nothing. I still don't want you and that won't change. Ever."

Jason turned on his heel and walked out of the bar. He needed a fight, a good old-fashioned brawl. He wanted to kill something with his bare hands. His rage was so overpowering he let out a roar, letting loose all his pain, rage, and despair. Slamming the door to his truck, he peeled out of the parking lot and headed for home.

Pregnant? She was pregnant? Mother of God, he had not seen that coming.

He pounded his fist on the steering wheel. What the fuck?

He needed to calm down, and he needed a plan. Lila obviously had her own plan and it was in full gear. He couldn't see her plan's path, and it killed him to have to wait it out.

He should not have let his emotions get the better of him back there, but she'd just pissed him off by throwing the baby card in his face. How dare she?

What did she hope to gain? He'd never even shown her a moment of affection, never led her on, never flirted with her—not even inadvertently. Was she so loony that it didn't matter to her?

For God's sake, she was Emily's cousin. Who did this to their own family?

Aw, shit! If Emily heard about this "pregnancy," it really would be the end to them. Was that Lila's ultimate plan? Maybe he was an innocent casualty in all of this and her real target was Emily. Did Lila's hatred for Emily really go that deep? And if so, why?

How could he keep Emily from finding out about it until he was sure one way or the other? And what would he do if it turned out that Lila was really pregnant and it was really his?

Jason pulled into the driveway, cut the engine, and punched the steering wheel again. Blowing out a breath, it occurred to him that beating the shit out of his truck wasn't going to fix anything. He stormed into the kitchen and got a beer out of the fridge. The beer wouldn't fix anything either, but he hoped for a bit of amnesia.

He wandered out to the back porch and sat in the lounge chair. He kept the lights off, hoping he could fool the mosquitoes into thinking he wasn't there.

What the hell was he going to do? Emily had been adamant that she didn't want him, didn't want to see him or be with him. How did you change someone's mind when they had it made up so thoroughly?

Maybe trying to woo her back was the only way? He could make phone calls, send flowers and gifts. Sure, it was going to be long-distance and that was going to make it all the more harder, but he had to try.

How long until he could know for sure whether Lila was pregnant? And did it really matter? Emily would flip out if she found out, and that would definitely be a thorn in their reconciliation. But how could he be sure it really was his? He didn't remember anything from that night, and he sure didn't remember whether he and Lila had gone all the way. He'd been so drunk he couldn't imagine they had gone all the way. Surely he would have passed out before anything serious happened.

He'd found no evidence of a wild, sexy night. He'd been sure to check when Clint had come by that morning hell-bent on beating the crap out of him. Sure, he'd been down to his boxers, but he hadn't woken nude, which would have been a given if he'd had sex that night.

He sat forward and set his beer on the ground. A smile broke across his face. Lila had to be lying, but how would he get her to admit it? Or how would he catch her in the lie? She was probably expecting her news to drive him into her arms, especially with Emily so inaccessible.

He didn't need another complication to getting Emily back, but he definitely had to get this nipped in the bud. He drained the rest of his beer and set the empty bottle on the floor next to the lounge chair. Standing, he paced the length of the porch and made a plan.

First, he had to confirm Lila's pregnancy, but he had no idea how. Second, if she was pregnant, he had to get a DNA test done . . . it wasn't his and he had to prove it. Third, and he hated that this was third on the list, he would start his wooing campaign of Emily right away by sending flowers, and he'd call her this weekend to say hi. And he should go shopping for a Christmas gift for her, and it had to be good.

He was a man of action, and action was what he needed right now. Actions spoke louder than words, right? Well, he hoped that was true.

"Knock, knock," Jason said, rapping his knuckles against the screen door. He'd stayed up late into the night making plans to catch Lila in her lie, and then he'd moved on to how he was going to win Em back.

He was tired, heart sick, and not ready to face the day. It was already scorching hot and it wasn't even nine o'clock in the morning.

"Come in," Grace said pleasantly, handing him a steaming mug of strong, black coffee as he walked through the door.

"Thank you," he muttered against the lip of the mug as he took his first sip of coffee of the day. He propped a hip against the counter and smiled at Grace. "How are you today?"

"I'm good. Getting geared up for the trip to Boston. We're leaving bright and early tomorrow morning."

"How long will you be gone?"

"I will most likely be gone until after the baby is born; Clint will be home Monday afternoon." She puttered around the kitchen, pulling out plates and homemade cinnamon buns. "Sit down," she gestured toward the table. "I'm sure you haven't had breakfast yet."

"Nothing as delicious as what you're about to serve me." He laughed, helping himself to a bun. He moaned in delight with his first bite. Nothing in the world tasted better than Grace's cooking. She had a gift. "Will you let me know when the baby is born?"

Grace nodded as she took a sip of her coffee. "Of course." She smiled.

"Do you think it would be a bad choice to fly out and see the baby?"

Grace grimaced and stared hard at her coffee mug.

"So, I take it that's a yes," he muttered, nodding toward the look on her face.

She sighed and raised her eyes to meet his. "No," she said slowly. "No, I think that would actually be a good idea."

"You do?" Jason asked incredulously.

"Yes," she said brightly. "The more I think about it, the more I think that seeing you so soon after the birth might help open her eyes. I'll call you once the baby arrives and you can make arrangements to come out to Boston." A bright smile lit up her face. "Yes, I think this is a great idea!"

Jason grinned, relieved that Grace was on his side for this. He fell silent, finishing up his cinnamon bun and wondering how to broach the subject of Lila.

"You look like you have something on your mind," Grace prompted, reaching across and serving him a second helping of cinnamon buns.

"You always could read me like a book," Jason teased. "But yeah, I do." The color rose in his cheeks, evidence of how uncomfortable this conversation was going to be.

"Spit it out, then. The sooner it's out, the sooner we can deal with it."

He proceeded to explain the situation he had found himself in upon his return from Boston. He made sure to stress that he was one hundred percent positive it wasn't his but didn't have the guts to go into the gory details.

"Definitely is a pickle you're in, isn't it?"

Dropping his chin and turning his head to the side, he nodded. He drained the last of his coffee and then went over to the coffee pot to fill their cups. "Can you help? What should I do? How do I prove she's lying?" he asked, sitting down at the table again.

"Either set it up yourself or have her set up an appointment with a doctor. A quick exam, plus some blood work will sort it out pretty quick. And if that's inconclusive, just get an ultrasound."

"I do have a friend from college who's an intern at an OB/GYN office. I wonder if he'd make time for me?"

"It's worth a try. What if it is true?" At Jason's sharp look, she raised a hand and shook her head. "I don't mean whether it's yours or not. What if it's true that she's pregnant?"

"I'll demand a DNA test. I know it's not mine, and I refuse to be tricked into it. I'm not responsible for her bad choices, and I won't be held accountable for them."

Grace smiled. "Good for you."

He spun the mug around on the table. "I saw her Sunday," he said quietly.

"Who?"

"Emily."

"You did?" Grace asked, a smile breaking out on her face. "How was she?"

"She seemed to be doing well," he answered, hanging his head. "But not thrilled to see me on her doorstep."

"How'd you figure out where she was?"

"Process of elimination. She wasn't here, nor at Gina's or Phoebe's. I called some friends in Santa Fe. Called a few hotels, checked in with some family members I know of. But Hope hasn't returned one phone call, and she was the last holdout."

"Smart boy," Grace smiled, patting his hand. "Did you explain?"

"I tried. She barely looked at me. She just wanted me gone."

"She'll come around, but you can't force it. You'll only drive her away further. Give her time, woo her, show her how much you love her, show her how wrong she is despite what she saw with her own eyes."

Jason sighed. "It sounds like you want me to start all over again."

Chuckling, she tapped her fingers on the table. "It's not as if you had to try in the first place. You two have been thick as thieves since you were babies; your relationship has just moseyed down the natural path of things. Neither of you have had to work for your relationship; it's been easy."

He nodded.

She stood and put her mug in the sink. "And now you have to decide: Do you fight, tooth and nail, for her or do you let her keep her misconceptions and walk away? And it wouldn't just be Emily you'd be walking away from. It would also be that sweet baby."

Jason shot to his feet. "Whoa, who said anything about giving up? Certainly not me," he said, taking his own mug to the sink. Turning to face her, his eyes bored into Grace's. "I'm fighting, tooth and nail. I won't give up on her, on us, on our family. I know it's not going to be easy, but I'm not a quitter. She's the love of my life, Grace. Always has been."

A brilliant smile lit up Grace's face. She pulled him in for a hug and patted his back. "I knew it, but I had to be sure. I'll help you as much as I can." She stood back and poked a finger into his chest. "Don't screw this up, though. It won't just be Clint you have to worry about if you do."

Chapter Eight

"I can't be on bed rest! I have too much work to do."

"Your blood pressure is too high, Emily. Any higher and I'll have to admit you to the hospital. There's protein in your urine and you have too much swelling. You've been pushing yourself too hard and now you have no other choice."

"But I have to pick up my parents at the airport this afternoon."

Dr. Robbins shook her head. "Not going to happen. Find someone else to pick them up. You are to go straight home to bed. I shouldn't even let you drive yourself home."

"I suppose my sister can pick them up. Can I work in bed?"

"I'd prefer you didn't. Watch television, read a book, sleep. You need to relax. No stress. If you don't rest, I'll have to admit you."

Emily sighed and hunched her shoulders. "How dangerous is it?"

"Preeclampsia is very serious. If not treated properly, it can lead to eclampsia. Seizures, coma, death. You need to take this seriously, Emily."

"Death?"

Dr. Robbins nodded. "Call your office and tell them you're taking maternity leave now. Pass off all your work. Go home and rest."

"What should I be aware of?"

"Blurred vision, severe weight gain, headache that won't go away, pain in your abdomen or in your shoulder. If it seems wrong, call me. I'd rather you call me and it be nothing than to take a chance with your life and Baby Girl's."

Emily slid to the floor and gathered up her things. "I'll be home in bed in a half hour. I promise."

"Good."

After checking out and making her appointment for the following week, Emily hurried to the car and drove home. Walking into the apartment, she dropped everything on the dining room table and went straight to her room. Changing into her pajamas, she slid under the blankets and called Hope, who assured her she'd pick up Clint and Grace at the airport and they'd bring something home for dinner.

Next she called Kendra, who agreed with Dr. Robbins that Emily had been pushing it too hard. She told Emily not to worry, that she'd done an amazing job training Phil, and Kendra had no doubt that everything would go smoothly.

She decided to take a nap and woke a few hours later to the sound of voices in the foyer. Rubbing the sleep from her eyes, she sat up in bed, surprised she'd slept so long.

"Emily?"

"In my room," she called out.

Grace poked her head in the door. "She's decent," she announced as she walked into the room, followed closely by Clint. Grace sat on the edge of the bed and reached out to hug her.

"Darling girl, how are you?"

"I'm okay, Mama G. Just took a nap. Doctor's orders."

"That's good. You've been pushing yourself too hard lately."

"I know, I know. I brought this wretched bed rest on myself."

"It'll do you good to lie about," Clint said sternly.

Grace nodded. "Dad and I will get Baby Girl's room ready."

"I was planning to wow you with my turkey dinner. Who will cook now?"

Grace turned a hard stare on Emily. Despite her confused thoughts and frazzled emotions, Emily chuckled. "I know you can cook it, but I didn't want you to. You're visiting."

"Emily," Grace began in an exasperated tone, "I'm here to help, in any way I can."

"I'm so glad you're here." Emily smiled warmly. "And I have news."

"News?" Clint asked.

"Hope!" Emily called out, waiting for her to hurry into the room.

"What's up?"

"I've finally picked a name for Baby Girl!"

Clint whistled, Grace squealed in delight, and Hope gasped.

"About time!" Hope cheered. "Well, don't keep us in suspense!"

"Sadie Violet."

"Oh, it's lovely," Grace approved, smiling brightly.

Hope nodded. "I agree. It was worth the wait."

"Nice work, kid," Clint said. "I like it. Now point me in the direction of Sadie's room and I'll get to work."

Emily laughed. "I love the way her name sounds. It's definitely the right one."

"Daddy, I'll show you, and then I need to run to the agency for a little bit," Hope said.

"Why?" Emily and Grace asked simultaneously.

"Just some last-minute paperwork I need to finish up before the holiday. I should be back in a couple hours. Do we need anything while I'm out?"

"I bought everything we need for dinner last night, so I think we're good to go," Emily said.

"All right. I'll see you later."

Emily sighed and leaned back against her pillows.

"Can I get you anything, dear?"

"I'm okay, Mama G," Emily grinned. "But I'm already sick of being in bed."

"I'm sure you can lie on the couch, too, if you need a change of scenery."

"I feel bad. I was hoping to go sight-seeing with you."

Grace rose from the bed. "We'll have plenty of time to sight-see once Sadie comes."

Emily nodded. "True."

"How are you doing? I mean really doing?" Grace asked.

Emily closed her eyes. She'd known this conversation was coming.

"I'm good. I have a stable job, a place to live, my independence, and Hope."

"None of those will keep you warm at night. Nor will they be a father for your little girl."

"I know," Emily said softly, wrapping the blanket around her fingers. "I'm not ready."

"Ready or not, the baby is coming. That baby's arrival marks the end of life as you know it."

"I know all of this," Emily said defensively, anger flashing in her eyes.

"You think you know it. But you really don't. Do you really think you're going to be able to work twelve or fourteen hours a day anymore? You think you're going to get eight solid hours of sleep every night? You think you're going to be able to do what you want, when you want?"

"Of course not."

Grace walked over to the bedroom window, staring unseeing at the street below. "He comes to the house every day."

"He came here the other night," Emily said softly.

"He was here?"

Emily nodded. "I sent him away."

"Oh, Emily," Grace said sadly.

Emily sniffed. "I don't know how I could have been so wrong about him. I grew up with him. I lived with him."

"I have my own opinions of what happened that night. I don't think you're giving Jason the fair shake he deserves. Did you at least let him explain?"

"He claims he doesn't remember anything." Emily turned her face away from Grace's prying eyes. "I can do this. I'll be a good mother, and I'll make this work. Sadie will be happy and healthy."

"I know you can do it, and I know you'll be a wonderful mother. I just wonder what will happen to you in the process. What will you lose?"

"Lose?"

"You and Jason belong together, Emily. You always have been together."

"He ruined that. I can't go back."

"That's one of the things you're losing, don't you see? You've banished yourself from your home. You've left the wide open spaces and traded it for the cramped, busy city life. You'll deprive your daughter of it, too."

"I don't understand why you're coming down so hard on me. I'm not the one who cheated. I'm not the one who threw away our future just hours before our wedding."

"Aren't you? All I see here is a woman determined to make it on her own, to forget the love of her life, and to prove to all that she can do it alone. I see a woman who can't swallow her pride long enough to listen to an explanation from a man she professed to love with her whole heart."

"You see a man who actually did wrong and yet you're blaming me!"

"Not the way you think. Jason wasn't the only person you cast out of your life, Emily."

Emily gasped. She never thought of it that way—that she'd not only left Jason but also her family and friends behind. Before she could stop them, tears fell from her eyes, coursing down her cheeks. Her heart broke a little for the pain evident on Grace's face. Pain that would only increase when Sadie arrived and then when Grace had to leave.

"I'm sorry, Mama G."

Grace shook her head. "I'm not looking for apologies. I just want you to open your eyes, Emily. It's not just about you."

Grace sighed and walked over to the bed. Reaching out, she slid her fingertips down Emily's cheek and cupped her chin. "You should rest. I'm gonna go see if your father needs help." She leaned down and kissed the top of Emily's head. "I love you."

"Love you, too, Mama G."

Emily watched her stepmother walk down the hall to Sadie's room. Grace had given her a lot to think about.

Was she scared of being a single mother? She was terrified. Her days would never be the same——replaced with sleepless nights, diaper changes, and feedings, and she was okay with it.

Rubbing her belly, she grinned. She couldn't wait to meet Sadie. Couldn't wait to hold her in her arms. To look into her eyes and know that Sadie was her own little princess. She couldn't wait to rock her to sleep, to bask in her presence and watch her grow.

It would be the end to life as she knew it—Grace was right about that. But it wasn't a life that Emily thought she'd miss. She was looking forward to her new life as a mother too much to mourn the old one.

Chapter Nine

Jason pulled up outside Lila's house and grimaced. As with her own appearance, her home was decorated to impress. Flower pots full of fall mums lined the front steps and her house was already decorated for Christmas. They made the house and its occupant look cheerful and full of Christmas spirit. He knew the truth, though; she was full of anything but Christmas spirit. More like hate and dissension. Although, it cheered him slightly to think that since Santa knew all, Lila was sure to only receive coal this year . . . as she probably had every year of her existence.

He put the truck in park and walked up to the door. Knocking lightly, he waited impatiently for her to answer. He wanted this done and over, and the sooner he could trick her into going with him, the sooner he'd have his answers. The sooner he could move on and forget Lila and her deceptions.

"Jason!" she exclaimed, opening the front door and motioning for him to come in.

"Hi, Lila," he said pleasantly, opting to stay on the front porch. "I was hoping you'd like to go on a drive with me."

"Sure," she said, smiling brightly. "Let me grab my purse and jacket." She turned to get both off the rack behind the door. "I knew you'd come around eventually," she said as she closed and locked her door. "I'm so happy!"

Jason nodded and led the way to his truck. Even though she didn't deserve it, he opened the truck door for her and helped her up inside. It made his skin crawl, but he would do what he had to in order to get her cooperation.

"Where are we going?" Lila asked.

"I thought we could get some lunch, drive around, and talk. Make some plans about our future."

"Oh, Jason! I'm so glad you've come to your senses," Lila gushed, caressing his arm.

Jason faked a bright smile. "I've done some thinking the past few days, and I came to the conclusion that you're probably right. She obviously doesn't love me; otherwise, why would she leave without letting me explain myself? Right? And then I thought, well, Lila's into me and she's right here in Mosquero. Why not give this a chance?"

Lila clasped Jason's free hand in her own and squeezed.

"Where would you like to go to lunch?" Jason asked.

"Let's go crazy and go somewhere special to celebrate," Lila said. "Do you have to be back anytime soon?"

"Nope."

"Let's go to Tucumcari. There are some fabulous restaurants there."

"Great idea, I was hoping you'd want that," Jason smiled shyly. "I made a reservation at Connor's Seafood."

"You didn't!" Lila screeched. "That's my favorite!"

"I know," Jason grinned. "Why do you think I chose it?"

"How did you even know?"

"I have my ways."

"You're so sweet!"

Jason settled into silence while Lila chatted on, making plans for them and building a future Jason knew would never come to fruition. He responded when warranted and let her dig her own grave on the two-hour drive to the restaurant.

After lunch, that's when the fun would begin. He had plans to take her to the OB/GYN office down the street from Connor's and strongly suggest she take a pregnancy test. He'd make sure to put it across to her as if he was concerned for her health and the health of the baby and how good prenatal care shouldn't be avoided. He hoped the lunch, plus the concern, would be enough to get her to agree.

Then, once they knew the results, he'd be able to move on to the next phase. Either cutting her off or somehow getting a DNA test. He hoped and prayed it didn't come to that because he knew that would be harder to accomplish than a simple pregnancy test.

When they pulled into the restaurant parking lot, Jason continued his chivalry and opened the truck door, holding her hand all the way into the restaurant. He gave his name to the hostess, and she seated them right away at a table by the window.

She handed them their menus and told them their server would be right with them.

"I was so busy cleaning my house and doing laundry this morning that I forgot to eat breakfast. I just realized how famished I am!" Lila said.

"Mmm," Jason acknowledged, trying to figure out what would be the least likely to cause him heartburn or nausea. Maybe a meal wasn't the best idea when his stomach was churning with nerves.

"Oh, I think I'll get the salmon salad and a cup of chowder," Lila said, closing her menu. "What looks good to you?"

"I can't decide. It all sounds good."

"I know what you mean. I bet you were up with the sun and have already worked a full day," Lila said soothingly. "You should get the steak and lobster platter and put back some of those calories you burned off this morning."

Jason nodded, but the thought of so much food made his stomach churn even more. If he didn't order and eat it, Lila would know something was up. And he wasn't sure he could pull off the "I'm just nervous" act to explain his not eating.

"It's a good idea, but I think I'm more in the mood for some pasta. It's been a while since I had a meal of carbs."

When the server returned, Lila put in her order and, to Jason's surprise, ordered a glass of white wine.

"Just one to celebrate." Lila winked.

Jason nodded and ordered the seafood pasta, thinking it would have the least effect on his churning stomach, and also requested a glass of wine.

The server brought them their wine and a basket of dinner rolls. Jason raised his glass. "To our future happiness," he said, tapping Lila's glass.

"To us!" Lila corrected. "Finally!" she said as she took a sip of her wine.

The food was delicious; Jason couldn't fault them that. But the service was exceedingly slow. At least, it seemed that way to him. He was about to get up and pretend to use the restroom just so he could talk to the manager about it, but realized if he did, the server or manager might make a special trip to their table and mention it. Plus, he was supposed to be here celebrating with Lila, and she'd be plenty suspicious if he complained. The waiting was driving him nuts though, and when the bill was finally paid, it took all his willpower to let Lila decide when it was time to leave.

"Will you do something for me?" Jason asked, once they were driving out of the parking lot.

"Of course, my love. Anything for you!"

"I have a friend here in town, he's an OB. I don't know who you've been seeing, but Mosquero is tiny and Doc Martin is old. I'm concerned for your health and the health of our baby. Would you mind if we popped in to see him?" Jason clasped her hand and squeezed. "I worry and I want this to work out. Do you mind? It shouldn't take long."

"I doubt we can just walk in to see him," Lila hedged.

"He's a good friend of mine from college. I bet he'd make an exception for me."

Jason could see the wheels in her head turning, trying to figure out whether he was sincere and if there was a way out of this for her. He had a moment of panic when it looked like she was going to decline, but then he saw her face clear as if she didn't think he was trying to trick her and that she didn't have anything to lose.

"Well, I guess we can try. I don't want you to worry and have our afternoon of celebrating ruined."

Jason smiled. "Thanks, Lila."

He drove down the street and, after four blocks, pulled into a parking lot behind a tall brick building. Still pretending to care, he went around to the other side of the truck and helped her down. His hand on the small of her back, he guided her through the doors, across the lobby, and to the elevators.

Jason gave his name to the receptionist and joined Lila in the waiting area. He looked around at all the women in the room, most of them pregnant, and wondered how many more of these visits he'd have to make with her. He hoped this was the first and last.

When their name was called, they followed a nurse back to an exam room. She took Lila to the restroom for a urine sample and stopped at the scale on the way back for a current weight. When Lila entered the room, the nurse took her blood pressure and temperature and then asked Lila a bunch of questions relating to her last menstrual cycle and her current symptoms.

Other than feeling slightly nauseous in the morning and being tired throughout the day, Lila said she felt great most of the time.

The nurse wished them congratulations and left, indicating the doctor would be in soon.

Five minutes later, a knock on the door alerted them to the doctor's presence, and Jason bid him enter.

"Jason! So good to see you," the doctor greeted, holding out his hand.

"Tim, man it's been a while! How's it going?" Jason asked, returning the hand shake.

"Good, good. Getting set up here and loving life. Living the dream, you know?"

Jason nodded, smiling. "Tim, this is Lila. Lila, my friend Tim from college."

Tim shook Lila's hand. "Nice to meet you, Lila."

Thankfully, Jason had had the insight to call Tim ahead of time—not only to set up this appointment but also to tell him the situation. It would have been awkward if Tim had come in expecting Emily and found Lila.

Tim put Lila's chart on the counter and sat down on the stool. He quickly opened the chart and scanned through the information the nurse had gathered, along with the urine sample results. His brow furrowed, he turned to Lila.

"Lila, when did you say your last cycle was?"

"September first," she answered.

"Hm. That would put you at around ten or eleven weeks right now, but the urine sample is negative." Tim stood up and walked over to the examining table. "Lie back, let me do an external exam."

Lila did as she was bid, raising her shirt. Tim palpated her stomach and shook his head.

"I'm not feeling your uterus, and I should be at this point. Would you mind if I did an internal exam?"

Lila glanced at Jason. "I'm scared." She pouted. "Did I lose the baby?"

Jason stood and took the three steps necessary to get to her side. He clasped her hand and gave it a quick squeeze. "There's only one way to find out," he said. "Let Tim examine you and we'll get to the bottom of it."

Lila sighed and nodded.

Tim pushed the button for the nurse. "I need to do an examination on her. Please help her get ready." Turning to them, he pointed at the door. "I'll be back in a moment."

The nurse removed a gown from under the exam table and explained to Lila that she would need to remove all her clothes. Jason followed the nurse out of the room while Lila changed, and Tim was there waiting.

"She's not pregnant," Tim confirmed. "It's as you suspected. I'll do an ultrasound on her, but I already know what I won't find."

Jason's eyes lit with a burning rage. "I knew it," he said, clenching his fists. "Wouldn't she be showing at this point, anyway?"

"Not necessarily, every woman's body is different. Some don't start showing until their sixth month. If Lila were pregnant, she'd still be in the first trimester, and other than feeling tired and sick, most women aren't showing yet. Especially first-time moms."

Jason nodded. "Is it time to go back in?"

Tim nodded and motioned for the nurse to follow with the ultrasound machine. He opened the door and walked inside, followed by Jason and the nurse.

Jason took up his spot next to Lila and reached for her hand. The nurse hooked up the machine and then retrieved a sheet from under the table. She draped it across Lila's belly and legs and then lifted the gown to expose Lila's belly.

"Rather than go through the discomfort of an internal exam, I'm just going to do an ultrasound," Tim explained. "That will tell us all we need to know."

"Um, okay," Lila said uncertainly.

Tim squeezed the jelly on her abdomen and picked up the wand, rubbing it through the jelly.

"Ow!" Lila said, flinching.

"I'm sorry. I'm not seeing anything here."

"What do you mean?" Jason asked.

"I mean, I don't see a baby," he explained, wiping the jelly from the wand and putting it away. He turned to Lila. "Not even any evidence of a recently miscarried baby."

Lila sighed and rolled her eyes. She used the sheet to wipe the jelly off her abdomen and sat up.

"You're clearly not pregnant." Jason flung her hand away from him. "I knew you were playing me from the beginning, Lila. I knew I was too drunk to have done anything with you. And there," he said, pointing at the machine, "is my proof. You're not pregnant, you never were pregnant, and now this little game of yours can be finished."

Lila turned stricken eyes on Jason. "But what about us?"

"There was no us," he explained. "There was just me, trying to get to the bottom of this farce you've created."

"But, Jason, you said you cared and wanted us to work."

Jason shook his head. "Everything I said was to get you to agree to come here so I could prove you were lying."

Realization finally setting in, Lila glared at Jason. "You bastard!"

Shrugging, Jason turned from her. He reached out his hand to Tim. "Thank you, Tim. I really appreciate you fitting us in."

"What?!?!" Lila shrieked. "You set this up?"

Grinning, Jason turned to her. "Of course. The whole day was a setup, Lila."

Lila launched herself at Jason, fingers curled to claws as she raked them down his face. Tim circled his arms around her waist and pulled her off Jason.

Jason touched a finger to his cheek and saw blood on his finger when he looked at it. Nodding, he sighed and cast a pitying glance in Lila's direction. "Ah, there's the Lila we all know and despise."

Tim and the nurse opened the door to the exam room, and Jason followed them out only to stop quick and pop his head back in. "Tim and I are going for a drink. Find your own way home." With that he quickly shut the door and laughed when he heard something land against it.

Jason followed Tim to his office and sat down heavily in the chair. "Thanks, man, I owe you."

Tim shook his head. "Nah, I'm happy to help." He reached inside his desk drawer and pulled out a bottle of Scotch and two glasses.

"I thought that only happened in movies." Jason grinned, indicating the hidden booze. He toasted Tim with his glass before throwing the contents back. It burned its way down his throat, but Jason was glad for it. He needed it and as the Scotch warmed his stomach, a feeling of freedom exploded within him. He was so damned happy the situation with Lila was over.

Tim poured them each another glass, and sitting back against his chair, he studied Jason. "So, what are you going to do about Emily now?"

"I'm going to do my best to get her back."

"How?"

"No idea. But this should help," Jason said, raising the glass.

The nurse came in with cleaning supplies and sat down next to Jason.

Jason shook his head. "I'm all right."

"Let her clean them up. Who knows what kind of poison she has under her nails." Tim laughed.

"Good point," Jason acknowledged and tilted his head so she had better access to clean the wounds.

Forty-five minutes later, Jason practically skipped out of the office building to his truck. Slamming the door shut, he rolled down the windows to get rid of Lila's perfumey smell that had been trapped in there all day.

Relief flowed through him along with a new sense of purpose. He'd conquered one battle. But he still had the war to get through. It was time for him to finalize his plan of attack to win the love of his life back.

Chapter Ten

Two weeks later

Emily was beginning to wonder if Sadie would ever make an appearance. She was two days late and exhausted. Stepping from the shower onto the cold tile floor, she reached for her towel when she felt a trickle of something running down her legs. "Grace? Unless I just peed myself, I think we'd better head to the hospital!" As soon as the last word was out of her mouth, a flood erupted from her body, creating a puddle around her freshly showered feet.

"Okay, darling, stay calm," Grace soothed, rushing into the bathroom. "First babies usually take their time," Grace explained, guiding Emily into the bedroom.

"It couldn't have happened just thirty seconds earlier while I was still standing in the shower?" Emily asked as she started to pull on her clothes.

"Where's your Go Bag?"

"In the closet. My phone and charger are here, and my purse should be in the foyer." Emily pulled her hair into a bun and waddled out to the living room. "Do you feel comfortable to drive or should I call a taxi?"

"Let's call a taxi so I can focus on you during the ride."

"Sounds good to me. Ready?" Emily asked.

"As we'll ever be," Grace grinned.

At the hospital, they were first seen by a doctor who didn't seem older than a teenager to Emily.

"You're only three centimeters dilated so far," the young doctor announced.

When Dr. Robbins finally arrived, an hour later—thanks to another baby who decided to show up four weeks early—she did her own exam. "You're still at three centimeters, Emily. I think it might be a long night." She smiled.

"Are there any concerns about the preeclampsia?" Emily asked, twisting the blankets in her fingers.

"Yes. We want to keep you safe, which is why we've got the blood pressure cuff on to automatically check your numbers. And the fetal monitor will tell us if Baby Girl is under any stress."

"Can I get up and walk around once the pains start?"

"I'd rather you didn't. I don't want another excuse for your blood pressure to go up."

When Dr. Robbins slipped out, Emily rested her head against the pillows and closed her eyes. There was no pain yet, and she figured she'd better get some rest now.

Grace walked over and placed a cool cloth on Emily's forehead. Emily smiled and reached for Grace's hand. "I love you, Mama G."

Just then, pain, unlike anything she'd ever known, ripped across her stomach. Gasping for air and clutching the blankets, she panicked. Alarms started to sound, the noise doing little to calm Emily down.

Grace shot to her feet and grabbed Emily's hand. "Breathe, Emily. In through your nose and out through your mouth."

Emily sucked in air and let out a whimper as the contraction subsided.

The nurse barged into the room. "What's going on?"

"I think Emily had her first real contraction," Grace told the nurse.

The nurse took Emily's vitals, checked the printout on the fetal monitor, and set the blood pressure cuff to start. Three seconds after the cuff started to constrict, another contraction ripped across Emily's stomach.

"Ahhh!" Emily yelled.

Grace got up on the bed and sat behind Emily. Pulling Emily against her body, she spoke firmly into Emily's ear. "Breathe, Emily."

Grace glanced up at the nurse and mouthed the words requesting Dr. Robbins's presence now. The nurse nodded and quickly left the room.

Grace poured some of the ice water on a washcloth from the bedside table. She held it to the back of Emily's neck for a few seconds and then moved it to Emily's forehead. Back and forth she went until the next contraction.

Emily squeezed Grace's hand and the bed railing, bending and raising her legs. "I want to push," Emily moaned.

"Not yet. Wait for the doctor."

"I can't!" Emily yelled.

A few minutes later, Dr. Robbins walked into the room. "Doctor, please," Emily begged. "I have to . . . Owwww!" Another contraction ripped its way across her abdomen. Gritting her teeth, she couldn't wait another second. Bearing down, she pushed with all her strength and shrieked with the effort.

"Emily!" Dr. Robbins yelled. "Stop pushing!" She stuck her head between Emily's legs while the nurse called out the blood pressure numbers from the past thirty minutes. She quickly and gently checked Emily's progression. "You aren't fully dilated, Emily. You have to stop pushing or you'll rupture."

"It hurts," Emily wailed. "Oh God, it hurts!" she screamed as another contraction took hold.

"Doctor, this isn't normal. What's wrong?" Grace asked urgently.

Dr. Robbins put her hands on Emily's belly to feel the position of the baby and then checked the fetal monitor print out.

"I'm going to set up an O.R. The baby is in distress, and we need to get the baby out. I'll be right back."

Dr. Robbins rushed out of the room, and the nurse began to prep Emily for surgery. "Ma'am, I need you to get off the bed," the nurse said kindly to Grace.

"Mommy!" Emily shrieked. "Oh God! Please make it stop!" Emily hunched over her belly, hoping the new position would lessen the pain. One second it felt as if she was being torn apart from the inside out and the next there was nothing but sweet oblivion from the pain. Emily sighed with relief and turned her head to the man sitting beside her. "Who are you?" she asked in a hoarse whisper.

"Dr. Stark. I'm your anesthesiologist."

"She's looking a little green, Stark," Dr. Robbins said.

Dr. Stark whipped a bowl in front of Emily's face to catch the vomit just as Grace walked into the O.R. She raced to Emily's side.

"Is she okay?"

"Yes," Dr. Stark assured her. "It's a fairly common reaction to the anesthesia."

Grace stood by Emily's head and held her hand. "I'm here, darling," she whispered in her ear.

"Emily?" the doctor asked.

"Hmmm?" She smiled up at her.

"I'm going to start now. You're numb from the chest down. Can you feel this?"

Emily felt a slight tugging but no pain. She shook her head and closed her eyes. "Whatever you say, Dr. R. I trust you." Emily smiled, eager to meet her precious daughter. Dr. Robbins nodded and got to work.

The next thing Emily heard was the sweet, sweet sound of her daughter's cry. "Sadie?"

"Indeed she is," Dr. Robbins announced happily. "You have yourself a beautiful daughter."

Dr. Robbins raised Sadie over the barrier, and Emily smiled. "Can I hold her?"

"For just a couple seconds," she said, placing Sadie on Emily's chest before closing up Emily's incision.

Emily felt her heart explode with love as she gazed at her daughter. "Oh, you're so perfect," Emily said softly. She trailed a finger along Sadie's cheek and circled the impossibly tiny ear. What a miracle.

This tiny, perfect human belonged with Emily. She was Emily's special gift from God. A gift she'd never take for granted. She fell in love with her princess at first sight. Nothing and no one would ever come between them.

A nurse came to collect Sadie, and Emily's arms tightened involuntarily when the nurse tried to take her. "No, not yet. Please?" Emily pleaded.

"I'm sorry. I'll bring her back in a couple of minutes."

Emily forced herself to relinquish Sadie.

"She's beautiful, Emily. You did amazing," Grace gushed.

"She's perfect, Mama G."

At this moment, she didn't know what the future held in regards to her friends or family, her new life in Boston, or even with Jason. What she did know, though, was that her heart belonged to Sadie, and she made a promise to God, right then, to love, cherish, and protect the miracle gift He had bestowed on her.

*****

"She's resting now. The baby, oh my gosh, the baby! Sadie is just beautiful, Jason," Grace gushed.

"Do you have a picture?"

"Yes, I'll send it right now. I don't know why I didn't think of that sooner!"

"I'm online now and there's a flight, a red-eye, tonight. I have plenty of time to make the flight."

"What time does it arrive in the morning?"

"A little after nine."

"That will work. I can pick you up on my way to the hospital."

"I'll be a mess. Maybe I should catch a cab, get cleaned up at the hotel, and then make my way to the hospital?"

"If you'd rather, that would be fine."

"I think so. I don't want to look like a bum when I see my daughter for the first time."

Grace laughed. "Fair enough."

"Oh, Grace, she really is beautiful," Jason said with awe.

"I know. Just wait till you see her in person. And hold her. She's darling. Just the most perfect thing ever."

"I wish I was already there." He sighed. "See you tomorrow."

"Fly safe."

"Oh, Grace," Jason said quickly before she had a chance to hang up.

"Yes?"

"Thank you." He hoped she understood. She was his lifeline, his partner in crime, even though she didn't have to be. Her allegiance was to Em, but she was helping him. He owed her more than he'd ever be able to repay.

"You're welcome."

Jason hung up, a huge smile stretched across his face. He had a baby girl. She was finally here, healthy and safe. He couldn't wait to see her.

And he couldn't wait to see Emily. He prayed this would be the boost he needed to win her back.

Chapter Eleven

"Landed," Jason texted to Grace. "See you in about 2 hrs. Less if I can manage it. Will text when I get to hospital."

He'd carried his luggage on so he didn't have to wait around for baggage claim. As soon as the plane stopped, he unbuckled and stood. He reached above his head and brought down his suitcase. Glancing at the little old lady he'd had the *pleasure* of sitting next to the whole way from Santa Fe, he reached up again and brought down her carpet bag. Not even kidding, straight out of *Mary Poppins*, she carried it with two hands.

He put his book in the front pocket of his suitcase and put his phone and headphones in his front pocket. He'd sure gotten his money's worth out those headphones by listening to music and pretending he didn't notice the little old lady's attempts at conversation. He'd obliged her for the first half hour of the flight, but when she'd gotten up to use the restroom—a total of ten times!—he'd put those babies in his ears and done his best to tune her out. He pulled out his wallet to double-check he had his driver's license and, once satisfied, put his wallet back in his pocket and waited for his turn to deplane.

Ever the gentlemen, he waited for the little old lady to walk out in front of him and cursed his manners as he had to walk behind her extremely slow gait the whole way up the Jetway. Once out into the terminal, he double-timed his pace and rushed outside to hail a cab to the hotel. He gave the cabbie the address to his hotel, not far from the airport, and settled back into the seat to take in the scenery. Only his second trip to Boston, it was still new to him and took his breath away. The ocean blew his mind. It was incredible and he was in awe of the beauty of it. The dark blue water, the disappearing horizon, the ships, some of them massive but yet gliding gracefully across the choppy surface. It was an overcast day, much different than the bright sunny day during his first visit, and he was amazed at the difference in the shade of the water color.

Ten minutes later, the cabbie pulled up in front of his hotel. He paid his fare and jumped out of the cab, dragging his suitcase behind him. Once checked in, he rushed across the foyer and hopped on the elevator. He barely cast a glance about his room. He deposited his suitcase on the nearest bed, removed his toiletry bag and a change of clothes, and hurried into the bathroom to shower, shave, and get dressed.

Thirty minutes later, clean, refreshed, and clean-cut, he slipped out of the room and made the journey back to the lobby. It was then he realized he had no idea where he was supposed to go. What hospital were they at?

He pulled out his phone and texted Grace. "Where am I going? What hospital?"

He waited for what seemed like forever before Grace replied.

"Oops, that would be helpful, huh? Brigham & Women's Hospital - 75 Francis St."

"Thanks! OMW!"

A short ride later, he pulled up outside the hospital entrance. Not wanting to show up empty-handed, he ducked inside the gift shop and found a beautiful Christmas cactus, in full bloom, for Emily. He thought it would be better than his usual bouquet of flowers, something that wouldn't die after a week, and something, other than their daughter, to remember this special day by.

He chose a small pink and white teddy bear for Sadie. It had the year stitched into the foot and a bright yellow bow around its neck. Its long fur was as soft as an angora sweater.

After paying for his purchases, he went to the info desk and asked for directions to the maternity ward. He was surprised to find a high level of security awaiting him. Gone were the days when anyone could venture to the nursery and moon over the babies. Nope, now it was a lot like trying to get into Fort Knox.

After showing his ID, calling Grace down to vouch for him, signing a form, having his picture taken, and then being issued his own hospital ID, he was finally on his way to meet his daughter.

"Emily's showering and then her doctor should be in to check her incision. Sadie's in the nursery, so let's go see her first."

"Works for me," he replied, slowing his gait to match Grace's. No need to rush now that he was here. "How's Em doing?"

"She's sore, as expected. The birth was hard, and no one was expecting an emergency C-section to be necessary. She'll have a longer recovery time now."

"Are you planning on staying?"

"Yes, as long as she'll have me."

"You know she'll have you forever." Jason smiled.

"I know, but how long do you think Clint can manage without me?"

Jason nodded. They stopped in front of the nursery windows, and Jason scanned all the bassinets. Grace had texted a picture of Sadie to him, but he couldn't distinguish one baby from another—other than to know the pink hats were girls and the blue hats were boys.

"There she is." Grace pointed.

Jason followed her finger and saw a baby with a polka-dot pink and white hat. His heart skipped a beat and then melted into a puddle at his feet. There she was, *his* baby girl. Sadie. She was the most precious and beautiful thing he'd ever laid eyes on.

"Can I hold her?" he breathed, not wanting to take his eyes off her.

"Not here," she replied, patting his back. "Rules and regulations. You have to wait until we're in Emily's room."

"Will Em even let me in?"

"Good question. I haven't told her you're here, yet."

"Of course not, I just got here."

"No, I mean, I haven't told her you're here. In Boston."

"Graaaaace," Jason exclaimed. He swung his eyes to her face and stared hard.

Raising her hands in defense, she shushed him. "Surprise, Jason. We need the element of surprise."

He shook his head. "Uh, uh—she's going to be pissed."

"Probably," she agreed. "But this is the best way, trust me. She won't have had time to think about it, won't have had time to come up with excuses or a chance to forbid your presence here."

"This seems wrong," he hedged.

"It'll be fine. I'll make sure you get to stay at least long enough to hold your baby girl. I promise." She smiled and squeezed his arm. "Let me go down and see how she's coming along. Stay here and ogle your baby."

He nodded and watched her walk away, knowing this was the wrong path but unable to stop the hurricane that was Grace Camancho.

He turned back to the window and placed a hand on the glass. It made him feel closer to Sadie, and until he got to hold her, it was as close as he could get.

She looked impossibly tiny in the bassinet, despite being swaddled. The blankets seemed to swallow her up, just her tiny face was visible. And that cute hat. He looked around, no other child had a hat like it, so he figured either Grace or Emily brought it with them from home.

He stood like a statue, staring at this baby. He couldn't wait to hold her. He hoped Emily would let him stay so he could get to know the baby. There wasn't much happening around the ranch right now, so he could stay indefinitely. The only request his father had made was for lots of pictures to be sent his way. Sadie was his only grandchild, and it bothered him greatly that there was so much distance between where she would be growing up and where he lived.

No, Jason's mistake hadn't only ruined his life. It had rippled out too many others'. Jason was all his father had left, and Joe had been over the moon about the wedding and the baby. His wish had been for Em to have lots of babies and she'd seemed to be on board with that wish.

But then he'd gone and gotten piss drunk with the guys and Lila had happened. He hadn't lost control like that since. A beer or two with dinner or while out with the guys was all he would allow himself.

Argh. Would Em ever forgive him? He was betting on no but wishing on yes.

"She's just finishing up with the doctor," Grace said, breaking him out of his reverie. "Let's sign Sadie out of the nursery and bring her down to the room so you can hold your little darling."

"Maybe you should give her a little warning."

"She doesn't need a warning. And besides, I've just had an epiphany." She grinned hugely. "You're this baby's father. You don't need permission to be here."

He felt like his eyes were getting a workout with all the eye rolling he was doing today. He loved Grace, he really did, but sometimes he wondered whether he should even listen to her advice.

But it didn't matter now anyway because they were at Emily's door, and Grace was opening the door and walking through, pushing the bassinet.

He held the bear and the cactus in front of him, a peace offering of sorts. It wasn't what he wanted the gifts to be, but he had a feeling he was going to have to use them as such.

She didn't notice him at first as she only had eyes for Sadie. He was glad for it as it gave him a chance to drink her in. She certainly didn't look like a woman who'd just given birth, and a difficult one at that. Her hair shone in the fluorescent lighting, she wore a light application of makeup and had on a stretchy pink tank top and a pair of black yoga pants. Her toenails were painted a bright and cheerful pink.

As she held Sadie, her face was a picture to behold, full of awe and gratitude. She stroked one finger down the baby's face, across her nose, and down the other side. She traced Sadie's ear and gently caressed her bald head. She tucked her finger inside Sadie's hand and placed a sweet and gentle kiss on her forehead.

When she glanced up, he could see tears in her eyes and just like that, the moment was gone.

"What are you doing here?" she growled. "Mama G, did you know he was here?"

"Of course I knew, I invited him. Not that he needed an invitation, mind you. He is the father, after all."

"I don't want him here." She turned her eyes to him and glared. "I don't want you here."

"I came to see the baby, Em. Our baby."

Her eyes went to slits, and he knew, if she weren't holding the baby, she would have launched herself at him.

"Get out," she hissed. The baby must have sensed Emily's distress because she began to fuss. "Now look what you've done."

"He hasn't done anything," Grace chided. "She's reacting to your emotions. Calm yourself down and the baby will relax."

"I'll calm myself down once he's out of here."

"He's not going anywhere, and you're going to grow up. You're a mother now, stop acting like the baby you're holding." Grace gently took Sadie out of Emily's arms and walked her over to Jason.

"Uh," he mumbled, trying to decide what to do with the gifts he'd brought.

"Set them on the table over there and then have a seat. It's time you met your daughter."

"Mama G," Emily began.

"Hush, child. He's traveled a long way. It's his turn."

Emily huffed and leaned back against her bed. She folded her arms against her chest and glared at her lap.

"Support her head," Grace instructed. "There ya go. Just hold her gently, close to your body. You got it." She removed her hands and stepped back, a bright smile lighting her face. "You're a natural."

"Oh, I don't know about that. This is awkward, to say the least."

He stared down at her face and had an urge to trace Sadie's face, just as he'd seen Em doing moments before. Unable to help himself, he was surprised at how soft her skin was. And her head wasn't completely bald; she had the fairest peach fuzz he'd ever seen. Her eyes were a deep, dark blue, and he secretly hoped they'd stay that way.

She stopped fussing and stared at him for the longest time, and he reveled in it. She was so precious. He couldn't get over how tiny and perfect she was. He could sit here forever just holding her. She closed her eyes and turned her face into his chest.

And that was what did it. He completely lost his heart for the third time in his life. This tiny baby, less than two days old, had completely and irrevocably stolen his heart and wrapped it around her impossibly tiny finger.

He glanced up at Em. "She's . . . she's just . . . I can't even."

She offered a small smile. "I know."

Chapter Twelve

June 2010

18 months later

It was noon, and even though Emily had a to-do list a mile long, she took a break to call her sister. Hope was due home at the end of the week, having been away for a modeling shoot the last two weeks. Opening her grilled chicken salad at her desk, she dialed her sister's number.

"Hello?"

"Hey, Hope, how's it going?"

"The shoot is going fine, and we're on schedule. Here's hoping we stay that way!"

"That's great. We miss you."

"I miss you guys, too. Anything new?"

"Nah, same stuff, different day." She took a bite of her salad. "Are you okay? You don't sound quite yourself."

"Derek called."

Emily groaned quietly, praying Hope had *finally* made a decision where her long-term boyfriend was concerned.

"I told him I was out of town for the week," Hope said smugly.

"What are you going to do?"

"I don't know. He's a nice guy, and I really like him. I probably even, you know, L-O-V-E," she whisper-spelled, "him. But I just don't think I'm quite there yet."

"You can't leave him hanging much longer, Hope. You have to give him an answer, one way or the other."

"I know."

"Can you see spending the rest of your life without him?"

"I don't know."

"Hope," she said sternly. Hope's problem was she continuously held out hope that something better, bigger, and brighter would come along. She never settled for anything. But in this case, Emily didn't see how anyone better could come along. Derek was a grounding influence on Hope, and everyone could see that Hope was in love with him. Emily's fear was Hope was going to make the wrong choice and end up miserable. Emily knew Derek wasn't the type who would welcome Hope back when she realized her mistake.

"I know, Em," Hope whined. "I'm just scared. So scared."

"Scared of what?"

"What if I make the wrong choice?"

"He loves you, he treats you like a princess, and he's so good for you. It's your life, but I think you're making a huge mistake by waiting and considering saying no. He won't stick around, Hope. If you tell him no, he'll walk away and that will be that."

"You really think so?"

"Yes. If you tell him no, there won't be a second chance."

"You make him sound like an Alpha with no heart."

"Honey, he is an Alpha. You just don't see it because he treats you so well. Have you never seen the look in his eyes when you're out together? The man shoots laser daggers at any man who looks at you."

"That's ridiculous!"

Emily laughed. "It's the truth. It's a love that will carry you through anything."

"I should call him."

"Yes, you should. Ask him to pick you up from the airport, and when I see you on Friday, there better be a ring on your finger!"

"Okay," Hope squealed with excitement. "Oh my God. I'm going to do it. Oh shit! I'm getting engaged. Emily, I'm freaking out!"

"You don't say?" Emily laughed.

"Okay, okay. I need to chill. I still have so much work to get done."

"I'll let you go," Emily said. "I'm so happy for you, Hope!"

"Thanks, Em. See you Friday!"

Emily hung up and tried to settle herself. She truly was happy for Hope, but a part of her was envious, too. Would it ever be her turn?

Ten seconds later, the phone rang and Emily smiled when she saw her best friend's name on the caller ID. "Hi, Gina."

"Are you okay?"

"Yeah, glad to hear your voice. How are you?"

"Good, but enough about me. What's with the melancholy I hear in your voice?"

"Oh nothing. Just a lot of my mind."

"Like . . . ?" she prompted.

"I have a lot going on at work, Hope's probably getting engaged on Friday, I'm debating letting Sadie go out and stay with Jason during Labor Day weekend."

"Whoa, I don't even know where to start with all of that."

"I know."

"I guess I'll start with the exciting part. Hope's getting engaged?"

"I hope so. She's scared to commit, scared she'll make the wrong decision. But he loves her and she loves him. And if she waits too much longer, he'll be dust."

"Holy crap. I'm so happy for her."

"Me, too. Probably means Sadie and I need to start looking for our own place though."

"Speaking of," Gina hinted, "maybe you should move home. Less to decide regarding Sadie and Jason if you're already here."

"Ha. You know I couldn't live so close to him."

"No one says you have to live with your parents."

"I think even being in the same town would be too much. Seeing him at the bank, grocery store, gas station. No thank you."

"Hasn't enough time passed? It's been two years."

"I know exactly how long it's been, right down to the second. But I dream of him, still. My body longs for his touch. My heart yearns for his love. I can't live there with those feelings still swirling around."

"I hate the distance. And I know you do, too, but I just wish things were different."

"Me, too."

"You're sure it wasn't just a misunderstanding?"

Emily snorted. "It's hard to imagine his tongue down her throat being a misunderstanding."

"Maybe we could run him out of town? Phoebe and I can do pretty amazing things once we put our mind to it," Gina said. Phoebe was the fourth of their group and the most eccentric of them all.

"You'd have to run *her* out of town, too. I'd probably kill her if I laid eyes on her."

"I haven't seen her in a few weeks. I wonder if she's been in Boston."

"Wouldn't know."

"Fred said she called into the station last week. He wouldn't tell me why, though."

"Probably something petty." Emily paused to take a sip of her Dr. Pepper. "So, how're things with Fred?"

"Freaking fantastic," she gushed. "Well, when I see him anyway. He's been picking up some extra shifts at the station to make up the time he took off for the wedding and honeymoon."

"Have you decided whether you're gonna start a family right away or wait?"

"No. He still wants to start now; I want to wait. I don't even know why. I just know that I want, *need*, a little time first. I want to enjoy being married, enjoy having the house to ourselves, before we start filling it with the pitter-patter of little feet."

"Well, whatever happens, I know you'll both be wonderful parents."

"Thanks." Gina paused and then released a sigh. "Okay, I'm just going to come out with it. I can't hold it back anymore."

Emily grinned and, shooting to her feet in excitement, shouted into the phone. "Oh my God! You're pregnant already!"

"Uh, no. That's not it, so settle down," Gina said matter-of-factly. "I bumped into Jason Friday night. Phoebe and I were at The Dustbowl and he was there with the guys. When Phoebe went to the restroom, he came over."

"I hope you told him to go to Hell," Emily said firmly, dropping down into her chair.

"You know I didn't," Gina admonished. "Anyway, he asked how you and Sadie were doing. Wondered if you've thawed yet. I think he might be contemplating another trip east."

"Not necessary. I haven't changed my mind."

"Em . . ."

"Tyler says he's dating her," she said derisively.

"More like she stalks him and shows up wherever he's at," Gina said with heat. "She showed up at The Dustbowl and spent the whole night throwing herself at him while he tried to avoid her at all costs."

Emily snorted her disbelief, but if it had been anyone else telling her this, she would have laughed in their face. "He was probably putting on a show for you." She wrapped the cord around her finger and sat back in her chair. "Tyler saw them in Tucumcari a couple of months ago. They were walking down the street hand-in-hand."

Gina groaned. "I don't know what that was, but I'm sure it's another case of not what you think."

"You really think that?"

"You're too hard on him." She drew in a deep breath and continued, "Listen, we're best friends, and of course I'm on your side, if that's what you want to call it, but he's miserable and he wants you back."

"I can't, Gina," Emily said, wrapping a lock of hair around her finger. "It would hurt too much to see him." She paused to gather herself. She didn't want to cry, hated to cry, had promised herself she wouldn't shed another tear over him. "He should have thought about that before he played tonsil hockey with Lila," Emily scoffed.

"He loves you," Gina said simply.

"Marriage has made you soft," Emily said. "And you know how I feel about this whole thing. Sure, he's miserable—because he got caught. The only thing that surprises me is the fact that he's still trying to get me back."

"He loves you," Gina repeated.

"Yeah, you keep saying." Emily sighed. "I think you're just seeing the world through newly wedded love-tinted sunglasses."

"Maybe."

Emily's voice broke. "It was the night before our wedding, Gina. The. Night. Before." She enunciated each word, putting a fine point on the end. What was it about this situation that no one seemed to understand? "What if you'd caught Fred kissing someone the night before your wedding?"

Gina sighed into the phone. "I don't know. Maybe I would I have barged into the room and demanded an explanation right there."

Emily laughed harshly. "But that's you to a tee."

"Yeah, that's true. Listen, just give it some thought. Think for a minute that maybe you walked in at just the wrong moment. Maybe *she* was kissing *him* and not the other way around."

"You think I haven't thought of that in all this time? I know how she is. I've seen her operate. And that thought has crossed my mind. But why wasn't he pushing her away? Why didn't he step back and tell her off?"

"He was drunk, Em. He'd just gotten back from the bachelor party. I'm sure his reflexes weren't the best."

Emily groaned. "Let's just drop this."

"Fine."

"I don't want to fight, Gina."

"I know, but sometimes you're just so stubborn."

"How's married life?" she asked, trying to change the subject.

"You already asked me, but we'll do this again. And don't think this conversation is over, either. Anyway, married life is great and Fred is wonderful," Gina replied in a singsong voice.

"Have you christened every room of the house yet?"

"Like three times already!"

"Better be careful or that five-year plan is gonna go out the window!"

"Ha, says you. We're careful, and I'm going to get an IUD put in next week."

"I thought you already had one?"

"I did, but they're only good for five years. It's time for another one."

"I didn't know that. Huh, learn something new every day."

"I'm getting the eye from Fred. Think I need to go," Gina said, giggling. "Stop, no tickling!"

Emily grinned as Gina's giggling turned into peals of laughter. She was so pleased Gina had found someone to make her happy. "All right, go have fun. Talk to you later!"

"Bye," Gina said breathlessly.

Hanging up, Emily sighed wistfully. Oh to be in love and carefree. She finished her salad and went to the kitchen to refill her water mug. Returning to her desk, she tried to push the envy she felt for her sister and best friend out of her heart. She had so much work to accomplish, but as hard as she tried, she couldn't dislodge it. Packing up her briefcase, she decided to take an extended lunch break. She had a few things to pick up from the store, and then she thought she would treat herself to the fabulous view at the apartment and work from home for the rest of the day.

Chapter Thirteen

He drove into town for his weekly errand run, driving on autopilot, his mind on what more he could do to win back Em's heart.

For her birthday this year, he'd sent tickets to the ballet, *Onegin.* He had heard through the grapevine that she really enjoyed going to shows like that and tried to attend them as often as possible. When he'd researched the shows playing, this one had called out to him. So he'd read the background and, with more than a little devil in his eyes, bought the tickets. The ballet was about love triangles, unrequited love, and the hard lessons learned from it. He'd hoped she'd find the humor in what he'd done, but other than thanking him and telling him she'd enjoyed the show, she hadn't mentioned anything else about it.

For Christmas, he'd sent her a necklace with hers and Sadie's birthstones inside an eternity symbol. And again, though she'd thanked him for the gift, that had been all there was to it.

He was hoping one of these times something would help him break through the ice and get her to acknowledge him and his efforts. A few months ago, Grace told him that Em was stressed out—between work, Hope being out of town again, and Sadie being a typical toddler—Emily was at her wit's end. So he'd phoned their babysitter and set up a spa day for her over the upcoming weekend. But she'd canceled the babysitter and had yet to put the spa day package to use, saying things at work had come up and she hadn't been able to get away.

He sighed and parked outside the florist shop. He sat in his truck for a moment, wondering if he should even bother. He couldn't figure out where the negative feelings were coming from. Maybe just frustration. Maybe because he missed her. Missed Sadie. Maybe because he wanted to turn back time, not go out with the guys for his bachelor party, and be in a completely different spot in his life. He shook his head. He couldn't give up now. Maybe this would be the thing that made her realize he was sorry.

He opened the door and got out of his truck. He fed the meter and looked up, right into the eyes of the person who'd made his life a living hell.

"Hi, sugar," Lila said, sidling up to him and resting her hand on his arm. "Missed you at the bar this weekend."

He ground his teeth together. "Lila." He pulled away from her hand and started toward the florist shop.

"You don't have to buy me flowers." She giggled. "You're more than enough."

"They aren't for you."

"It's too bad."

Falling for the bait, he turned toward her. "What's too bad?"

"That you feel like you have to resort to this kind of thing. She should just love you for you," she looked down at her feet and whispered coyly, "I do."

He closed his eyes and tried to count to ten. But all he could envision was strangling her. He jumped when he opened his eyes and found her a hair's breadth away from him. She moved quickly and silently.

"It could be great with us," she purred. "I don't require strings, Jason. Just you."

"Lila, I've said this before. I'm not interested. Not in you. Not in the future you think you'd have with me. Not with anything to do with you. Not interested."

"I'm a patient woman, Jason. I'll wait as long as I need to."

He rolled his eyes and turned his back on her. He strode into the florist shop and tried to put Lila and her craziness out of his mind.

"She still annoying you?" the clerk asked, nodding toward the front windows.

He nodded and glanced over his shoulder. He let out a deep breath of annoyance when he saw she was leaning up against his truck. "Martie, this town is too small. I can't get away from her."

"Looks like she's waiting for you."

"She's going to be waiting a long time. Not interested."

She laughed. "What'll it be this week?"

"Roses, I think. Those thornless, purple ones. Two dozen."

"Anything for the little girl?"

"Nah, I have something for her already."

"How old is she now?"

"Eighteen months."

"No kidding? Really?"

"Yeah, can you believe it? Time is flying by too fast."

"Come back to me when she's getting married and having her own babies. Being a grandparent is the best way to see time fly by." Martie chuckled.

Jason inwardly cringed at the thought of Sadie having her own babies but laughed with Martie. She was a sweet woman. She ran the florist shop in town with her husband. She tended the stop and he worked the flowers. They had their own greenhouse in the back of the shop and they lived above it.

"I see the look of fear in your eyes. Savor all the moments because she'll be grown and having her own babies before you know it," she said wistfully. "Sometimes I wish we could travel back in time to our favorite moments. And those moments we don't remember anymore. The ones you tell yourself you'll never forget, but after a time, they fade away to nothing."

"I already have some of those."

"I bet you do. And you'll have more before it's said and done. Even now, with the boys all grown and married— I still have moments with them that fade to dust." She finished filling out the order form and passed it across the counter for him to review.

"Looks good," he said, barely glancing at it.

"They'll be delivered tomorrow."

"Perfect." He handed her his credit card, signed the slip, and tipped his hat in her direction. "Thank you, Martie."

"Anytime, cowboy. See you next week."

He nodded. "You know it." He walked out the door and ignored Lila. Turning, he headed for the bank. It didn't take long for her to catch up to him.

"Wait up," she huffed.

"I have things to do," he growled. "I don't have the time, nor the inclination, to wait for you." He increased his stride and hoped he could just outpace her. She wouldn't get the hint; she was too obtuse for that. But if he could outpace her, then he wouldn't have to listen to her.

When he reached the bank, he didn't even glance at her. He opened the door and walked inside. He knew his mother would be rolling in her grave because he didn't hold the door open for her. But he didn't consider her a lady and thought if his mother knew exactly what he was dealing with, she'd maybe let it slide. But on the off chance she wouldn't, he silently apologized to her, God rest her soul.

He stood in line, waiting for his turn. Lila waved to him as she walked into the back. He assumed she'd been on her lunch break, and he breathed a sigh of relief that her break was over. He'd be able to get the rest of his errands done without her tagging along. If he thought a restraining order would do any good, and wouldn't embarrass him in the process, he'd head over to the Sheriff's office right now and get it done.

He knew people in town saw her with him. Knew she did it on purpose. Knew she used the town gossipmongers to her benefit. Knew that Emily was aware every time he was seen with Lila and knew that each of those instances were taken out of context. But, in a way, it didn't matter because Emily saw what she wanted to see. And all she saw was Jason with Lila.

Once out on the sidewalk, he stood for a moment, staring out at the open fields across the street. It was time to try to visit Boston again. He was running out of ideas on how to fix this. She continued to keep him at arm's length, and it drove him crazy. If he went, he'd be able to count on Em not spending any time with him. And that would suck, but he had a bright shining light at the end of that particular tunnel. He'd get a lot of one-on-one time with Sadie.

He could take her to the aquarium, and they'd spend some time at the park. There was so much to see and do, he and Sadie never got bored. Well, he never got bored. She was still a little young for most of the things. But she loved the park and would toddle around for hours on the equipment.

Mind made up, he finished the rest of his errands and headed back out to the ranch. He was walking up the steps to the house when his father came around the corner.

"Cows getting out somehow. Clint's foreman just called and said they had three of ours in their back forty."

"Great, there goes the rest of my day."

"Probably the rest of your week." Joe laughed.

"Hopefully not. I was just gonna go inside and make arrangements to go to Boston for a few days."

Joe shook his head. "Do you really think this time will be different?"

"No."

"Waste of time."

"I get to see Sadie, at the very least."

"Bring the child out here for a visit. Just fly out, pick her up, and bring her back." Joe kicked at the dirt in the driveway. "I'd like to see my first and only grandchild in person, at least once before she's all grown up."

"That's a great idea, Dad. I'll call her tomorrow and run it by her."

"How can she say no? And don't let her."

Jason nodded. "I'm gonna head out and see about those cows."

He went to the barn and saddled his horse. He could take the four-wheeler, but he felt the need for horseback. He needed simple. He needed peace and quiet. He needed to think.

Chapter Fourteen

"You have one new voicemail message. Emily, it's Jason. Just checking in. Hope you and Sadie are doing well. Call me when you can. I love you, Em. Always."

Emily leaned her head against the back of the couch and closed her eyes. Every message ended the same. I love you. She didn't believe him. In her opinion, he said it out of habit, a last-ditch attempt to win back her affections. Life would be much easier, for everyone involved, if he'd just stop. She wasn't interested, and rumor had it he was seeing the very reason they'd split in the first place.

"Sadie!" she called. "Come FaceTime with Daddy." She smiled when she heard her daughter toddle down the hall. It was past dinner time, closing in on bath and bedtime. She'd been working long days to finish a project that was due at the end of the week, so they hadn't spent a lot of time together lately. Emily was planning to rectify that this weekend with a special trip to Splash!, an outdoor water park.

Emily had worked her way up, rather quickly, to lead designer. She'd interviewed for the position when she'd first moved to Boston and she loved her job. Her boss, Kendra, was a dream to work for, and she enjoyed the freedom that Kendra gave her to make the clients happy. The firm was bursting with work and Emily was busy all the time, and while she loved her job, she sometimes resented how it got in the way of spending valuable time with her daughter.

Sadie didn't seem to mind, but then she didn't know any different. This was the only life she knew. Sadie had daycare, she had her friends, and usually she had either Emily or Hope. Hope, who had accepted Derek's proposal and was now slowly freaking out about planning a wedding. Mama G wanted Hope to get married in New Mexico, but Hope wanted it in Boston. The possibilities for locations were endless, and as Hope had rediscovered her roots, she really wanted to honor them, and her father, with her wedding. Emily could understand both points, and she knew Mama G would bow to whatever Hope wished for, eventually. But until a final decision had to be made, Mama G would continue to press her wishes. She couldn't wait to start helping Hope plan the wedding. When Hope got home from her latest shoot in two weeks, they were going to tour a few venues to get a feel for what Hope was looking for and also for pricing.

Breaking herself out of the wedding fog, she pulled Sadie up onto the couch with her and dialed Jason's number. He picked up on the first ring, and Emily quickly shifted the phone's camera to Sadie's beaming face.

"Daddy!" Sadie squealed. She grabbed at the phone and poked Jason in the eye. Emily bit back a bark of laughter.

"Hi, Sadie-girl, how are you?"

"Sadie good," she replied, continuing to poke at Jason's face on the screen.

"Be careful," Emily whispered to Sadie. "You'll accidentally hang up on Daddy."

"Hi, Em," Jason called out.

"Hello," she replied through gritted teeth. Why couldn't he just talk to Sadie and leave her alone? "Thank you for the flowers. They're lovely," she said, referring to the beautiful purple roses. "I wish you wouldn't send them, though. Save your money or use it to buy things for Sadie."

"I like to buy you things," he began.

Emily quickly interrupted. "But I don't. We aren't together, and it makes me uncomfortable to receive gifts from you. Please stop."

Jason sighed.

"Talk to Sadie. I have some things to do. If she hangs up on you before you're ready, just call back and I'll set it up again."

"Em, we need to talk. I have an idea I'd like to run by you."

"I'm done talking," she replied tersely. She stood and looked down at Sadie. "Talk to Daddy, I'm gonna get your bath ready." She ran her hand over Sadie's blond curls and hurried off to the bathroom.

She could hear Sadie's babble and Jason's responses and questions. Why did he have to fight her on everything? He hoped and wished for them to get back together, but it wasn't going to happen. Why couldn't he see that? Why couldn't he accept that? It had been almost two years! He really needed to get the hint already.

Shaking her head, she gathered up a wash cloth and towel for Sadie and set them on the counter. Then dropping a color fizz into the tub, she turned on the water. While it was filling, she set out Sadie's pajamas and her clothes for tomorrow. She hoped it would give them an extra few minutes in the morning but knew they would be just as rushed as every other morning. Nothing she tried ever made their mornings go smooth.

Turning off the water, she walked back to the living room to monitor and hurry the video call along.

Jason's face was no longer the star of her phone. He'd been replaced by Emily's father, who was laughing and making faces, which in turn was making Sadie laugh.

"Hi, Dad!" Emily said, sitting down next to Sadie and popping her face into the camera view.

"Hello! Sadie just phoned me. She was saying Daddy when I first picked up."

"Oh, she was on the phone with Jason. She must have hung up on him. You know how she likes to press the buttons."

"Well, it's a nice surprise," he chuckled, sticking his tongue out at Sadie.

"How's Sophie?" Emily asked, referring to her sister-in-law who was hours, if not minutes, away from giving birth to her fourth child.

"Uncomfy is the word I hear," he replied sheepishly.

"I bet she is. Give her our love."

"I will."

"I hate to break up the comedy party, here, but Sadie needs a bath and bed. We'll call you this weekend."

"Sounds good. Good night, my princesses."

"Night, Dad."

"Night, Gamps!"

Forty-five minutes later, Emily had Sadie in bed and a silent apartment all to herself.

Hope would be back soon. She loved her sister, enjoyed living with her, was so grateful to have a place to live, but it was moments like this—when she was alone, with no one to entertain, no one to converse with, no one to intrude on her solitude——that she was at her happiest.

Hope had plans to go to Mosquero for Labor Day weekend, and Emily was contemplating letting Sadie go with her. She was old enough to sleepover at Jason's with minimal fuss, and she knew her parents would relish the time with Sadie. She planned to stay in Boston to work, relax, and enjoy some alone time. Phoebe, who was currently single, had mentioned coming out, and Emily thought that might be a good time to suggest a visit. She wouldn't hold her breath, though. Phoebe was in and out of relationships quicker than most changed their socks.

She slowly walked down the hall, knowing she should clean up from dinner but quickly losing her ambition. All she really felt like doing was sitting on the couch and moping. She was still irritated about her quick conversation with Jason earlier and his nerve at sending her those beautiful roses.

Sighing, she decided to clean up the kitchen and the clutter around the apartment. The messiness stressed her out. Yawning, she mentally added exhaustion to her list of reasons. A good night's sleep would do wonders for her. She had to get out of this funk.

Exhausted and hoping that was the real reason for her mood, Emily climbed into bed three hours later. She'd cleaned the kitchen, done a load of laundry, spent time on her work projects, and then taken a warm shower. She placed her tea on the bedside table and turned on her Kindle. She opened the latest release by Tess Gerritsen and started reading where she'd left off in chapter five. But as she read, she couldn't remember what she'd read before and realized it had been weeks since she'd given herself time to read. Sighing, she went back to the first chapter and began again, promising herself that she wouldn't let time get away from her again.

Groggy and disoriented, Emily startled awake. She glanced at the clock and was surprised to see it was a little after midnight. Her Kindle laid next to her, and Emily realized she must have fallen asleep while reading, confirming her earlier assumption that she was exhausted.

She couldn't figure out what had woken her so she put her Kindle next to her untouched cup of tea and turned out her bedside light. Closing her eyes, she was just drifting off to sleep again when she heard what must have woken her in the first place. The message ringtone on her cell phone. Someone must have called. She threw off the covers, knowing that if someone had called her at this time of night, it couldn't be good.

She unplugged her phone from the charger on her dresser and checked her caller ID. It was a call from her brother, Tyler, and Emily felt a jolt of excitement run through her. His wife, Sophie, must have had the baby—or they were at least on the way to the hospital.

She quickly dialed his number and waited for him to answer with the exciting news.

"Em?"

"Tyler! Oh my gosh, I'm so excited! Is it a girl?"

"What? What are you talking about?"

"The baby! Is it a girl? Did Sophie give birth?"

"Emily," he said slowly, "didn't you listen to my message?"

"N-no, why? Is everything all right? Are Sophie and the baby okay?"

"Sophie and the baby are fine. But Mama G isn't. She was in an accident tonight. She's in the hospital, and they don't expect her to make it. How soon can you get home?"

Emily's knees buckled, and she dropped to the floor. "What? What?" She couldn't wrap her mind around what he had just told her. "What happened?"

"Drunk driver. She swerved to avoid and lost traction on the gravel. Her car flipped and hit a tree. She's in surgery right now, but from what we understand, she had a lot of trauma to her head and they don't anticipate her waking up."

"Oh my God," she gasped. "Oh my God. Um, okay." She took a shuddering breath and tried to calm herself down. "Okay. I'll call the airlines now and see about tickets. I'm sure I can get something for the morning. Do you want me to call Hope or are you? She can probably get her flight changed easily, too."

"If you could call her, that would be helpful. Dad's not doing well, and I don't want to be away from him for long."

"I understand. I'll text you when I know our flights. Don't worry about picking us up, we'll rent a car. What hospital?"

"She was airlifted to Santa Fe General."

"Okay. See you soon."

She hung up and rested her head on her knees. There would be no more sleep tonight; she had a lot to do and little time to get it done. Dragging herself to her feet, she rushed over to her desk in the corner of her room. Sitting down, she pulled out a piece of paper to start a list. She wrote: call Hope, change flights, call Sadie's daycare, rent car, book hotel in Santa Fe, call Phil, pack clothes, pack work . . . she was sure there was more to add, but she stopped there and began.

She dialed Hope's number while she pulled up her favorite airline website. She selected flights and compared the prices and times to other airlines while she waited for Hope to pick up. As groggy and disoriented as Emily had been, Hope had just as much trouble as Emily had deciphering what was being said to her.

"What do you mean?" Hope asked. "This doesn't make sense."

"I know it doesn't. She was in an accident, Hope, and they don't think she's going to make it. You have to get home, now!"

"Are you going?"

"Yes. I'm working on flights now."

"I need to call Derek."

Emily could hear the tears in her voice and wanted so badly to be there to comfort Hope. "You do. Call him, he'll want to know. And no doubt he'll be able to meet us in New Mexico to be with you."

"You think so?"

"Yes. Call Derek and then call the airlines. Then call me when you know your flight info. I'm going to rent a car so don't worry about that. I'll either wait for you at the airport or come get you. Mama G is at Santa Fe General, so I'll try to get a hotel close by. Do you want your own room or do you want to share with us?"

"Sharing is fine," Hope said quickly. "Oh my gosh. What am I going to do without her? She's too young, Emily. What if she doesn't make it? She'll miss my wedding," Hope's voice broke and then she gasped. "Sadie and I were supposed to go dress shopping over Labor Day weekend with Mom. We were going to go out there for the long weekend."

Emily could hear Hope's soft cries over the phone but didn't know what she could say to help Hope.

"Oh my God," she croaked. "I haven't even had babies yet! She'll never get to meet my babies!"

"I know, Hope. Let's try to think positive though, okay? At least until we get there and know what's what. Let's focus on getting there and being with her. Okay?" Emily took

Hope's sniffle to mean yes. "Call the airlines and then call me back. I love you, sis. We'll make it through this."

Emily spent an hour on the phone with the airlines getting their flights arranged. While she'd been on the phone, and on hold a dozen times, she'd gotten a car rented and hotel booked. She reserved two rooms, knowing that if Derek was able to go out to New Mexico, they'd want their own room. She'd also sent an email to Phil with a promise to call him as soon as he made it into the office later that morning.

Now that the flights were arranged, she texted her brother the information and walked back to her room. It was almost two in the morning, but she knew sleep was still out of reach. She pulled her suitcases from the closet and began to pack.

When she was finished with that, she packed her briefcase with her current projects and her laptop and set everything by the door. She went back to her desk and crossed the completed items off her list—the rest would have to wait until later in the morning. Their flight didn't leave until one, so Emily would have plenty of time to get phone calls made, the rest of the things they'd need packed, and get them both over to the airport.

She only planned to rest on her bed for a couple minutes, let the situation sink in and then get back to organizing and getting ready to leave, but the next thing she knew, Sadie was shaking her awake.

"Mama!"

Emily blinked and sat up. Eyes darting to the clock in panic, she sighed in relief when she saw it was only four in the morning. "What is it, Sadie?"

"Pee bed, Mama. Sadie sorry," she said, lip quivering and tears ready to spill.

"Oh, it's okay baby," she soothed, drawing her in for a hug. "Let's get you cleaned up."

Sadie was basically potty-trained during the day; she did great and barely had any accidents. It was a feat Emily knew was unusual for a child Sadie's age. Not unheard of, just unusual. But they struggled at night. Sadie refused to wear a diaper or Pull-Up because she was NOT a baby, but she was a deep-sleeper and couldn't wake herself up until it was too late. Emily was grateful for the plastic mattress covers they had now. They made the middle of the night cleanups much easier.

She got Sadie cleaned up and into dry pajamas. She stripped Sadie's bed, cleaned the plastic cover, and remade the bed. Sadie went right back to sleep, thankfully, and Emily took the soiled sheets and threw them in the washer. She made a mental note to remember to throw them in the dryer before they left.

Heading back to her room, she picked up her phone and texted Phoebe and Gina with the news and her flight and hotel information. She was sure she'd hear from them as soon as they saw her messages in the morning.

She picked up her Kindle and tried to focus on her book, giving up after reading the same paragraph five times.

While she waited for the TV to turn on, she quickly ran out to the kitchen with her cold tea and reheated it. Then she laid back down in bed, flipping through the channels and waiting for the morning to arrive so she could get home to her family and Mama G.

Chapter Fifteen

Jason glanced at his phone. Eight o'clock and he was just now sitting down to dinner. The repairs on the fencing ate up his day, and by the time he was chased home by the descending darkness, he'd been too tired and too lazy to make dinner. So, he'd taken himself to The Dustbowl, his favorite haunt (and really the only option that wasn't at least an hour away), for dinner. They served typical bar food and Jason opted for a burger and fries. He ordered a beer to go with it but wished it was something stronger. He had more fencing to repair before winter set in and knew if he started on the hard stuff, he'd never be able to pull himself out of bed in the morning.

When Ben, the owner of The Dustbowl, set his beer down in front of him, Jason took a long drink and let his thoughts have free rein . . . not that he was in charge of them anyway. He freely admitted he spent way too much time coming up with plans to get Emily back, but lately, he'd run out of ideas. After his initial visit a few months after she fled

Mosquero, he'd returned to Boston four times but hadn't taken the chance to interact with Emily. Instead, he let the calls, gifts, and actions make his point. He was religious about sending cards, flowers, and gifts for both Emily and Sadie. He made sure to send Emily a check every month even though she never asked for help.

Every Tuesday, he stopped in at the Camancho ranch and had breakfast with Grace. She updated him on Emily and Sadie, shared pictures and anecdotes. It had taken Grace a while to warm up to him after Emily left, but daily visits back then had finally worn her down. He remembered the morning she'd relented. About a month after Emily left, the morning started out rough. He'd tried for the zillionth time to call Emily. Straight to voicemail, so he'd thrown his phone against a wall. It shattered and he cursed a blue streak. He tried to brew some coffee but the damn thing shorted out and a small fire broke out. Giving up, he went outside only to see it raining sheets. There went his plans to get any major work done that day. He turned to go back inside the kitchen when his eyes had fallen on Emily's house on the other side of the line of trees.

Stiffening his spine, he stormed off his porch and stomped his way to the Camancho home. He pounded on the kitchen screen door and waited for someone to answer.

Grace came to the door and all of Jason's pent up worry, rage, and confusion came pouring out. "I still love her. You're supposed to be a mother—how can you ignore me like you've never met me before? Has our relationship meant nothing to you over the years? Where is she? I still love her!"

Grace had kindly shown him in and sat him down at the table with a towel and a hot cup of coffee. She had sat at the table with him and listened as all his feelings came pouring out. She hadn't told him where to find her, but she had told him that Emily was doing okay. And every Tuesday, from then on, Jason had shown up at the kitchen door and had breakfast with Grace. She told him bits and pieces of Emily's life, things that were of no serious consequence, but things that Jason drank in. And once Sadie had been born, she'd been a fount of knowledge giving him all the growth and physical milestones as well as giving him a plethora of photographs.

He needed to see them in person, again. The FaceTime chats with Sadie were a treasured treat, but he needed more. Especially for times, like tonight, when he and Emily had a difference of opinion. He had to make his case, face-to-face, to Emily. How much longer could this go on? Maybe Emily just didn't realize how incredibly serious he was about getting her back. Maybe she thought he was just going through the motions. Though, how she could believe that was beyond him.

Ben set his dinner in front of him, and nodding his thanks, Jason dug in.

"Hello, handsome," a silky smooth, yet grating, voice greeted him.

"Lila." He acknowledged her presence with a curt nod and pulled his arm away from her touch. He went back to his food, praying she'd get the hint even though he knew better.

"Will you be here Friday with the guys?"

Jason shrugged, but knew if she was going to be here, he sure as hell wasn't.

"Why won't you talk to me? You know how I feel about you." Lila pouted.

"Lila," he growled between bites. "We've been down this road. Go away."

Eyes going to slits, Lila's true nature spilled out. "Obviously, she doesn't want you back. You're wasting your life."

"It's mine to waste," Jason warned, taking another long gulp of his beer.

"Did you hear about Aunt Grace?" Lila asked innocently, inspecting her cuticles in the dim light.

Jason whipped his head around, his burger and fries forgotten. "No."

"She was in a car accident this afternoon."

"What?" Jason asked, straightening up on the barstool, alert and worried.

Lila nodded. "People have been coming in to the bank all afternoon talking about it. I don't know all the deets, but people are saying she was hit and the car rolled. She's at the hospital right now."

"Shit!" Jason stood and threw a twenty on the bar. "Which hospital?"

"Santa Fe General," she said, placing her hand on his arm again. "Where are you going?"

"To the hospital," he growled.

"Don't be ridiculous. It's two hours away, and you know they'll never let you see her," Lila said with a smirk.

"We'll see about that," he replied over his shoulder, already jogging to the door.

He sent a prayer toward heaven for Grace. She was more to him than just his only connection to Emily and Sadie. She was like a mother to him. No, she *was* a mother to him. His own had died when he was two and taken his little sister to heaven with her. Living next door to the Camanchos had been a blessing, and when Grace joined the family, she'd welcomed him into her heart with open arms, long before he'd seen Emily in any kind of romantic light. She'd bandaged his skinned knees and elbows, helped with homework, and fed him almost nightly. His father had more than enough on his plate with running the ranch and overcoming his devastating loss, and he knew his father credited Grace for turning him into the man he was.

Arriving at the hospital, he headed straight to the gift shop, hoping they were still open at this late hour. He would not show up empty-handed . . . at the very least he could buy her some flowers. She loved flowers, and Jason had bought her a bouquet every year for Mother's Day and for her birthday, ever since he'd gotten his first paying job. Before that it had been random weeds and wildflowers picked from the fields and the sides of the road. Even these past few years when tensions were strained, he never failed to give her flowers. Only instead of bringing them to her in person, he now sent them from the flower shop.

He stopped at the information desk to find out which room Grace was in, surprised to learn she was in the ICU. After wiping his suddenly sweaty palms on his jeans, he pressed the button for Grace's floor. He didn't know how they would react to his arrival, but he hoped they could see and remember how much Grace meant to him.

The nurses' station was right outside the elevator, so Jason walked up and asked for Grace's room. The nurse smiled up at him and pointed him in the direction of her room. Jason thanked her and continued down the hall.

Arriving at Grace's room, Jason knocked on the door and waved to Clint through the window. He watched as Clint rose from his chair and met Jason in the hall.

"Jason," Clint said, holding out his hand.

"How's she doing?" Jason asked, shaking Clint's hand.

"Not good," Clint answered, his worried eyes scanning his still wife through the window.

"What happened?"

Clint sighed and motioned toward the flowers in Jason's hand. "Can't have those in the room."

Jason set them on the floor in the hall and followed Clint into Grace's room. It was quiet, save for the occasional beeping from the machines. Clint motioned for Jason to sit in the chair he'd just vacated. Sitting down, Jason held Grace's hand in his own, marveling at how small her hand seemed next to his own. *Had it always been so small?* He never remembered that. Grace had always seemed larger than life to him. Of course, you always thought of your parents being so much bigger, even when you were fully grown.

"Drunk driver was in her lane. We think she swerved to avoid him, skidded on the gravel, flipped the car, and landed in a tree."

"Where's he at?"

"The police station, sleeping it off in a jail cell. Sheriff Fred said he found him about a half mile down the road in a ditch, passed out. Not a scratch on him, either."

"Is she going to be okay?"

Clint sighed. "Doctors aren't optimistic. She's had a lot of trauma to her head. There's swelling, and she's in a coma."

Jason nodded and squeezed Grace's hand. He knew visiting times were limited in the ICU, so he stood, leaned over, and kissed her cheek. "Get well soon, Grace. I love you," he whispered in her ear. He shuffled toward the door and looked Clint in the eye. "I've been out fixing fences all day. I just found out when I stopped at The Dustbowl for dinner. I had to come and see her for myself." Jason shook Clint's hand. "If you need any help at the ranch, don't hesitate to call."

"Thanks, Jason," Clint said, resting a hand on Jason's shoulder. "I appreciate it."

Jason's eyes found Grace, so pale beneath the blankets. "She's always been kind to me."

"She has a soft spot for you." Clint chuckled. "Not that I blame her. You've always been a good boy."

Jason smiled. "Will you let me know how she's doing?"

Clint nodded. "Sure. Glad you stopped in."

Jason cast one last glance at Grace and then silently walked out the door.

He meandered down the hall, nodding to the nurse at the station and then slipping into the elevator. His hands were shaking as he pressed the button for the ground level. He didn't know what he expected, but it wasn't the easy acceptance he'd received. He was happy it hadn't been awkward and figured Tyler's absence helped in that respect. He still had an immense amount of respect for Clint, even more now. Clint allowing Jason in the room, giving him a chance to sit and hold Grace's hand, just reinforced that.

When he got to the truck, he rested his head against the steering wheel for a moment. He missed them and he hadn't really realized how much until this moment. It had almost felt like old times for a few minutes there. That, as much as anything else, made his resolve to get Emily back even stronger now.

He drove for an hour and then pulled over in a rest stop to get a little sleep. Resting his head against the headrest, he was almost asleep when a thought made his eyes pop open. As it gained traction in his mind, his heart rate sped up. There was no way she could stay away, not with Grace in such bad shape. Could she? Could it be possible that Emily would be coming home?

Chapter Sixteen

After getting Sadie settled by the window, Emily pulled out her cell phone and dialed the office to check in before her flight. Between getting calls made and the packing finished, the morning had flown by and she had completely forgotten to call Phil. But she and Sadie were one of the first on the plane, so she had just enough time to get it done before takeoff.

"A Touch of Flair. This is Phil, may I help you?"

Emily smiled, it was nice to know that the employees were professional and polite even when she wasn't in the office. "Hey, Phil, it's Em. Just wanted to check in before this flying deathtrap takes off."

"Jeez, Em, try some positivity. Bad things happen to people who envision bad things," Phil warned her.

"You know I don't like to fly," Emily said, cringing when she realized there was just the tiniest bit of whining in her voice. Clearing her throat, she continued, "How are things?"

"Ugh, horrible. Jenny's sick as a dog, and she won't go home. I'm afraid to get within ten feet of her."

Rolling her eyes, Emily sighed. This was the last thing she needed. The owner of the company was away on a months-long trip across Europe with her husband and children. Emily was in charge, and she needed both Phil and Jenny in the office this week, especially now that she was heading home for who-knew-how-long. Emily was Kendra's backup, and Phil was hers. There was no backup for Phil. She couldn't risk Jenny infecting Phil and then having no one in the office.

"Tell her to go home and email me the new project from Friday. I can sketch it out and get it started while I'm in New Mexico."

"You tell her; she's not listening to me."

"Are you crazy, Emily?" Jenny shrieked into the phone. "There's too much to do around here, I can't go home!"

"You have to go home, Jenny. I can't afford for you both to be sick. Take a project home with you and work on it there. Phil can handle the office by himself."

"He's sticking to his side of the office and he's wearing a face mask. I'm fine. I'm just a little stuffy," she said, dissolving into a coughing fit.

"Uh-huh. Just a little stuffy. Go home, Jenny!"

"Fine, I'll go."

Emily heard the unmistakable sound of an aerosol spray across the line.

"Thanks, Em! I didn't think she'd go."

"Did you just spray Lysol on the phone?"

Phil laughed. "Yes. I've been spraying everything she touches since she came in this morning."

"Nice." Emily chuckled. "Is she going?"

"Yeah, she's packing up her desk."

"Email me the project notes, and when I get to the hotel this evening, I'll start working on it."

"Are you sure you'll have enough time to work on this stuff? Shouldn't you focus on your mom?"

"The ICU only allows five- or ten-minute visits every hour. I'll have a lot of downtime. Just do what you can this week, Phil. When I get back, we'll update all the project plans and see what needs doing. You know we always manage to get it done. Somehow."

"Sounds good. Have a safe flight."

"Hm. I'll practice some of that positivity you like so much."

Emily hung up with seconds to spare. She was putting her phone back in her purse when the announcement came over the loud speaker to turn off all electronic devices. She watched as the flight attendants went through the safety procedures, but it did little to ease her mind on the safety and survivability of the aircraft. Sighing to herself and trying to calm her racing heart, Emily held Sadie's hand and rested her head against the headrest, closing her eyes and practicing deep breathing exercises.

A few minutes later, the plane taxied out onto the runway. "Mama, fast!" Sadie exclaimed excitedly, eyes glued to the scenery outside the window.

Unable to help herself, she gripped the armrest hard during the takeoff and didn't relax her grip until the plane leveled out. Who had the bright idea to invent planes? Weren't trains, boats, and cars enough? How much of the world was missed because people were too high in the air to see it and appreciate it. She wondered what life would be like if the airplane had never been invented. Would families have continued to live close? Would children be better adjusted? Would there be less crime?

Shrugging her shoulders, she pushed the thoughts out of her mind. They'd been invented, so there was no use imagining a world without them. She pulled out her copies of *US Weekly* and *People*, reading through both of them and then starting on the word find puzzles book she'd tucked into her purse at the last minute.

She was relieved when the plane landed with barely a bump in Dallas and was glad for the break, a chance to stretch her legs and get something to eat. Even better, a chance to use the restroom—one that wasn't cramped and impossible to maneuver in. Sadie had fallen asleep during the flight and was groggy and slow as they tried to deplane.

They quickly used the restroom and then stopped at a TGI Fridays for some food.

When it was time to board again, they gathered up their belongings. Emily was grateful that the airlines saw fit to let passengers traveling with small children board first. Settling into their seats, she made sure Sadie's bag was in easy reach yet still under the seat in front of her. Then she turned off her phone and pulled out the word find puzzles, tucking it under her leg for easy access. She leaned her head against the seat and closed her eyes. One more takeoff and landing. I can do this. When the plane had leveled out again, she slowly opened her eyes, peeking out the window. All she saw were puffy white clouds, a soft carpet beneath the plane. Deciding that wasn't as comforting as she thought it should be, she pulled out her puzzles and left the window gazing to her daughter.

It was close to ten when the plane landed in Santa Fe, and Emily was exhausted. Sadie had fallen asleep again and was now refreshed, wired, and ready to take on the world. A sharp contrast to Emily's travel fatigue, exacerbated by the little sleep she'd gotten the night before. She gathered their luggage from the carousel and walked over to the rental car desk. She'd be all too happy when they arrived at the hotel, were checked in, Sadie was set up with a movie, and Emily could fall asleep in a bed with no fear of falling out of the sky.

Hope wouldn't arrive until midday tomorrow, and Emily had promised to pick her up at the airport. The next few days were going to be excruciating, and she promised herself that that with all that was going on, she would push all thoughts of Jason to the farthest reaches of her mind.

Chapter Seventeen

"Emily Camancho, checking in," she said, barely able to keep her eyes open.

"Can you spell your last name, please?" the clerk asked.

Emily did as she was asked. "My sister is arriving tomorrow, I have a reservation for two rooms, one king and one with two double beds."

The clerk nodded and continued to type. "I'm sorry, ma'am, I'm not seeing a reservation here for you."

Emily sighed and bent over to find the printout of her reservation in her briefcase. "I just made this reservation early this morning. Here's the confirmation printout."

The clerk typed in the confirmation number and looked up at Emily. "It says this reservation was canceled."

"Canceled? By whom? It surely wasn't me, obviously, as I'm standing here trying to check in."

"I'm sorry, ma'am."

"Well, can I still get a room?"

"No, I'm sorry. We're completely full tonight."

"Are you serious?"

"Yes, ma'am. One of our sister hotels might have a room available, would you like me to call?"

"Please," Emily said, trying to keep rein of her emotions. Who would have canceled her reservation? It certainly hadn't been her, and other than her brother and father, no one knew she was coming. Hope wasn't in any frame of mind to cancel a reservation, and even if she had, she would have told Emily of the new hotel plans. Emily had been mindful of Hope's hotel preferences and booked them at a Hilton property, so she couldn't imagine Hope had been the one to tamper with the reservation. She shook her head; there was no use trying to figure it out. It was late, she was exhausted, and it was something she'd probably never get to the bottom of. It was probably some sort of computer glitch.

"I can get you into the Embassy Suites," the clerk told her, pressing the phone to her chest.

"Where is it?"

"Two streets over, four blocks down."

"Fine."

The clerk finished up the reservation and hung up the phone. "Here is the address and your new confirmation number. Do you need a map?"

"No," Emily said, shaking her head and leaning down to pick up her briefcase. "I went to school here. I'm familiar with the area."

"I'm sorry for the inconvenience."

"Have a good night," Emily said. She was in no mood for being placated, and while she knew it wasn't the clerk's fault for the mix-up, she wasn't in the mood to take the high road, either. She gathered up her suitcase and called for Sadie to do the same, then walked out of the hotel. She was happy to see that her car hadn't been valeted yet and walked over to the valet station, handing the boy her ticket. "Looks like we won't be staying here, after all. Thank you."

The valet offered to help with the luggage and Emily allowed him to. She settled Sadie into the back seat and tipped the valet when he closed the trunk. Ten minutes later, they pulled into the Embassy Suites, and leaving the car running, Emily ran into the hotel to make sure she was at the right place and that they did indeed have a reservation for her. She checked in with ease and then went back out to the car for Sadie and their belongings. She gave the keys to the valet and then headed for the bank of elevators.

Once they were settled in their room, Emily sent both Hope and Tyler a text with the hotel information, indicating she'd explain the snafu tomorrow, as well as to Gina and Phoebe.

"Glad you're here," Tyler texted. "Grace is still holding on."

"I'm going to bed. Beyond exhausted. What time do visiting hours begin?"

"7."

"See you then?"

"I'll be in a little later, chores to do in the morning."

"Okay."

Emily went into the bathroom to check on Sadie. "Everything okay?"

"Yes," Sadie said, hopping off the toilet. She assumed the position, and Emily quickly cleaned her up. They both washed their hands and walked into the room. Sadie stopped at her suitcase for the teddy bear Jason had given her the day she was born and then climbed into bed.

Emily turned on her bedside lamp and turned off Sadie's. "I'm just going to get ready for bed myself. I'll be out in a few minutes." She bent over to kiss Sadie's forehead and tucked her in. It might only be a little after midnight here in Santa Fe, but it was after two in the morning in Boston. Sadie should fall right to sleep, but there was a big difference between should and would.

As Emily got ready for bed, her mind raced with things she needed to do over the next few days. At the top of the list was to call Jason and make sure he knew they were in town and Sadie would be available for visiting in between things happening at the hospital. She'd wait until morning, though. She was way beyond exhausted, physically, mentally, and emotionally.

She climbed into bed and turned off the light, and when Sadie curled her warm body against her back, Emily sighed and let everything go, slipping off into a peaceful and dreamless sleep.

Despite the late night, Sadie was up early—even earlier considering they were two hours behind. Emily needed at least another hour of sleep, so she dragged herself out of bed and went out into the living room to turn on Cartoon Network. She set Sadie up on the couch with a pillow and blanket, some snacks, and then went back to bed. Now that morning was here, Emily was grateful for the mix-up in hotels; the suites part of Embassy Suites was very convenient for situations like this. She rolled over and closed her eyes, but after twenty minutes, she realized going back to sleep was not in the cards. She glanced at the clock. Six o'clock. She groaned and threw back the covers. The inclusive breakfast buffet didn't start for a half hour and visiting hours began in an hour. Too early to do anything but get a little work done. Especially since they'd gotten in so late and she hadn't had a chance to do much more than fall, exhausted into bed.

"Mama, sleep?"

"No, Mama is up!"

"Sadie hungry."

"We'll go down for breakfast in a minute; I just need to check in at work."

"Okay," she said, returning her attention to the television and her sippy cup of milk.

Emily tickled Sadie's neck and kissed her cheek, smiling in response to Sadie's squeals of delight. Sitting down at the desk slash table, she pulled up her email and found the new project Phil emailed her yesterday. He wouldn't be in the office for at least another hour, so Emily read the proposal and jotted down a few ideas she had for the project. Then she opened up her two current projects and lost herself, and the time, in sketching out ideas and designs.

"Mama," Sadie said, tugging on her arm. "Hungry!"

Dragging herself out of her creative space, Emily glanced at the clock on her phone and cursed under her breath. "Sorry, Sadie. I lost track of time. Let's get dressed and we'll go eat."

Twenty minutes later, Emily led Sadie down the hall to the elevators. She had to admit that she was pretty hungry, too, and the cooked-to-order omelet sounded divine. Knowing Sadie's preference for a carb-heavy breakfast, Emily made a tray of waffles and cold cereal. She set Sadie at a table within sight and then stood in line for the omelet.

She put in her order for a ham, Swiss, and mushroom omelet and then helped herself to some yogurt, coffee, and pastries while her omelet cooked.

When they finished eating, they headed back up to the room. Emily finished getting ready and then helped Sadie pack her backpack with her stuffed animals and fun activities to keep her occupied at the hospital. Emily packed her own briefcase as well. Grace was in the ICU and only one person at a time was allowed in. There would be a lot of downtime today, even though they'd be spending it all at the hospital. She checked to make sure her phone was charged and set a reminder to pick up Hope from the airport.

"Ready to go?" she asked, gathering up her purse and briefcase and helping Sadie put her backpack on.

"Yes."

Emily allowed Sadie to press the buttons on the elevator, one of Sadie's favorite things to do. When the doors opened, Sadie rushed out. Emily hurried after her and took hold of her hand.

They crossed the lobby, and she passed her ticket stub to the valet. A few minutes later, they were off to the hospital. She wanted to be positive, but the closer they got to the hospital, the darker she felt. The situation with Grace was serious and no amount of positive thinking could change that. It had to be very serious if Tyler had suggested Emily come home. He knew her feelings, knew where she stood, and for him to not only suggest it, but insist upon it, meant that this would most likely be the last time she saw her stepmother.

Chapter Eighteen

Emily had known what to expect.

She knew Grace would be hooked up to machines, knew there would be wires, knew even that she would be pale and lifeless. Knowing all of this, though, still hadn't prepared her for her first look at Grace. Tears immediately sprang to her eyes as she placed her hand on the glass window, wanting to be closer but scared at the same time. The nurse said her father had just gone in, so Emily had at least five or ten minutes to wait, and hopefully that would be enough time to compose herself.

She led Sadie down the hall to the waiting room and got her set up on the floor with her toys and activity books. No one else was in the room and Emily was glad. They'd have dibs on the TV when Sadie grew tired of the things surrounding her.

When Clint walked in fifteen minutes later, Emily jumped to her feet and gave her father a long hug. Neither said anything, letting the power of the embrace do what it could to heal and comfort.

"Gamps!" Sadie screeched, shoving herself between the hugging adults.

"Sadie-girl, look how big you've gotten!" Clint exclaimed, reaching down and picking her up into his famous Grandpa Bear Hug.

Sadie giggled and squirmed in his tight grasp.

"Such a little stinker, coming between a girl and her daddy!" Emily smiled fondly at her daughter then tickled her ribs.

"Help!" Sadie squealed.

Clint spun around, away from Emily's tickling fingers and sprinted to the opposite side of the room. He swung Sadie onto his back and put his arms out to ward off Emily's attack.

"Well now, I can see when I've been outmaneuvered." Emily laughed, breathlessly. She sat down and rested her head against the back of the chair. "Been working out much, Dad?"

"What do you mean?" Clint smirked.

"You're as spry as a teenager with those spinning moves and sprints."

"Nah, just playing with the boys. They're enough of a workout for anyone!"

"Will Tyler bring them today?"

"I doubt it. Sophie is staying home with them so they can go to school. She's having a hard time getting around now, anyway, so close to her due date. Tyler said she'll come Saturday with the boys." Clint put Sadie down and she walked over to the chair to watch TV. He sat down next to Emily. "Not sure there'll be a reason for her to come on Saturday, though."

Emily grasped his hand. "Do you really think that?"

Sighing, Clint nodded. "They aren't detecting any brain activity. It could be a fluke, maybe she's way down deep in the coma, but there should be some sign, right?"

"Tyler said it was bad. I guess I was hoping he was exaggerating."

"The nurses move her around; she hasn't moved an inch on her own since she arrived. She doesn't react to my touch or my voice. Ten minutes an hour barely gives me enough time to tell her a story or a memory. We were supposed to have more time. I want more time, dammit!"

Emily didn't know what to say, so she squeezed her father's hand and rested her head on his shoulder. She couldn't fathom what he was going through, the prospect of losing his second wife had to be soul crushing.

"Hope should be here around lunchtime," she said quietly.

"What about Derek?"

"I don't know. Last I heard from her, he was still working on getting his schedule under control."

Clint nodded and raised a brow, finally noticing the pile of stuff Emily had on the table.

"I've brought plenty to keep me occupied in between visits. Is there anyone I should call or visit? Anything you need me to do while I'm here and at loose ends?"

Clint shook his head. "Jason stopped by last night. It was good to see him and kind of him to drive all the way out here for ten minutes."

"He loves Grace, always has."

"Just as he loves you and always has."

"Dad," Emily warned.

"You wanted to know if there was anyone you should call or visit or anything I need you to do while you're here," Clint began. "Well, there is. You need to talk with him, reconcile with him."

Emily shook her head. "Dad, please don't."

"It's been left unsaid for far too long, Emily. You push and push and push him away, and yet he still holds out hope. Even if he was in the wrong, no man waits around two years if he doesn't truly love a person. If he were a terrible person, he'd have given up on you a long time ago."

Emily sighed and pulled away. She sat back in her chair and crossed her arms in front of her. "This isn't the time or place," Emily said, indicating Sadie's presence at the table.

"Bologna. She's as much a part of this as you are. Maybe more so."

"They have a great relationship, Dad. I've made sure of it. I don't deny her any chance to speak with him, or even to video chat with him. I repeat, they have a great relationship."

"There's no denying that, but it could be better. You know that. It should be better. It should be *more*."

"Found your opinions, did you, Dad?" Emily stood up and paced across the room.

"You know I've always had them, Emily Rose. I'm just particular about when I air them."

"You've picked a real fine time to air them now, haven't you?" Emily stopped her pacing and glared at her father.

"Seize the day, child."

Emily growled and resumed her pacing.

She was saved from further discussion when the timer on Clint's phone went off.

"Visitor time."

Emily's heart started racing, and her palms grew clammy. Until this moment, she'd been able to compartmentalize the situation. She'd had her to-do lists to fall back on, the traveling, the checking in to the hotel, making sure Sadie was taken care of and had things to keep her busy. But now, it was time. Her turn to visit. And in this moment, it hit her. Grace was in a coma and not expected to live through the week. She needed a moment, but there were no more moments to have, so she walked down the brightly lit hallway.

She took a deep breath and pushed the door open. She paused just inside the door. There was a stillness to Grace that was unnatural. Emily had never seen her so still. Grace was always in motion, always. She slowly ambled to the side of the bed and slid down into the chair. Taking Grace's hand in her own she traced the veins that stood out in sharp relief, their blue-purple color bright against the pale translucency of her skin. She studied Grace's appearance. Up close, Grace was paler than she looked from the window. The sheets surrounding Grace had more color.

Her face was riddled with bruises, and Emily assumed those were from the accident. Grace's left arm was in a cast and her left foot was raised with two pillows propped beneath it.

The room itself was bright and white. Emily quickly shut down a train of thought of someone waking from a coma only to fall right back in, sure they were at the gates of heaven. She understood why the room was as it was, but it didn't change the fact that, at this moment, it seemed cold and uninviting. Nothing graced the walls except equipment, monitors, and a white board. The sheets and blankets were white. The tile was a blueish tan color, really the only thing of color in the whole room, besides the red dry erase writing on the white board.

Emily leaned forward and brushed her fingers across Grace's brow. "Mama G? It's Emily. We're here, and we're praying for you to come back to us. We're not ready to let you go; there's still so much for you to see and do. Hope will be here in a few hours. I love you, Mama G. Please get better," Emily whispered this last sentiment against Grace's ear, tears leaking from her eyes.

Emily sat down and held Grace's hand. She started to hum the lullaby Grace would always sing to her whenever she was sick or sad. Two verses into the song, Grace's hand twitched and Emily sucked in her breath.

She pressed the call button on Grace's bed. Was it a fluke? Had she just imagined that? Her father said Grace hadn't moved on her own the whole time.

"Ma'am?" the nurse asked, sticking her head inside the door.

"My mom. Her hand. It just twitched in mine while I was singing to her. Can you call the doctor? Maybe this means she has some brain activity after all?"

"I'll page the doctor, but I wouldn't get my hopes up too high."

"I understand," Emily replied.

She continued to sing, but no further movement happened. It was probably a fluke, if Grace hadn't moved for her husband, why would she move for Emily? And besides, if she was going to move for anyone, wouldn't it be Hope, her daughter? Suddenly, she was impatient for Hope's arrival. Maybe all Grace needed was the people who loved her best surrounding her and pulling for her and showing her how much they loved and needed her.

Chapter Nineteen

"I know you want to think it was brain activity in response to your singing, but I have to tell you to be cautious. We will, of course, run tests, but you need to prepare yourself."

"I understand," Emily muttered. Could this doctor be any more doom and gloom? Grace's hand had moved. Shouldn't they be celebrating?

They entered the waiting area and Clint jumped to his feet.

"It's not bad, Dad," Emily hurriedly assured him. "I was humming our lullaby and Mama G's hand twitched in mine. I asked to speak with the doctor."

"That's the first sign of voluntary movement since we got here," Clint exclaimed. "What does it mean?"

"I don't know," the doctor replied. "It could be nothing. The human body, especially in a coma, is a mystery. It could have been a reaction to the singing, or it could have been completely random with no meaning."

"Are you going to run some tests?" Clint asked.

"Yes, of course. She's due for another brain activity scan, and we'll check on the brain swelling as well."

"When?"

"As soon as I can get the orders written up, we'll take her down. Probably right after lunch."

Clint nodded.

"How long do the tests last?"

"It should take an hour or two," he replied.

Emily glanced at the doctor's face and silently shook her head. He, Dr. Mosler, looked to be in his early twenties. He may be brilliant, but he certainly didn't instill trust when you first spoke to him. He had a hard time keeping eye contact, and his quiet manner made you think he wasn't confident in his work. Emily knew he was the best in the area and one of the five top neurosurgeons in the country. She knew they were lucky to have him on Grace's side, overseeing her care, but when you had to speak with him, it certainly left you wondering.

"Her, our daughter, Hope, will be arriving around lunchtime. She'll be anxious to see her mother. I know the tests are important, but would it be possible to delay them until after Hope has had a chance to see Grace?"

"Do you have a time of arrival for her?"

"Her plane lands at eleven. I doubt she checked any luggage, so we should be back here no later than noon," Emily explained.

"I'll schedule the tests for one, if that's all right?" he suggested. Clint and Emily nodded. "I'll see you then. And if any more movement happens, please don't hesitate to let the nurses know."

Clint watched Dr. Mosler walk away. "What do you think?"

"I don't know, Dad. I want to be optimistic, but I am out of my depth here."

The rest of the morning went by fast with Emily and Clint alternating visits with Grace. Try as she might, though, Emily couldn't concentrate well on her work. She took a break outside to speak to Phil, explaining the situation.

"Emily, this is a delicate time. Do what you can, isn't that what you always tell us?"

"I know. I just feel like I need to be able to do it all. Kendra is counting on me."

"That's ridiculous and you know it. We're all a team, and besides, Kendra would be the first to tell you to take it easy and focus on your family."

"How's Jenny today?" Emily asked, changing the subject.

"Still sick. She called me this morning and I told her to stay home and work."

"Did she argue?"

"Of course she did, but I told her you'd fire her if she came in."

Emily laughed. "Good call."

"It worked, so I consider it a win for everyone."

"Has Kendra called in?"

"She left a message on the answering service last night. Said she was just checking in and she'd be in touch at the end of the week. I sent her a quick email and told her you'd send one of your own once you got settled and knew what the lay of the land was."

"Thanks, Phil. I'll work on that email to her tonight."

"We got an inquiry this morning. A business this time. They want us to completely redesign their lobby waiting area. And if they like what we come up with, they want us to redo the conference rooms, too. I think we could have the opportunity to redo the entire office space."

"Wow, that's fabulous. Kendra was saying she'd like to branch out into the commercial arena. She'll be so excited."

"We need to answer them. Should I send them an acceptance letter and tell them we'll work on a proposal?"

"Yes, that would be fantastic. When do they want proposals?"

"End of the month. We have a little time. Kendra will be back by then, right?"

"Doubtful, they plan to spend the whole summer away."

"I thought they were coming back at the end of June?"

"They were, but the kids are having fun and everyone is getting along. And the grandparents have begged for more time."

"The proposal is due on the thirtieth."

"We'll get it done, no worries. I'm sure I'll be back by then, and if not, we'll still blow them away."

"All right. I'll send out the acceptance letter today and let them know to expect our proposal on the thirtieth."

"Great, anything else?"

"Not that I can think of. Want to speak at lunch tomorrow and go over the Thompson and Trudeau projects?"

"Sure, sounds good. I'll let you know if anything happens and I can't make that meeting."

"Okay. Talk to you tomorrow. Keep your chin up," Phil advised.

"I'm doing my best to keep positive thoughts in my head."

"Good, they go a long way."

Emily hung up and breathed in a few deep breaths of fresh air. She missed the clean, desert smell and knew it would be even stronger at her father's ranch. She liked the briny ocean scent in Boston, but nothing beat the smell of the desert.

"Emily?"

Emily's heart stopped and her mouth dried up. She closed her eyes and waited a beat or two before turning. She wasn't ready. So often, over the past twenty-four hours, things were happening before she was ready for them.

She turned and there he was. Time had been good to him; she couldn't deny it. His eyes were still deep chocolate, his dark blond hair still full and unruly and a little longer than was decent. Sure, she'd peeked at his face during Sadie's video chats, but seeing him in person was so much better. He was taller and leaner than she remembered, but then again, she'd tried to block him from her heart for so long.

God! All she wanted was to walk into his arms and listen to his heartbeat. She cleared her throat and stiffened her spine. She was hopeless. She was not going to fall back into his trap.

"Hi, Jason," she breathed, annoyed her voice didn't come out strong and brisk.

"How's Grace?"

"About the same. They're running tests on her this afternoon because her hand twitched in mine earlier. I'm choosing to look at it as a positive sign, but the doctor is being cautious."

"How are you?"

"Hanging in," Emily said as she looked off into the distance. It hurt her heart to see him, be near him, even just talking to him. "I was going to call you later today to set up a visit with Sadie. She'll be excited to see you."

"I'm happy you're both here, even under the circumstances." Jason brushed his fingers across her forearm. "I'm happy to see you, Em."

She moved away from his touch, noted his pained expression as she did so. "I'm here for Grace, nothing more," she said firmly. "And when it's time, you should know we'll be returning to Boston."

"If I didn't know any better, I'd say you were warning me off."

Emily nodded and turned to walk inside. Jason fell into step beside her and reached out to open the door before she had a chance. Deep inside, she was pleased. Outside, she fumed. The last thing she needed was Jason getting ideas of wooing her back and thinking she'd stay. She meant what she said two years ago when he had showed up at her apartment door before Sadie was born. Nothing had changed. Not then, not when he'd visited after her birth, or the third time last summer. In her eyes, he was still a cheating jerk and that was something she didn't think she'd ever be able to get over.

They reached the elevator and Emily pressed the button, tapping her foot as the elevator seemed to be taking longer than usual to arrive. When the doors whooshed open,

Emily all but ran into the elevator and pressed the button for Grace's floor.

"In a hurry?" Jason asked.

Emily made a noise in her throat, half hum, half growl.

"Is this toe-tapping thing new? I don't remember it," Jason said, a smirk gracing his beautiful mouth. "Must be the city living."

"I'm just anxious to get back upstairs. I've been away too long."

"I'll say," he agreed.

"And we know at whose feet we can lay that blame, don't we?" Emily snapped, striding off down the hall as soon as the doors opened.

"Yep, but it's not who you think. Or who you blame," he muttered, following closely behind Emily's stiff back.

"Daddy!" Sadie shrieked, leaping into his arms.

"Hey, Buttercup!" Jason twirled her around and gave her a big hug. Kissing her cheek, he looked her in the eye. "How are you?"

"Sadie good. Happy see you!"

"Have you had lunch yet?"

"No."

"Good, I'm hungry," he said, nibbling on her neck. She squealed with joy and wiggled in his arms. Holding her close, he whispered, "I've missed you so much." He glanced at Emily. "Mind if I take her to lunch?"

"I have to leave soon to pick up Hope from the airport."

"I'll keep her until you get back," he said.

"Jason," Clint interrupted, turning off the visiting alarm on his phone. "You want to go in and see Grace? It's time for a new visitor."

"Sure, give me one second?"

Clint nodded and picked up his book as he sat back down in the chair.

"I'm gonna go in and visit with Grace, and then I'll take her out. Can you wait a few minutes to leave?"

"Yeah."

"Do you want her back at any specific time?"

"No. They're taking Grace down for tests after Hope has her visit. They should take an hour or two, but there's no reason Sadie has to stay in here, cooped up. Just let me know what you're going to do and we'll go from there."

"K." He waved to Sadie and left the room.

Emily watched him go and sighed.

"You still love him," Clint observed.

"Don't be ridiculous, Dad."

"Didn't think I was." He chuckled. "Pretty sure that's what most folks call being observant."

"Well, your skills need honing," she said, concentrating on her laptop.

"They do not. It's as plain as the nose on your face."

"Dad, I really don't want to discuss this. It's over and has been for a long time."

"It won't *ever* be over. You've loved him since you were twelve years old. You have a child together. You're tied to him for the rest of your life. That kind of love never goes away."

"He messed up. It's plain and simple."

"Did he? Or was he tricked? Have you even given him a chance to explain?"

"I saw it with my own eyes, Dad. I don't know what he can say that will absolve him of that."

"Are you serious, child? Was he not drunk as a skunk? Was it not pitch dark inside that room? Was he not expecting *you* to be there?"

Emily scrunched up her face. "How do you know all these details?"

Clint sat back in his chair, folding his arms behind his head and resting it on the wall behind him. A self-satisfied smirk gracing his face, he winked at his daughter. "Because I have a wife who has made it a priority to have coffee with him every week."

"She never told me!" Emily exclaimed, annoyed at having her personal life be fodder for gossip between her parents.

"Why should she? You weren't listening to either of them. You've got your mind made up and no one, but no one, is changing your mind. You saw all, you know all."

"Well, that's just fabulous. It's no wonder he won't leave me alone. He's got you and Mama G in his pocket, cheering him on. I'm surprised he hasn't made more trips out to Boston."

"He's wanted to, but we suggested he wait. Course, the waiting has been driving him a little crazy, and I'm pretty sure he was out there last fall but kept his distance. He's a man of action, and he's been feeling like his small actions aren't doing the job. Certainly haven't thawed your frozen heart, have they?"

"That's rude, Dad."

"How's it rude when it's the truth? He's been giving and giving for years. What have you done in return?"

"I've given him visitation rights to his daughter. I let her video chat with him whenever they want. I allow her to call and video chat with him whenever she wants. I don't restrict their time in anyway."

"Don't you? You live in Boston, and he lives in Mosquero. She deserves to have a full-time daddy. And he deserves to *be* a full-time daddy."

"What do you know, Dad? Seriously! You weren't engaged to the man. You didn't walk in on him and Lila. The night before we were to be married. You weren't there, you didn't see, and you sure as hell didn't feel my heart shatter. It's still in pieces and I'm not sure it'll ever get put back together."

"Em?" Jason asked from the doorway, eyes wide.

"Mama mad!" Sadie announced, hopping off the chair and walking to Jason.

Emily watched as Sadie reached up, wanting to be held by her father.

"Are you kidding me?" Emily shrieked, staring at her father. She darted furious eyes in Jason's direction. "How long have you been standing there?" She jumped to her feet, and even though it killed her, she walked over to Jason and gave Sadie a hug. "I'm sorry for yelling, Sadie. Mama needs a time-out. Go have a fun lunch with Daddy, and I'll see you when you get back. I love you," she said, kissing Sadie's cheek.

With one last furious glare for her father and Jason, she fled the room. Her heart and soul had been ripped open and Jason had been there to witness it. He had to know he'd hurt her that night, but damn if she'd wanted him to know just how deep it went. Why had her father brought all this up? All her life he'd been content to let her mother or Mama G do the serious talking. Now, all of a sudden, he had sage advice and wanted to butt into her personal life.

Mortified, she fled the floor and burst out of the lobby doors, breathing deeply of the fresh air. She felt as if she were suffocating, the pain and agony of that night sucking the life out of her again. Would she never get over it? Would the images that tortured her dreams never fade?

She had to pull herself together. She had to go back in there and do so with her head held high. She could still pretend he didn't matter, could still pretend she wasn't scarred for life. She would deal with him as she always had, at arm's length and with latex gloves. She could chalk the outburst up to exhaustion and worry about Mama G. He didn't have to know that all those emotions were purely because of him.

She really had to get herself under control. She had to leave soon to pick up Hope, who was sure to be a basket case. Hope never dealt well with emergencies of any kind.

Shaking her head, she couldn't force herself to reenter the building. She sat on the bench just outside the doors and covered her face with her hands.

She had to take some time for herself. She needed to find her happy place and visit it for a while. If she went back into the hospital now, she'd really lose her cool and that wouldn't be a good thing. She had to remind herself why she was here. She was here to support her father, sister, and brother. She was here to help Sadie say her good-byes. She was here to bury Mama G when the time came. And then they would leave. They hadn't even been here for twenty-four hours and already she could see what it would be like if they lived here. Jason would show up at the most inconvenient times, and she'd never be able to get away from him.

No, Boston was where she should be. It was good for them there. Sadie had many friends, loved her daycare, and was happy there. Emily missed Mosquero, missed her best friends, but with technology today, you were never that far from friends and family anymore. And besides, her happiness didn't matter as much as Sadie's. Boston was the only life Sadie had known. And Emily didn't think it would occur to Sadie to want or wish it any different.

*****

"Should I be worried?" Jason asked.

"No." Clint chuckled. "She's stubborn, and she thinks she has everything figured out. But she's wrong and someone needs to make her see that. Hope hasn't. Gina and Phoebe haven't. You haven't. Grace hasn't. It's time someone got in her face and made her see it with her own eyes."

"She won't. I think I understand that now. She's hell-bent on believing what she saw and she's not going to let that go."

"She will eventually. I'm not saying you didn't make a mistake. You did. But you can't be wholly to blame for it. You were drunk, Lila was hiding in your room and naked. And you were expecting Emily."

Jason's face turned bright red. "Uh, about that."

Clint put his hand up. "I don't want what you're selling. You think I don't know what goes on behind closed doors? Obviously you'd already done the deed since she was pregnant then. That's not the point anyway. The point is, she assumed and she's made an ass of herself. The sooner she owns up to it, the sooner she sees how wrong she is, the sooner you all can be one big happy family."

"But is this the right time to force her to see all that? She's got to be in high distress over Grace. Hell, she hasn't even been back here since she left. I'm just not sure if forcing her to see all this now is a good idea. What if she loses it?"

"When would be the right time? And what else do we have but time. There's fifty minutes of every hour where we're just sitting around here with our thumbs up our asses. Grace has wanted this fixed since it happened. And if that's how we're spending our time in between visits, I know Grace wouldn't complain."

"I guess you'd know for sure."

"Bet your ass I would." Clint sighed and took a seat. "Listen, even when she does see the light, you're going to have some hard work to do. But you've been fighting for a long time, and I know how much you love her. Any fool can see she still loves you; it's written all over her face every time she looks at you. All we have to do is knock that wall down she's got erected around her heart and you should be good to go." Clint paused and pointed his finger in Jason's face. "So long as you don't screw it up again!"

"No, sir."

"I'd suggest you make yourself a permanent fixture around here the next few days. Get in her face as much as possible."

"Yep, got someone hired on for the next few weeks to take care of the ranch. Soon as I got back from seeing Grace the other night, I made arrangements. I plan to be here as much as possible."

"I knew you were a smart man." Clint laughed.

"Figured it was my best shot at getting her to see me. To talk to me. To let me explain. She's not going anywhere, not with Grace laid up here," Jason said, face reddening. "Shit, I didn't mean that the way it sounded."

"I know you didn't. But it's the truth."

Jason sat down hard on a chair. "I didn't realize you knew so much of what happened. I guess I should have figured Grace would have discussed it with you. And here I've been avoiding you for fear you were disgusted with me. Or planned to finish what you started that morning," he said, referring to the morning of the wedding and Clint's powerful right hook.

"I was at first, no denying it. But once you found out the truth, I couldn't hold you fully accountable. Lila played a mean and dirty trick, and I'm sure she'll play some more before it's all said and done. Especially once she finds out Em is back in town."

"I stay away from Lila as much as I can in a town this small. But she knows my habits, knows my haunts. You'd think a victim of stalking would know when she's doing it herself."

"Yeah, well, she's a little touched in the head. Probably wouldn't hurt her any to spend some time in the mental hospital. Some of those meds could help, I'm thinking."

Jason laughed. "Do you know where they're staying? Figured I'd get myself a room here so I'm not wasting time driving back and forth."

"Some kind of suites place. I'm not sure, but I can find out from Hope when she gets here."

"Thanks." He looked over at Sadie. "Are you hungry, Buttercup?"

"Yep."

"Let's go." Jason stood and held out his hand. "I guess Emily isn't coming back anytime soon. So, we'll go get lunch, and then I have no idea what we'll do. But we'll be back here around five. Maybe we can all get dinner together or order pizza and eat in here."

"Sounds like a good plan. See you then."

Clint watched them leave, a smile on his face. "I feel good about this Grace. I feel like this will be solved soon and they'll be coming home." Clint nodded his head, and when the alarm on his phone went off, his steps were a little lighter on his way to visit with his wife.

Chapter Twenty

"He just appeared?" Hope asked, eyes wide with incredulity.

"Yeah, out of the blue. He's all 'Hi, Emily. Long time no see. Let's pretend the past didn't happen.' It was ridiculous."

"What are you going to do?"

"Ignore him as much as possible. Then go home."

"Sounds like he wants you back."

"Surprise! Of course he does. He's been spending all this time trying to get me back. Now I'm here, in his territory, so of course he's going to try even harder. But it's not going to work."

"What if he's sincere?"

Emily snorted. "Please."

Hope rolled her eyes and changed the subject. "So, how's Dad?"

"Hanging in there, honestly. He's being a good sport about sharing the visiting times with us. I haven't seen Tyler yet, but I imagine he'll be arriving shortly. He said he had a lot of chores to get done today."

"I'm sure between Mom and Sophie, he's got to be boiling over with stress."

"True. Sophie is planning to come here on Saturday with the boys."

"How's she feeling?"

"I don't know. Haven't seen or talked to her. Just been busy since we got here." Emily glanced over her shoulder, and seeing nothing in her way, she changed lanes. Their exit was coming up, and she needed to get over to the far right lane. The traffic wasn't cooperating though, as the big SUV next to her wouldn't move. "Have you heard from Derek?" she asked after speeding up enough to squeeze between the two SUVs, earning a loud horn blast for her efforts from the SUV that was next to her.

"Yes, he was able to get everything mostly rescheduled. He said he'd have to do a few conference calls, but he's on his way."

"When does he arrive?"

"I'm not sure. He's flying standby, so it's anyone's guess." She played with the engagement ring on her finger. "He said he'd get his own rental since he's not sure when he'll arrive. He doesn't want to inconvenience anyone."

"It can't hurt, though," Emily said, maneuvering the car onto the exit ramp. "The more cars we have the better flexibility we have to get where we need to." She took a right at the end of the ramp and quickly got into the left lane for the hospital.

"So he'll meet us at the hospital?"

"Yeah." She sighed, glancing up at the massive brick structure that was the hospital. "Guess I better reserve him a room, he could get in in the middle of the night."

"Oh," Emily said, smiling slightly. "I already took care of that."

"What do you mean?"

"I got you two a room, in case he was able to make it. Figured you'd rather share a room with him than with us."

Hope nodded. "Yeah." She grinned. "Thank you. Hey, so what happened with the hotel, anyway?"

"Beats me. The clerk said it was canceled. But she got us a room at the Embassy Suites, and it's still a Hilton property," Emily said positively. "More geared toward families but still Hilton. And their breakfast is phenomenal."

"Doesn't matter to me, though I do appreciate you taking care of me and my silly idiosyncrasies. I'm just glad to be here and to be here before anything more tragic happens."

"I know what you mean."

"I was so scared, Em. So scared I'd be too late," Hope said softly, gazing out the window and wiping a tear from her eye.

"You're here now, put it away. We need positive thinking."

"I know, you're right. Damn." Hope blew out a deep, cleansing breath. "I'm here, and it's all going to be okay."

"They won't take her down for the tests until after your visit. Being her daughter, you might get a reaction out of her, too."

"I hope so. Anything would be nice. I hate that they think she has no brain activity. Doesn't that mean life support and then major decisions about taking her off?"

"She is on life support, Hope. She has machines and wires and all that. As far as taking her off, I have no idea how that works. But I doubt Dad would let that happen."

"Me either. Not if there's a chance."

Emily nodded and took the exit for the hospital. "Are you hungry?"

"No. I couldn't eat right now, anyway."

"There's a reasonable cafeteria in the hospital. Food isn't terrible, surprisingly."

"Where's Sadie?"

"With Jason. He took her to lunch."

"That's nice. The hospital has to be boring for her."

"Yeah, there's only so much we can bring in to keep her occupied. Unfortunately, she has the attention span of a fruit fly."

"I bet she was excited to see him." Hope smiled.

"Yeah." Emily nodded. "It was good to see. And I have to admit, he makes a pretty good father. He was very concerned about how she was doing and feeling." Then she snorted. "Dad went all Mother Theresa on me while Jason was visiting with Mama G."

"What do you mean?"

"Well, you know how he keeps his opinions to himself usually and lets Mama G do the hard talks?"

"Yeah . . ."

"Well, he wasn't holding anything back today." Emily went into the conversation, doing her best to be as accurate as possible in the retelling.

"Well, that's nothing you haven't heard before from Mom, me, or Gina."

"I know, but I guess I didn't know he knew. And since when does he have an opinion on it?"

"I guess since now. But seriously, what are you going to do?"

"I told you. Ignore him as much as possible and then go home."

"Doesn't sound like Dad or Jason are going to let you go without a fight."

"Nope, but I can handle it." *I hope*, she added silently to herself.

"So, is the general consensus that Lila staged the whole thing, and since Jason was drunk, no one really blames him?"

"Pretty much. They think I should give him a pass."

"You have to admit, it sounds plausible."

"If it were anyone else, yes, I suppose it would. But it's not, and I'm not, and here we are." Emily banged her hand on the steering wheel. "I just wasn't expecting it from Dad. And the worst part?"

"What?"

"The worst part was Jason showed up right after my angry outburst. After I'd just poured out how shattered I was. Like I wanted or needed him to hear that? Or Sadie, who was quietly watching television? I forgot she was even there. I can't believe I lost control like that!"

"Oh shit," Hope breathed. "What did you do?"

"I shrieked, apologized to Sadie, and then stormed out. Went outside for about a half hour and tried to find my happy place. Jason and Sadie left while I was outside."

"Did you find your happy place?"

"No," Emily admitted. "I imagine I won't find it again until we get home to Boston."

"That could be a while."

Emily nodded. They drifted into silence until they reached the hospital. Clint was waiting for them in the waiting room, and Hope went straight to his arms. "Aw, Daddy," she sighed against his chest.

"I'm glad you're here. When you're ready, you can go in to see her."

"I thought I was ready, but it turns out I'm just a big chicken."

Emily walked over and placed her hand on Hope's back. "You're not. This isn't a moment you ever thought you'd have to face. Take some breaths, and when you're ready, go in. They'll wait until you visit. I'll make sure of it."

Hope nodded and continued to hold on to Clint. "I feel like I'll crumble into pieces if I let go right now," she whispered.

Emily could feel the tears brimming in her own eyes, and she wrapped her arms around everyone. "Group hug," she choked out.

She recognized her brother's cologne a second before she felt his arms come around them. "Family hug," he corrected.

They stood together, wrapped in each other's arms. After a few minutes, Hope broke free. "I guess I better get in there. Do you want to come with me, Ty?"

"I've seen her and been in with her. You haven't yet. Go." He motioned toward the door. "Have your time with her. I'll visit after the tests are over."

Hope nodded and walked out of the waiting room.

Emily launched herself into her brother's arms, giving him a tight squeeze. "You're here!" Emily said happily through her tears.

"Finally. Got up early to get the important chores done."

"How's Sophie?" Clint asked.

"She says she's feeling good, but I know she's exhausted."

"Does she need anything?" Emily asked.

"Just for the baby to arrive," Tyler said, grinning. "She just wants her body back, sleeping with a watermelon in your stomach doesn't lend itself to a lot of rest. Or so I'm repeatedly told throughout the day when I suggest she rest."

"She's right, but your heart is in the right place." Emily laughed.

They sat around chatting while Hope had her ten minutes with Grace. When she poked her head into the waiting room, the three of them jumped to their feet and followed her into the hallway. "They're ready for her." Hope motioned to Grace's room.

They stood in the doorway of Grace's room while the nurses prepared Grace to be moved.

"We'll come tell you when she's back," one of the nurses told them. "She should be done in a couple hours."

As she was wheeled down the hall and into the elevator, the four of them followed Grace with their eyes, praying the tests revealed what their hearts yearned for most. That she would come home with them soon.

Chapter Twenty-One

"I'm sorry for yelling at you earlier, Dad."

Clint nodded and pulled Emily in for a hug. "I'm sorry for embarrassing you in front of him."

"I need you to understand, though, that we're not getting back together. It's beyond repair, and when I no longer need to be here, Sadie and I are returning to Boston."

"I hear you, but you need to understand that I don't agree with your decision. I don't want to make you any angrier, but I will not give up trying to persuade you to stay."

"Well, so long as we understand each other." Emily smiled.

"Indeed." Clint smoothed a hand down Emily's face. "Jason and Sadie are bringing pizza back with them this evening, and we're gonna eat here before dispersing to our respective hotels."

Nodding, Emily sat down at "her" table. "Sounds good."

"I'm going to run out and do some errands while Grace is in testing. Call me if I'm not back by the time she's done?"

"Sure, Dad. Is there anything I can do for you?"

Clint shook his head. "No, I just need a haircut. I'm going to pick up some toiletries. I don't like what they have in the hotel. And see if I can find a couple more books to read." He pulled on his button shirt. "Anything is better than sitting around here waiting. I think I've had enough of that to last me a lifetime."

"I'm just going to sit here and try to get some work done. I'll let you know if I hear anything."

Clint nodded his thanks and walked out of the waiting room.

Emily was deep in conversation with Phil when Hope and Tyler returned from lunch. She had designs spread all over the table and three chairs lined up by the table.

"No, Phil, I just don't think that's going to work. She hates pastels; it's written clear as day on this order."

"But maybe she doesn't know she likes pastels. I'm telling you, we need something to soften up the room."

"I agree, but we're going to have to figure it out without the use of pastels."

"What if we give her two options? One with pastels and one without? And we don't even have to use a lot of pastels, just a pale yellow or green would go a long way to softening up that room."

"I guess that would be okay, but we offer it as a last resort. You know if we offer it first, she'll close her mind to it as soon as she sees the pastels and that'll be the end of the presentation."

"Works for me."

"I hate this room. Who designs a room with barely any windows? It's a nightmare."

"You can only add so many lamps to the room before it becomes too cluttered."

"Exactly. Okay. Well, you come up with the design using pastels, and I'll work on mine. We can talk later and compare notes." Emily took a sip of her Pepsi. "Did you send out the acceptance letter?"

"Yeah, it went out with this morning's mail run."

"Have you heard from Jenny? How's her project?"

"I haven't, but I'm sure she's working away on it."

"Yeah. Okay, we can talk about the rest tomorrow. But this one is due tomorrow, so let's get it done."

"I love having a plan for my afternoon. Talk to you later."

"Bye." Emily hung up and eyed her siblings. "What's so funny?"

"Nothing," Tyler snickered.

Hope shook her head and tried to hide her smile.

"What?" Emily asked again.

"It's just you've turned this waiting room into a conference room-type place, your papers are everywhere, and have you seen your hair, Medusa?"

"What?!" Emily shrieked. She ran out of the room and straight to the bathroom. Between the wind and her hands, they were right. She looked like a nightmare. Doing her best to repair her hair, she returned to the waiting room. "Anything good to eat down there?"

"The usual hospital cafeteria fare," Tyler replied. "I had a greasy cheeseburger with fries, and this one," he said thumbing Hope, "had a nice healthy salad."

Hope stuck her tongue out at him. "There's a nice selection. You can pretty much find whatever you feel like."

Emily nodded. "Okay, I guess I'll go eat before I begin working on this project. I need some fortification. You guys need anything?"

"Nah," they said in unison.

"Okay. Dad went out to run errands. He wants a call if we hear anything ahead of when we're supposed to."

Tyler saluted her. "We'll be good soldiers and guard the situation. Never fear, fearless leader, we've got this!" he mocked.

Emily's smile was tight. "Good. See you in a bit."

When he was sure Emily was out of earshot, he turned to Hope. "What's her problem?"

"What are you? An idiot? She's in close quarters with Jason. Dad's being relentless in his pursuit to keep her in Mosquero, and I'm pretty sure he's pushing hard for her to patch things up with Jason."

"Seriously? *Dad* is doing this?"

"Yeah, it's weird, I know. But Mom being here must have opened his flood gates of opinions. She told me they got into a huge argument before she came to get me at the airport. And apparently Jason heard some of it."

"Oops."

"Yeah. She was mortified."

"Well, can't say I disagree with Dad."

"Me either."

"Do you think we should get involved?"

"I'm not getting involved. You do what you want, but I'm staying out of it. I live with her, no way I'm taking a public stand. Nope!"

Tyler laughed. "Smart. I might join you and just sit back and watch the fireworks. There's bound to be some more."

"Yep."

Thirty minutes later, Emily swung into the room. She threw a bottled water to her sister and a Mt. Dew to her brother. "Figured after your gossip session, you'd be parched."

Tyler raised his eyebrow and Hope's jaw dropped.

"Please, you think I don't know? My ears were burning the whole way through lunch."

"You give yourself way too much credit," Tyler said. "You only took up about a minute of our conversation."

"I bet," Emily said and crossed her arms in front of her chest. "So, whose side are you on?" she asked, swinging her eyes from one to the other.

"I don't know what you mean," Hope said.

"Really?" Emily lifted an eyebrow and tapped her foot.

"We're on the winner's side." Tyler laughed. "We're total bandwagon groupies."

"Funny." Emily smirked.

"We just want you to be happy," Hope said in a calm voice.

"Oh, I know," Emily said sarcastically. "Everyone just wants me to be happy and somehow they think that involves moving back here and taking up with the cheating jerk."

Hope sighed.

Emily waved her hand in the air. "Well, it doesn't matter."

"May the best man win!" Tyler shouted.

Emily laughed and shook her head. "You're so weird," she said, sitting down at the table. She pulled up her email and tried to block out Tyler and Hope's conversation.

Their easy banter made it hard to concentrate and left her wanting to join the conversation. It wasn't often that she felt left out, but today was one of those days. Between Jason sneaking up on her and her argument with her father, not to mention the conversation she was sure Tyler and Hope had had about her, she was feeling off. Left out. Out of the loop. However you wanted to phrase it, she didn't feel right and it bothered her.

She normally would be fine, setting up her *office* and getting her work done. Ignoring the easy banter of her siblings. But today was impossible, and it was the worst possible day for it. She needed the escape and this project was not only due next week, but she and Phil still had so much to do. The client would be coming into the office on Wednesday at 2:00 p.m. and Phil would be presenting their designs.

From the beginning, Emily knew this project would be trouble. Maryanne Thompson was the client, and she was fairly well-known and hoity-toity in Boston. They were old money, and Maryanne was not shy about informing anyone who would listen about how her husband's family had made a mint in the railroad business and miraculously kept it by diversifying their investments. They'd been smart, she'd often say. They hadn't taken their newfound wealth for granted and because of that, look where they were.

She had a very narrow view of design, and Emily couldn't fathom why she'd chosen their firm for her design needs. They were anything but old-fashioned, their tastes running toward modern and contemporary. The thick draperies and wallpaper of long ago held no desire for anyone in their firm, but it was what appealed to Maryanne Thompson, and by all that was holy, she'd have new everything—drab as can be.

Emily was determined to give Maryanne what she wanted, but modernized. Instead of wallpaper, Emily was experimenting with different paints and paint designs. As for the draperies, Emily couldn't see any way around them. There was one window in the room, nothing spectacular. It seemed to Emily that it was added as an afterthought, with no real thought to the aesthetics. She was hoping Maryanne would be amenable to having a slight remodeling project to make the window bigger and grander. Opening up the room and letting in more light.

Which the room could definitely benefit from. And if she felt like being unkind, which when she had to speak with Maryanne was quite often, the room's owner could benefit from more light as well. Brighten up that dark and drab personality.

Emily shook her head and pulled up her design plans. Phil would be presenting three designs, though he didn't know it yet. There was his design, incorporating the pastels Maryanne despised. Emily's first design, which basically is a mirror of what is currently there, just new. And her third design, with the bigger window, new paint, and no draperies.

She hoped Maryanne liked the designs they offered but was prepared for a negative reaction. She just hoped, if Maryanne did indeed hate the designs, she didn't go spreading it around like wildfire. Especially with Kendra out of the country and unable to help with staving off the bad review.

Taking a deep breath, she tried one more time to dive into her work, but she just couldn't concentrate. And when her father walked in a couple of minutes later, she knew it was over for good. She'd just have to work tonight, after Sadie and Hope went to bed and burn the midnight oil to get it done.

She closed her laptop and put it in her briefcase and then rolled up the design plans, putting an elastic around them and setting them on the chair next to her briefcase.

"Done working so soon?" Clint asked her.

"Not exactly, but I'm having a hard time getting into the groove. I'll work tonight after Sadie's in bed." Emily stood and stretched. "Did you get your errands done?"

"Your hair looks nice, Dad," Hope gushed. "Where'd you go?"

"Some quicky haircut place down the street. It was next to the drug store. Got my toiletries and some books. Counting it as a win." He sighed and glanced toward the door. "Your mother's not done yet?"

"Not that we've heard or seen," Tyler answered.

Clint looked at his watch. "Guess it's only been an hour and a half." He sat down heavily on the chair and opened his book. "Maybe they'll be done with her by the time I finish this book."

No one knew what to say, so they sat in silence as Clint read, lost in their own thoughts.

Forty-five minutes later, the doctor came in. "Mr. Camancho?"

Clint shot to his feet, the book falling to the floor next to him. He bent down to pick it up, holding it nervously in his hands. "Yes?"

"I've reviewed all the results and I'm sorry to say that there is still no brain activity."

"But how is that possible? She reacted to the song," Clint asked.

"We think that was an involuntary movement," Dr. Mosler explained. "The next step is discussing removal of the life-support systems and letting Mrs. Camancho go."

"What?" shrieked Hope. "No, no, no. That's not an option. She could still get better!" She turned to Clint. "Couldn't she, Daddy?"

Tyler and Emily wrapped their arms around Hope, shushing her while the doctor continued to speak with Clint.

"I understand this is not what you were hoping to hear. It's certainly not what I was hoping to convey to you this afternoon. Mrs. Camancho has sustained a large amount of trauma to her brain, and it is our opinion that she will not recover from it."

"What about a second opinion?" Emily asked.

Dr. Mosler nodded. "I would be happy to provide you with the names and contact information of several neurosurgeons."

"Assuming we don't obtain a second opinion, when would you recommend disconnecting my wife from life support?"

"That is completely up to you, Mr. Camancho. I know this is a difficult time, and I know that a decision of this nature is not made lightly. She is in no pain, so if you need a day or two, I'm happy to accommodate you."

"Can we have a few minutes to discuss this?" Clint asked.

"Of course. Just have the nurses page me when you're ready."

Clint nodded and sat down on his chair. He dropped his head in his hands and took a shaky breath.

"Daddy! Please don't. Please don't make this decision without a second opinion. I mean, that doctor doesn't even look old enough to be out of high school!" Hope pleaded. She was on her knees in front of him, hands wrapped around his forearms.

Emily and Tyler stood just behind her, eyes wide and hearts breaking.

"I want a second opinion, child. But I fear any doctor we speak to will tell us the same thing."

"But she's all I have left," Hope keened.

Emily dropped to her knees beside Hope. "You have us, Hope." Tears coursed down Hope's face, and while she accepted her embrace, Emily knew Hope was lost in her grief. They'd been a family since Hope was seven years old, but Emily could understand Hope's pain at losing her last biological parent.

"Hope?" a gruff voice asked from the entrance to the waiting room.

Hope raised her tear-stained face and glanced at the door. "Derek," she cried, voice breaking. She continued kneeling on the floor, unable to gather the energy to greet her fiancé.

It didn't matter. Derek dropped his briefcase on the closest chair and rushed to her side. He pulled her up into his arms. "Babe, what's going on?"

Hope buried her face in his chest, the tears turning to sobs.

He turned worried eyes on Emily, who quickly and quietly told him what was going on.

"You'll be getting second and third opinions, right?" he asked, holding Hope tight against his chest.

Emily glanced at her father, who slowly nodded his assent. His face was full of despair, heartbreaking to see.

Derek turned back to Emily, inclining his head toward Hope. "Has she been like this the entire time?" he mouthed the words so Hope couldn't hear.

Emily shook her head. "Just since this news," she mouthed back.

He nodded, and after kissing the top of Hope's head, he pulled back to look into her eyes. "Babe, let's get some air," he suggested, leading her toward the door.

Once they were out of earshot, Clint glanced up. "I'm glad he's here for her."

Emily and Tyler nodded.

"She needs him," Emily whispered.

"Especially if she thinks she's all alone," Tyler said sadly.

"She doesn't. Not deep down. She'll remember we're family and that we're here for her. She just needs some time," Clint said.

They fell silent for a few minutes until Emily remembered Dr. Mosler was waiting for their answer.

"Dad, Dr. Mosler is waiting," she reminded him.

Clint sighed, his entire body seemed to deflate.

"Dad," Tyler said forcefully. "Let's get those second opinions. I'll go get the info from Dr. Mosler."

Clint glanced up, noted Emily and Tyler's hopeful faces, and said "Yes" on a sad sigh.

"I'm so sorry, Dad," Emily said, laying a hand on his shoulder.

"Me, too," Clint mumbled, voice cracking in pain. "Me, too."

Chapter Twenty-Two

The next couple of days flew by. Three doctors from across the country came to give their opinions on Grace's condition. But every one of them said the same thing. "No brain activity."

By Sunday evening, they had no choice but to accept the truth. Grace would not be coming back to them.

Emily tried to offer comfort to Hope as best she could, but Hope was inconsolable. She refused to eat, spent all her time with Grace, and exiled herself to the room she shared with Derek at the hotel when they weren't at the hospital. Derek did his best to coax her to eat, but he didn't have any better luck than Emily.

Clint was just as wrecked. He barely ate, and unless Sadie was in the room, he didn't have anything to say.

Neither of them were capable of making decisions, too lost in their grief. Tyler wasn't much help, either, not with Sophie so close to giving birth. He was splitting his time between the ranch and the hospital, the two-and-a-half-hour drive exhausting him.

That left Emily. She was the one signing paperwork, speaking with the insurance companies, preparing things for Mama G's death, and organizing the funeral arrangements.

Sophie had opted to stay at the ranch to get things prepared for the funeral. She thought keeping the boys at home amidst all the devastating emotions was for the best, and Emily couldn't blame her. If she had her choice, Sadie would be as far away as possible, too. As it was, Sadie was spending a lot of time with Jason—away from the hospital. And though she'd never admit it, having Jason at the hotel *had* been a blessing.

Oh, she'd been plenty pissed when he'd pulled up into the hotel parking lot behind her Friday night. And she'd had a good many words to say to that effect right there in the parking lot. Not that it had mattered. He'd sauntered right into the lobby and up to the registration desk, all while she glared death and destruction at him.

The creep had even reserved a room near theirs, on the same floor, and had grinned the whole way up the elevator. Meanwhile, she was seething and Sadie was happier than a pig in mud.

Nope, as the minutes passed, Emily was feeling the last of her support system wither away in favor of Jason.

Seriously, what was wrong with her? She shouldn't be feeling this way. She was a grown woman for goodness' sake. She'd been living on her own, raising her daughter, and succeeding at her job.

If she didn't know herself better, she'd say she was jealous. But that couldn't be right, could it? Jealous of Jason? Sadie was glued to him. Clint and Hope, and now even Tyler, seemed to be taking up his "Win Emily Back" cause. She hadn't yet seen Gina, but she could well imagine what Gina would have to say. Hell, Gina had been saying it all along.

Emily shook her head. She really needed to get a grip on herself and this crazy situation. Just because everyone else jumped off a bridge, did that mean she had to do it, too?

No. And she was going to stand firm on that one fact. She didn't have to jump off the bridge and she wouldn't.

Dr. Mosler would be taking Grace off life support in the morning, and once she was cleared, the funeral home director would be arriving to transport Grace back to Mosquero.

She pushed thoughts of Jason and his cause out of her mind, instead focusing on the options in front of her for Grace's funeral. Who knew there were so many? She closed her eyes and circled her finger around the page, letting it drop where it landed. On this page were the options for the coffins and Emily cringed at the one her finger had landed on. It was a dull pine, with no embellishments. It was obviously their lower end and Emily couldn't picture Grace spending eternity in it. Sighing, she chose the maple casket. She liked the color of the wood and it was neither ostentatious nor dull.

The options for the service blew her mind. Traditional service in a funeral home or at the church; a memorial service; a viewing and then a funeral service; a graveside service. How was she to know which option Grace would have preferred? She sorely wished Hope or her father were in a better place to help her with this. Tyler was as clueless as she was. She tried asking his opinion and had been disappointed when he'd been no help, either.

"What's the point?" he had asked.

"What do you mean?" Emily asked, frustrated.

"I mean, she's dead." He crossed himself. "God rest her soul."

"But we should still honor her."

"Yes, but I have no opinion here."

She could understand where Tyler was coming from, and there was a part of her that understood funerals were done for the living, not the dead. But decisions and plans had to be made.

She opted for a traditional service at the church followed by a graveside service, and they'd have a viewing the evening before. Then they'd have a traditional gathering at the ranch after the services. She asked Sophie to arrange for house cleaning, neither she nor Hope were familiar with the companies in town that would do it on such short notice.

She knew from experience that they wouldn't have to worry about food as everyone who gathered would bring enough to feed an army. That, in itself, was a load off.

She'd stop at the liquor store on their way to Mosquero, and she'd also pick up a veggie tray and something sweet from the grocery store as well. That was more about her own pride than anything. She certainly didn't want the first guests to show up to an empty kitchen. And she didn't know about anyone else, but she was going to need a drink or two or three to get through the day.

When they arrived back at the hospital bright and early Monday morning, everyone looked as though they hadn't slept in a week. Emily knew she herself didn't look any different. She'd tried her best to fix the stress, devastation, and sleeplessness that showed on her face, but there was no help for it. She was heartbroken and there really was nothing that could be done for it.

Her father was already at the hospital when she arrived, and he was speaking with Dr. Mosler in the hallway. Emily walked into Mama G's room and sat down on the bed. She took her hand in her own and kissed the paper-thin skin. She was going to miss her. Mama G had been her anchor when she'd had left home . . . in fact, she'd been her anchor since joining the family when Emily was eight.

Grace and Hope had been new to town. Grace had gotten a job as the third grade teacher, and Emily was thrilled to have a new friend in Hope. They quickly became inseparable and would spend many afternoons together. With Gina and Phoebe joining them often, the fast friends quickly became known as The Four and it stuck the entire way through high school. Emily wouldn't be surprised if the folks in town still called them that.

Spending all that time with Hope was sure to bring their parents together, and that is exactly what happened. By the end of the school year, Clint and Grace were a pretty serious duo and by the following summer had tied the knot. Emily was delighted that her best friend was now her sister and they shared everything.

Grace had been there for everything, and now she was going to miss the best part. Emily felt the first stirrings of rage for the drunk driver that caused this wonderful, caring person to be lying here in this hospital bed so close to her last breaths. It wasn't fair! The boys needed their grandmother, Sadie needed her grandmother—Hope needed her mother! They all needed Grace, and Emily couldn't fathom what they'd do without her. There would be a huge hole in their family.

Emily laid her head on Grace's chest and let the tears flow freely.

She felt a hand on her back and twisted her head to see who it was. Hope. She had a wobbly smile on her face, and she sat on the opposite side of the bed. She rubbed Emily's back, giving comfort where there hadn't been any before.

"You haven't had a moment to grieve yet," Hope said quietly. "I'm so sorry everything has fallen to you."

Emily shook her head. "Don't be sorry." She sat up and wiped her eyes. "I was doing fine until this morning. Being here, having free reign of her room. It made it all too real. She's leaving us and there's not one of us who's ready for it."

"She visited me last night," Hope whispered. "It was during one of my snippets of sleep. She's so proud of us all, she said, and she loves us so much. She'll be watching us from above and she'll be waiting."

"Oh, Hope," Emily said, reaching out to hug her sister. "I'm so glad you got to speak to her one last time."

"It was something I needed," Hope nodded. "And whether it was really her or my subconscious dreaming it, I don't care. But I'm in a better place today, more accepting, though I really wish we didn't have to do this."

"Me neither."

Clint stepped into the room and came around to Emily's side of the bed. He grasped her hand and squeezed. "The paperwork is all signed. Dr. Mosler said we have a few minutes before he comes in."

Emily nodded, and Hope switched sides. She put her arms around Clint's waist and hugged hard.

"Where's Tyler and Derek?" Emily asked.

"Derek didn't want to intrude. He's finishing up some work this morning. He offered to come with me, but I told him I'd be okay. The visit last night helped," Hope explained.

"And Tyler said he couldn't watch this, so he left this morning to help Sophie with the last-minute preparations," Clint said gruffly.

Understanding, Emily nodded. She'd left Sadie with Jason this morning for the same reason. They would enjoy a leisurely breakfast, play in the pool, and Sadie would have good memories of today. Tonight would be the viewing and Emily had already decided to keep Sadie away. She was too young, and if she was honest, Sadie didn't need the closure, not at eighteen months old.

When Dr. Mosler came in a half hour later, they'd all had time to say their private good-byes. Now they stood around Grace's bed, holding hands and lost in their own memories of Grace. As Dr. Mosler began turning off machines, Hope began to hum "Amazing Grace," and with tears pouring down her face, Emily joined in. Clint took it a step further and added the words, and Emily couldn't think of a better send-off for their beloved Grace than this.

Chapter Twenty-Three

An hour and a half into the drive back to the ranch, Emily, Hope, and Sadie were driving through the main village of Mosquero. Derek had gotten pulled into a last-minute conference call, and rather than hold up the procession, he'd encouraged everyone to go on without him. Hope had offered to drive so Emily could keep Sadie, who had never been in a car for longer than a half hour, happy in the backseat. They shouldn't have worried. All the activity that morning had worn her out and she'd fallen asleep before they'd left the city limits of Santa Fe.

Despite herself, Emily was a little excited about being home. The village itself wasn't very big and consisted of less than two hundred people. It was one of those towns where everyone knew everyone, and all your private business was fodder for gossip among the locals.

She glanced out the windows as Hope drove through the village. It hadn't changed much and that was a bit of a comfort to Emily. The tiny grocery store that was a third of the size of the stores in Boston was still on the corner of Main Street. Mr. and Mrs. Addlemeyer were out front, Mrs. Addlemeyer sitting on her rocking chair waiting for customers and Mr. Addlemeyer sweeping the sidewalk. Emily smiled to herself; it was nice to see some things hadn't changed, but she felt bad for him. How many times had he swept that sidewalk throughout his life, only to have to do it again the next day? The dryness of the desert made the sand soar with the slightest of breezes.

Next, they passed the post office and the courthouse. Mosquero was the county seat, which was good because there were always land disputes to be dealt with, and it was so much easier to take care of those issues right here in town, rather than traveling an hour or more away to one of the bigger towns.

Next in line down Main Street was The Dustbowl, the cafe by day and bar by night, and next to that, the gas station.

A feeling of contentment settled over Emily as she took in these familiar sights. It was good to know that somewhere in the world things stayed the same.

"Can't believe how little Main Street has changed," Hope said.

"It makes me strangely happy," Emily said. "I feel like in all the chaos of our lives right now, some things are stable and we can count on them."

Hope nodded and went back to driving.

A farming community before the Dust Bowl drought, Mosquero was now a ranching community. Emily's family was no different from the rest of the village in that respect. They raised Black Angus cattle for the sole purpose of selling them to be processed for beef. The Camancho ranch consisted of a few hundred thousand acres, one of the largest in Mosquero.

Jason's family owned a ranch a bit bigger than the Camancho's. It bordered their ranch. To get from one house to the other, one would only have to walk across the yard and through a patch of trees. Emily recalled many afternoons when she would take that trip across the yards. There was a small creek that ran between the properties that all the children had played in during their youth. A small bridge had been added to the creek when Emily had been around six years old, but none of them ever used it, preferring to hop across the creek on the rocks.

Emily looked back into the back seat of the car to find Sadie still sleeping. She gently shook Sadie and told her that they were almost at the ranch.

Sadie was instantly awake. "How long, Gamps?" she asked with so much excitement that it brought a lump to Emily's throat.

"About five or ten minutes."

"Gamps! UncTy!"

"Gramps will be there, but I'm not sure about Uncle Tyler. He might still be at home with Aunt Sophie and the boys."

"Ride horsie?"

"Maybe in a little while."

"Sadie, look at the cows in the field over there." Hope pointed out the window. "Those are just like the cows that Gramps and Uncle Tyler raise."

"Mooooo," Sadie mimicked.

"Those are Black Angus. That's where we get our hamburgers and steaks," Hope explained.

"Look, here's the entrance to the ranch. Do you see the house?" Emily asked.

"Big!"

"Yes, it is. A lot bigger than our apartment, huh?"

"UncTy! UncTy!" she screeched, straining against her car seat buckles and pointing out the window at her uncle on the front porch.

"Hold your horses, kid, can I at least get to the house first?" Hope laughed.

The next minute, they were pulling up to the house and Sadie was bouncing in her car seat.

Tyler opened Sadie's door when Hope pulled to a stop in front of the huge wraparound porch.

"UncTy!" she squealed in delight when he unbuckled her and lifted her high in his arms.

"How are you doing, sport? How was the car ride?"

"Where's Dad?" Emily asked.

"He's in the kitchen."

"Down! Down!" Sadie said, wiggling in Tyler's arms. As soon as her feet touched the porch, she went flying into the house. "Gamps! Gamps!"

"Now, if that isn't the biggest bundle of energy I've ever seen, I don't know what is! What do you feed that child? Pure sugar?"

"No, she just woke up from a nap," Emily told her brother as she gave him a hug. "And besides, she doesn't have nearly as much energy as those boys you have. Sadie is positively peaceful compared to them!"

Tyler laughed and nodded, opening the screen door for Emily and Hope. "True story."

The interior of the house looked exactly the way it did the day Emily left. The front room contained the same furniture in the same place. The hallway still contained the little table that the phone rested on along with a vase of flowers. The same oriental rugs were in the hallway leading to the kitchen that had been there since Grace moved in with them. That memory brought tears to her eyes and she sniffed them back. She couldn't break down now. She still had so much to go through.

Emily followed behind Tyler and Hope down the hallway. When they got to the kitchen, Tyler stopped short and burst out laughing. Emily and Hope pushed him aside so they could see what he was laughing at. "Oh my," Emily murmured as the full scale of what she was seeing hit her. It wasn't another second before she and Hope were laughing as well.

Sadie was on the floor, trying to eat a cookie around one of the new puppies. Clint was covered in milk, apparently from a glass he had gotten for Sadie. And another one of the puppies was trying to lick the milk off Clint.

When they didn't move to help the two of them out, Clint snapped at them, "Do you think the three of you could stop laughing long enough to help with this mess?"

"Sorry, Daddy," Emily said as she walked over to the sink to get a washcloth. "But this wasn't exactly what we were expecting to see when we walked into the kitchen."

"Didn't know you were into milk baths, Dad," Tyler joked as he bent over to pick up one of the puppies and put him outside, then he picked up a towel and bent toward the floor to clean up the milk.

Hope picked Sadie up and put her on the counter so Emily could wipe the milk, chocolate, and puppy slobber off her face and hands.

"I'm glad you all find this so amusing," Clint said dryly as he picked himself off the floor. "I'm going upstairs to change."

"Doggie kisses," Sadie said gleefully.

Emily smiled and sat Sadie at the table to finish her snack.

"Tyler, did you check on our pregnant cow?" Clint asked, entering the kitchen with dry clothes on. He went straight for the coffeepot and poured himself a mug.

"Yeah. I'd say her time is near," he replied. "Probably tonight or sometime tomorrow."

"Terrible timing," Clint muttered.

"We'll just get one of the hands to watch her while we're busy. We have the vet on speed dial. As soon as she starts, we'll have them call Doctor Ed. He can be here in five minutes, and he's more than qualified to see a cow through a birth."

"You're right." Clint took a gulp of his coffee. "You girls get settled in your rooms, yet?"

They both shook their head.

"What time do we need to be at Dell and Sons?" he asked, referring to the funeral home.

"They said we should plan to arrive forty-five minutes early," Emily said. "So, I guess we need to be there around quarter after five."

Shaking his head, Clint finished off his coffee, and rinsing the mug out, he placed it in the dish drainer. "What the hell am I supposed to do with myself now?" He let out a deep sigh and walked out the screen door, heading for the barn.

"Should one of us go after him?" Hope asked.

Tyler shook his head. "Nah, let him go. He needs some time."

A few minutes later, they heard a knock on the door.

"I wonder who that could be," Tyler said.

"Probably someone wanting to give their condolences," Hope said. "I'll go find out."

As she neared the door, she couldn't believe her eyes. The woman had balls, she had to give her that. Her welcoming smile turned menacing, and without opening the screen door, she folded her arms in front of her, her eyes like glaciers. "What are you doing here?"

"I came to offer my condolences and to see if there was anything I could do to help," Lila said sweetly.

"Thank you and no. We have everything well in hand."

"She was my aunt, Hope."

"Yes, she was. But it doesn't change anything. Your parents will be here in a few hours, shouldn't you be on your way to pick them up?"

"They're renting a car," Lila said. "They need freedom to come and go as they please, and I have to work."

Hope nodded. "I'm sorry for your loss, too," she said sadly. "I'm sure we'll see you at the viewing tonight and funeral tomorrow, as we can't keep you away from those public events. But I'd appreciate it if you would stay away from the reception tomorrow. Your presence will only serve to bring more sadness."

Lila's eyes narrowed, and she took a step closer to the door. "I'm not welcome at the family reception tomorrow?"

"Correct. You've done enough damage to this family; it's best if you stay far away. Like I said, we can't keep you from the public events, but you are not welcome here tomorrow after the funeral services."

"This is about Emily, isn't it?"

"No, this is about you. You've made bad choices and those choices have consequences. This is one of those consequences. Don't come back here, again, ever. You are not welcome here."

With that, Hope took a step back and closed the front door in Lila's face. She took a minute to collect herself. She hated confrontations, they made her have tunnel vision and made her heart race. Tyler and Emily would want to know who was at the door, and she better not keep them waiting or they'd come out here to find out. She went back to the kitchen, knowing once she told them Lila had visited, they'd both want to race out and track her down. Neither would appreciate Lila's gumption. She knew Lila's visit had been a ploy; she didn't care about Grace. She wanted to see Emily and get Emily all riled up. That was her focus. How would they keep Lila away from Emily tomorrow? She'd have to figure that one out this afternoon. The last thing they needed was a confrontation between Emily and Lila.

Chapter Twenty-Four

"Mama?" Sadie asked from the doorway of the room they were sharing. It was Emily's childhood bedroom that she'd shared with Hope, and it hadn't changed since the day she and Jason had left for college.

When Hope had joined the family, they'd made a few adjustments to the room—adding a second twin bed, bookcase, and dresser, but leaving the decor the same. Once they'd grown up a bit, her parents had taken down the rose floral wallpaper and painted the room a pale lavender. The girls had gotten white comforters with lilac flowers on them and curtains to match. Her father had had someone come in to clean and wax the hardwood floor, making it glossy and smooth.

The floor was a bit worn after almost ten years, and the curtains and comforters, as well as the beds and furniture, were the same—if only a bit faded.

"Yes, sweetpea?" Emily was unpacking their suitcases and stowing them under the beds. It was unseasonably cool, so Emily had the windows open to air out the room.

"Have puppy?" she asked, eyes wide and hopeful. "Home puppy?"

"Maybe." Emily smiled. "We have to ask Aunt Hope, it's her apartment." She ran her hand down Sadie's hair and turned to finish unpacking.

Sadie wobbled to the bed and rubbed her eyes. Yawning, she stuck her thumb in her mouth and twirled a lock of hair around her finger. Emily glanced up and sighed to herself. Her poor baby. Crazy schedule, change of time zones, boring time at the hospital, and a normal toddler schedule gone straight to hell.

"Tired baby?"

Sadie shook her head. But Emily knew better. She picked Sadie up and pulled back the blanket and sheets on the bed. Tucking her in, Emily laid down next to her and rubbed her back. Not even two minutes later, Sadie was sound asleep.

Emily quietly got up and finished unpacking. She spent the day roaming the rooms and halls of the house. Venturing outside after Sadie woke from her nap, they saddled a horse and took a short ride around the ranch. Sadie loved the ride and spent the rest of the day talking about it.

When Emily laid her head on her pillow late that night, she wished for strong arms to hold her tight. Sadie was softly snoring in the bed next to her, and Emily's heart was breaking. She wanted to curl up in a ball and cry herself a river, and those strong arms would help to keep her from falling apart and floating down the river with her tears.

She didn't want to wake her daughter, so she turned over and resolutely closed her eyes. There'd be a time and place for her to grieve later. But as the minutes ticked by and she couldn't find a comfortable position, she wondered if sleep would be elusive for her tonight. Her legs were twitching, her mind racing with thoughts and memories of Grace, and the twin bed seemed so much smaller than it had when she'd been a teenager.

Sighing deeply, she flung the blankets back and quietly got out of bed. She pulled the blankets up on Sadie, who was a hot sleeper and routinely kicked her blankets off every night, then kissed her cheek. She snuck out of the room and went down to the kitchen. Pouring herself a mug of milk, she popped it in the microwave and stood in front of it waiting for the countdown so she could open the door before it dinged and woke the house.

She took her mug to the living room and sat on the couch in the dark. Sipping her mug of warmed milk, she glanced around the room and smiled to herself. She remembered the night her father had come home from a poker game and fallen head first over the couch that she'd moved earlier in the day. He'd been so mad and had made her promise to never change the furniture again without the express approval from both him and Grace. She'd agreed but been rather put out about it. She should have known even then that she'd become an interior designer later in life.

She pulled the afghan off the back of the couch and tucked it around her legs. So many cherished memories haunted just this one room. Many nights they sat around watching television together, Grace knitting and Clint reading a book. Endless board games between herself, Hope, and Tyler. Prom pictures. Homecoming pictures. Birthday parties.

And before Emily realized it, tears were pouring down her face. She set her mug on the coffee table and curled up on the couch, wrapping the afghan around her shoulders. She cried until she had no tears left, hiccuping softly and trying to calm her racing heart. She hated to cry, hated the feeling of being emptied and dried out. Hated the puffy, swollen eyes and the red, blotchy skin that always accompanied her bouts of tears. But the worst was that it never made her feel better. There was no cathartic well-being for her. All it did was leave her feeling wrung out and weary.

This time was no different. Wiping her eyes and face, she quietly blew her nose and then picked up her mug. She continued to sip the milk as her mind played through all her fondest memories.

"Can't sleep?" Clint asked quietly from the doorway.

Shrieking softly, Emily jumped and came close to spilling what was left in her mug. "Jeez, Dad, you scared the crap out of me."

"Sorry." He chuckled, sitting down on the couch next to her.

"It's okay. I just didn't hear you. You're stealthy." She smiled into the dark.

"You okay?"

"Yeah, just couldn't sleep. Couldn't get comfy and my brain wouldn't shut down." She motioned with her mug. "Was hoping some warm milk would help." With her free hand, she patted her father's arm. "You?"

"Bed was too empty for my liking. Figured I'd check on the cow."

"Have you been out to see her yet?"

"No, was on my way when I saw something moving in here."

"Do you mind if I come with you?"

"Not at all. Be glad for the company."

When they got to the barn, her father opened the gate to the stall where the cow was being kept. They went inside and found the cow laying down in the hay. Emily went straight to the front of the cow, stroking her nose and whispering soothing words. Clint passed his hands over her belly.

"Is she okay?" Emily asked.

"Yep, shouldn't be long now. She's secreting, and I can feel contractions. We'll have a calf by morning, no doubt."

Emily smiled and continued to pet the cow's face and head. Long before she'd had her own child, she was familiar with the birthing process. Many a night had seen her out in the barn with her father and brother, waiting for a new calf to be born. It had been something neither Hope nor Lila had cared for and Emily had always chalked it up to their city upbringings.

Emily settled down into the hay, leaning her back against the stall wall. "Guess there'll be no need for the vet?"

"Nope, this little mama is doing it right."

"Good. I always hated when the vet came. Meant there was trouble and danger."

"We've lost some pretty good cows through the years."

"Will you call Tyler?"

"No, she's doing well, and there's no reason to have him come over for an easy birth. Besides, Sophie needs her rest and I certainly don't want to call over there and chance waking her up."

"Good point." Emily laughed.

"How's your job going?" Clint asked, settling himself down in the hay.

"It's going well. We've got plenty to keep us busy and just got a new opportunity to send in designs for a business. Kendra should be back at the end of the month. One of her goals for next year is to pick up some more commercial business."

"Will you split the responsibilities?"

"What do you mean?"

"She does the commercial stuff and you do the residential stuff?"

"Oh, I don't know. She hasn't said anything one way or the other."

Clint nodded.

They lapsed into silence, lost in their thoughts and grief. The viewing earlier in the day kept running through Emily's mind like a track with no end.

Even though she'd been at the hospital when Grace had been taken off life support, it still hit her like a sucker punch when she saw Grace laid out in her favorite outfit, a light application of makeup, and looking all the world as if she were just taking a nap. It had taken all the air out of her lungs.

She dropped into the chair in front of the coffin, closing her eyes and praying this was a nightmare she would wake from. Eyes still closed, she pinched the inside of her arm. She blew out a long breath. It hurt, not just the pinch, but Grace's death.

"You holding up okay?"

She stilled. She felt his hand on her shoulder, felt the heat through her shirt, and wanted more than anything to melt into it.

Realizing where her thoughts and heart were headed, she stiffened.

"Fine, thanks," she said stiffly, pulling slightly away from his hand.

He took the seat next to her, staring at Grace. She could only assume he was consumed with much of the same thoughts as she had been. As much as Jason had hurt her, she couldn't ignore the pain he was feeling right now. He loved Grace very much and had relied on her as his mother for a long time. His weekly breakfast/coffee time with her over the past two years had most likely only strengthened their bond and Emily knew he had to be suffering right now.

"She loved you, you know," Emily said quietly, placing a gentle hand on his arm.

"I'm gonna miss her so much," he choked out.

"Yeah, me, too." Emily sighed and sat back in her chair.

"She's been there for me for so long. I have no idea what I'll do without her."

"We just have to keep moving on, living our life and keeping her in our hearts. She was so proud of all of us, and she loved us all very much. We have to keep that in our hearts, too, and take it out when we need it most."

"She's helped keep me sane since you left," he said quietly. He turned imploring eyes on Emily. "I probably would have been camped out on your doorstep, if not for her."

Emily flinched at the pain and conviction she saw in his eyes. This wasn't what she wanted to know or hear. She just wanted peace. It was all she'd wanted since that morning and what she'd been longing for for what seemed like forever.

"I haven't changed my mind, Jason. Grace's death doesn't change things for me. Sadie and I are still going back to Boston."

Jason nodded. He stood and walked over to Grace. Leaning down, he placed a gentle kiss on her forehead. He closed his eyes, bowed his head, and was quiet and still for a few moments. Then he pressed one last kiss to her forehead and slowly walked to the back of the room.

Seeing evidence of Jason's grief brought a tear to Emily's eyes, and unable to help herself, she turned in her seat to watch him. He stopped in front of Hope and gave her a hug. They spoke for a minute before, with one last hug, he moved on to Tyler. He shook Tyler's hand and offered what looked like cordial condolences before moving to Clint.

Clint shook off Jason's offered hand and instead wrapped him in a bear hug. They spoke for a few minutes, and then Jason walked out of the room. Not once did he look back to the front of the room . . . and the room seemed empty with his departure. She didn't want to dwell on that fact, nor how her heart had filled at the sight of him when he'd sat down next to her. She certainly didn't want to dwell on how much her heart hurt for him and how she'd had to force the words out to discourage him from ideas that she'd be staying in Mosquero.

No, she didn't want to dwell on Jason because it only caused her pain. She wanted to forget. She wanted to go home to Boston and go back to pretending she was fine and dandy.

She talked a good game, but she knew, deep down, leaving Mosquero would be hard.

"Looks like it's time," Clint said, standing and moving behind the cow.

Emily, startled from her thoughts, jumped to her feet. "What should I do?"

"Just keep soothing her," he said.

She nodded and sat down in the hay, petting the cow's face and humming a soft lullaby. Twenty minutes later, they had a brand new female calf and a tired mama cow. "She's beautiful," Emily said, speaking softly to the cow. "Great job, Mama!"

"Glad to have that over with before daybreak," Clint said wearily. "I'm gonna go get cleaned up and hit the hay."

"Me, too," Emily said. "I'll walk with you. Will they be okay?" she said, pointing at the new little family.

"Yeah. I'll leave them here in the stall for the rest of the night. Let them rest and bond."

Emily closed the gate behind her and wrapped an arm around Clint's back. "Good work, Dad."

"Thanks to you, it was easy. You've always had a way with them. Keeping the mom calm makes for a quicker and easier birth."

They reached the kitchen door and slid quietly into the house. Emily turned and kissed her father on the cheek. "Night, Dad."

"Night. Get some rest."

"You, too." Emily went into the living room and laid down on the couch. She didn't want to risk waking Sadie, and she knew she'd never fall asleep in that tiny bed anyway.

Helping her father with the birth had been fun and had taken her right back to her childhood. She loved living in the city but, oh, how she'd missed being here and part of the cycle of life on the ranch.

You can take the girl out of the country . . . Yeah, leaving here was going to be hard.

Sighing, she closed her eyes and willed sleep to come quickly.

Chapter Twenty-Five

  Emily awoke with a start and bolted upright, thinking she had overslept. She looked at the clock, and seeing it was only six thirty, she laid back down, willing her racing heart to settle down. She realized two things immediately: the first was the scent of fresh-brewed coffee wafting into the living room, and the second was the smell of bacon that was not far behind the coffee.

  She couldn't imagine who would be awake at this hour. She didn't think it was her father as they'd only gone to bed a few hours ago. There was no way it was Hope, the notorious beauty sleeper. She would have heard the front door open if Tyler had shown up, but he was no chef. The man could barely work the microwave.

  Curiosity getting the better of her, she got up from the couch and went upstairs to use the bathroom and to freshen up before making her way into the kitchen and whoever was working magic in there.

As she passed by her father's room, she could hear muffled sounds coming through the door. She paused outside, and when the sounds didn't cease after a few seconds, she carefully opened the door a crack to peer inside. It was a sight that almost brought her to her knees. He was lying on his stomach, face buried in a pillow, sobbing. She wanted to go to him, to offer comfort, but she knew he would never accept it. Nor would he appreciate having his privacy invaded. She quietly shut his door and continued down the hall toward the bathroom.

She knew she'd never forget the sight of her father on the bed. He was the strong, silent type, and she'd never seen him shed a single tear. Seeing it didn't diminish the strength her father projected, if anything, it only reinforced it. Everyone needed to experience the healing power of crying, and if Emily were a betting woman, she'd bet that this was the first time her father had addressed his grief since Grace's death.

When she was finished in the bathroom, she went into her room and noticed right away that Sadie wasn't in her bed. Where could she be? She wondered if Sadie had awoken in the night, worried that she hadn't been able to find Emily. What if Sadie had needed her while she'd been in the barn with her father? She threw on a pair of sweats and a T-shirt.

Dressed and barely presentable, she rushed from the bedroom and quickly searched the upstairs. Emily didn't find Sadie in the guest room where Hope was sleeping or in Tyler's childhood room. She hurried down the stairs, and reaching the foyer, she began a search of the rooms. She didn't see Sadie anywhere. When she got to the kitchen doorway, the sight that greeted her had her stopping in her tracks. Jason and Sadie were making breakfast, and Sadie was standing on a chair in front of the stove, watching Jason stir eggs in a pan. Emily stood where she was, taking in the sight, marveling at how the two of them meshed so well, despite how little time they got with each other.

"Should we add more cheese to the eggs?"

"More cheese!"

"More cheese it is then." He sprinkled the cheese into the egg mixture and ruffled Sadie's hair when he was done.

Emily smiled to herself as she watched them. What a pair they made.

"Daddy! Love Daddy!"

"And I love Sadie!" he said, hauling her up into his arms, squeezing her tight.

"Good morning," Emily said brightly, entering the kitchen and heading for the coffee pot.

"Mama!" Sadie exclaimed, jumping down from her father's arms and running to hug her mother.

Emily scooped her up and twirled her around the kitchen. "Working hard on the eggs, huh? Everything smells so good!"

"Make breakfast. Yum!" Sadie said, pointing at the stove.

Emily took her mug of coffee and sat at the table. "How long have you been here?"

"I got here at six," Jason said with a smile. "She was in here playing with the puppies."

"Six!" Emily exclaimed. "Well, at least she slept in a bit."

"Six is sleeping in?"

Emily laughed. "It is when you consider she's usually up at seven every day, our time."

"I see your point."

While Jason helped Sadie finish up breakfast, Emily got plates and silverware and set the table. Then she put bread in the toaster. While it was cooking, she retrieved the butter and Grace's homemade marmalade out of the fridge. Jason brought the eggs and bacon over to the table and they all sat down.

"This looks and smells delicious," Emily said. "Thank you for making breakfast."

Jason nodded, and they ate in silence for a few moments.

"I'm sure you'll be busy with all the funeral stuff. Are you planning to bring Sadie with you?"

"I was, yeah. I don't really have anyone to watch her."

"My dad said he'd be happy to take her until we all get back. He hasn't had a lot of time with her and he'd like some."

"He's not coming?"

Jason shook his head. "Not because he doesn't want to. We've got one pregnant cow and one sick one. He wants to stay close."

Emily nodded. "We just had a birthing early this morning." She took a sip of her coffee. "If he's willing and he doesn't think she'll be in the way, that would be a huge load off," she agreed.

"Great!" He turned to Sadie. "Want to hang with Papa Joe and play with the cows today?"

She bounced in her seat. "Yes! Yes!"

Grinning at Sadie's enthusiasm, she pushed her plate away. Out of nowhere, her grief reached out and pricked her heart. "I think I'm gonna go up and get a shower before Hope gets up and hogs it," Emily said, standing and taking her plate to the sink. "Thanks again for breakfast."

Jason stood and walked his plate to the sink. He brushed his hand down Emily's arm. "I'll take Sadie home with me now. Let me know if you need anything."

Sighing, Emily took a step away and watched Jason's hand fall to the side. Why did he insist on touching her all the time? It wasn't helping his cause and only made her uncomfortable because she wanted the past and the pain to disappear. His touch made her yearn for things she couldn't have. "I will." She turned and went to stand behind Sadie. Leaning down, she kissed the top of Sadie's head. "Be good for Papa Joe. I love you!"

"Love too!"

She left the kitchen and slowly climbed the stairs. She was glad Jason was around to help with Sadie, that more than anything was a burden lifted and one she truly appreciated. But it gave her a glimpse of what a true family life would be like and it hurt her heart. That glimpse was what their life should have been.

Jason ruined that and she needed to keep that in the forefront of her mind . . . and her heart.

Chapter Twenty-Six

"Are we ready to go?" Clint asked as everyone gathered in the foyer.

"Yes," Emily agreed, opening the door and walking out onto the porch.

The Camancho clan was not the first to arrive at the church. Many of Grace's friends were already there and eager to shake hands and offer their sympathies. They got out of the vehicle and headed toward the entrance. Elizabeth rushed to Clint's side and gave him a hug. "Thank you for being here, Elizabeth," Clint choked out. "I'm so lost."

Clint's sister, Elizabeth, and her daughter Chloe, had arrived late last night from California and were staying at Tyler's house. It had been at least ten years since Emily had seen them, and though the reason was sad, she was excited to see them.

Chloe came to Emily's side and gave her a hug. "I'm so sorry, Em."

Emily nodded and returned the hug. "It's good to see you."

They walked together into the church, but it was slowgoing because many of the people already in attendance stopped them to offer condolences and share stories. They finally made it to the front and filed into the pew. Gina and Phoebe joined Emily in the pew. Emily grasped Gina's hand. "I don't know if I can do this," she whispered in Gina's ear.

"You can do this," Gina said fiercely. "And tonight, when it's over and everyone has gone home, we'll go down to The Dustbowl and get shit-faced."

"Deal," Emily said, offering a small smile.

When the minister stood at the pulpit, all talking ceased. Emily sat back and listened as the minister, her father, and several of Grace's friends honored her. She was doing well until Hope went up to give her eulogy. Hope spoke of meeting Emily and Tyler for the first time, how happy she'd been to be accepted into their family. How the loss of her father had devastated her, but the love and acceptance from Clint, Tyler, and Emily had helped to heal not only her, but also Grace. The best decision Grace had ever made had come in the move to Mosquero. With tears in her eyes, she looked straight at Clint and thanked him for his love, acceptance, and his family.

"My mother was happier here than I'd ever seen her, even in Boston. She found herself out here in the desert and she bloomed. I'll miss her so much. She got cheated out of so much, but I know she's looking down on us," Hope said, smiling through her tears. "And she's at peace."

When the service ended, they all piled back into the cars and followed the hearse to the cemetery. The grave-side service was short, and all too soon, the casket was being lowered and they were taking turns throwing dirt down on it.

Friends, family, and acquaintances filed by to offer their condolences. Emily was itching to be gone, needing some time to process all the emotions she was feeling, before having to share her home and her stories with everyone. After what seemed like an hour, they were back in the SUV and on their way to the ranch.

What she really wanted was to saddle a horse and take a long, hard ride across the desert. She needed the wind whipping past her face, the chance to be alone, to lash out and expend some of the emotions swirling around inside her. She couldn't do it today, but she promised herself that first thing in the morning, she'd do just that.

They arrived back at the house before anyone else. She assumed most had gone home to get their food offerings and maybe even change into something a little more comfortable.

Emily went straight to the fridge to start taking out the food she'd purchased for today. She also poured herself a stiff drink, her standard rum and coke, and guzzled down the first glass without stopping for a breath. She poured herself another and set it aside while she prettied up the food.

Two more drinks later, people began to arrive and Emily had a good start on numbing her pain and grief. She wandered through the house, stopping every now and then to thank people for coming. Most gave her a hug and shared some tidbit about Grace. Most were happy or funny stories and Emily was able to keep her tears at bay.

She was sitting on the couch in the living room, chatting with Chloe, when Lila arrived. Hope had mentioned Lila's visit and her edict that Lila stay away from the reception. Without realizing it, Emily stood and stormed over to Lila. She reached back and slapped her in the face. "How dare you?!" Emily whispered urgently. "Get out!"

"Excuse me?" Lila said, reaching up and holding her cheek.

"You know you aren't welcome here. Hope made that plain. Get out. Leave!" Emily said, grabbing her arm and leading her toward the door.

"I'm here to pay my respects," Lila yelled, trying to pull her arm out of Emily's grasp.

"We don't want them!" Emily pushed open the screen door and hauled Lila out onto the porch. "Get off our property and don't come back."

Emily turned to reenter the house when Lila reached out and snatched Emily's arm. "You're the one who's unwelcome here," Lila sneered.

"What's that supposed to mean?"

"You broke their hearts when you ran away. How dare *you* come back here? You act like you never left, like you still own the town and the house."

Emily yanked her arm out of Lila's grasp and took a step closer to Lila. "Get out! You have no right to be here, you have no right to speak to me. You ruined our lives, every single one of us. You're poison, Lila. Go away."

Gina and Phoebe came out onto the porch and flanked Emily. "Problem?" Gina drawled.

Lila's fury shone bright in her eyes. She glared at each of them in turn and stormed off to her car.

Gina and Phoebe made a show of dusting off their hands and turned back toward the door. "Let it go, Em," Phoebe said quietly. "She did this on purpose, to rile you up and upset you more."

"She succeeded."

"Of course she did, it's what she does. But let it go for now. You can take it out on something later, but right now you have to go in there and act like the grieving daughter you are," Gina advised.

"I know, I know," Emily mumbled, blowing out a deep breath. "I just need a minute." She turned and sat on the porch swing. "Shit!"

Gina and Phoebe followed and sat down next to her.

"She'll come back," Emily said. "I doubt today, but she'll be back for her pound of flesh at some point before I go home."

Gina nodded. "And when she does, give her the hell she deserves."

"Why can't she just leave well enough alone? She got what she wanted. I left town and she got Jason all to herself. Why couldn't she have just left us alone today? Just one day. That's not too much to ask for, is it?"

Gina rubbed Emily's back and Phoebe stood, pacing in front of the swing.

"That's not who she is," Phoebe said. "She was put on the Earth to cause hate and dissension. She's at her happiest when she's bringing misery to everyone."

"And we have to do our best to take the high road and ignore her," Gina continued.

"But it's her aunt's funeral," Emily cried.

"Doesn't matter," Phoebe said. "She doesn't care about anyone but herself."

Emily sighed. "I know."

"What do you want to do?" Gina asked.

"I don't know. I need to go back in there," she said, pointing toward the door. "But I think I want to just catch the first plane home. I can't take this; I really can't. Between Grace's death, Jason's hovering, and now Lila—I just can't take anymore."

She really couldn't. Lila's appearance was the last straw. She knew Sadie wanted to stay, hell—*everyone* wanted her to stay. But she just couldn't see herself doing it. Not with Lila still living here. Or Jason, for that matter. How could she stay? He broke her trust and her heart. And the one he broke it with was making it her mission in life to make Emily's life hell.

Chapter Twenty-Seven

Two hours later, Emily was sitting with her aunt and cousin when Tyler appeared in front of her. "There's someone here to see you, Em. I put him in Dad's office."

A puzzled frown crossed her face. She wasn't expecting anyone and couldn't fathom who would be here for her. "Who is it?"

Tyler shrugged. "Don't know, but he said it was urgent and would only take a moment."

"Hm." Emily stood and went to her father's office. She opened the door and found a man standing by her father's desk. "Can I help you?" she asked.

"Hello, Emily." He walked toward her with his hand held out.

"I'm sorry, do I know you?" she asked, folding her arms against her chest.

"Not yet, but we're about to get very well acquainted."

Emily took a step back. "Listen, we're in the middle of a funeral. Whatever you have to say to me is nowhere near as important as that."

"I think you'll change your mind once you hear what I have to say."

Emily tapped a finger against her arm, eyebrow raised. "Then say it so I can get back to my guests."

"You need to come with me."

"Excuse me?"

"The life of your daughter depends on it."

Emily's heart stopped and she dropped her arms to her sides. "What are you talking about? What have you done?"

"She is safe right now, but if you don't come with me—quietly and willingly—then I can't promise her fate."

"Of course she's safe," Emily said with forced bravado. Sadie was still next door with Papa Joe, she had to be. He would have called her if Sadie was missing.

"No, that she isn't."

"Who are you?" Emily yelled.

"My name is Edward."

"What do you want? How do I get Sadie back?"

"Come with me."

Emily took a deep breath and nodded. "All right, I'll come. What do I need? Money?"

"No."

She followed Edward out of her father's office, down the hall, and through the living room. She kept her eyes on his back, knowing if she caught anyone's eye, she'd give up the charade and risk Sadie's safety.

Scenarios flew through her mind, all bad. She tried to tamp down the panic that was threatening to take over. Her mind was so busy on the worst case thoughts that she almost missed Sadie's giggle. But there it was, distinct and safe across the room.

She stopped in her tracks and quickly scanned the room. Her eyes almost immediately found Sadie, sitting on Jason's lap. Her panic dropped a half level. But she was still scared. Right on the heels of "she's safe" came "who is this man and why is he threatening us?"

She caught Jason's eye for a second, and he must have sensed something was wrong because he handed Sadie off to Phoebe and started in her direction. She averted her gaze and caught up with Edward who was just opening the screen door.

When he cleared the threshold, Emily closed the screen door between them. "I don't know what game you're playing, but it ends now. If you show your face around here again, I'll call the sheriff."

Edward walked to the screen door and tried to open it. "Your daughter's life is hanging in the balance, lady."

"My daughter is safe and sound, this I know as fact. Get off my property."

He opened his mouth as if to say something, but Jason arrived and stood like a sentry behind her.

"Problem?" he drawled.

"No, this man was just leaving."

Rage burned in Edward's eyes as he turned on his heel and left.

"Who was that?" Jason asked.

"I don't know who he was," she said, turning away from the door and moving into the living room. She scanned the room again, searching for Sadie. She needed, more than anything right now, to hold her baby girl. Who would threaten a baby?

She found Phoebe by Grace's piano. Tyler was playing one of Grace's favorite songs. Sadie was smiling, clapping, and dancing in Phoebe's arms.

"Mama! Dance!"

Emily smiled, tears brimming in her eyes. The sudden release of adrenaline made her weepy and even more out of sorts than she already was.

"Why are you crying?" Jason asked.

She jumped, not realizing he'd followed her. "You know why I'm crying," she said, keeping her face averted. She held out her hands and Sadie jumped into her arms. Emily buried her face in Sadie's neck, breathing deeply of her baby scent. Thank God she was safe.

Jason took hold of Emily's arm. Startled, she looked up and knew immediately that she'd given everything she was thinking and feeling away.

"What's going on, Emily?"

"I don't know!"

"Who was that man? What did he want?"

"Look, this isn't the time or place." She nodded toward Sadie.

"You're scared. I can see it in your eyes!"

Emily sighed. She nodded toward the kitchen and handed Sadie back to Phoebe. Emily walked through the kitchen and out onto the back porch.

"I don't know who he was. He said his name was Edward. He just showed up and told me to go with him because Sadie's life was in danger. He wanted me to believe he'd kidnapped Sadie. And I was on my way to go with him when I heard Sadie giggling across the room."

"And you didn't think this was important to tell me? She's my daughter, too."

"I know that. But it was over, he left. And Sadie is fine."

"But there was still a threat. A threat happened. One that you were gonna sacrifice yourself for." He reached out and pulled her to his chest. "When are you gonna realize you don't have to do this all alone?"

For a moment, she allowed herself to revel in the strength and comfort he offered. She'd missed this. She could admit it to herself. But never to him. She took a deep breath in, capturing his scent in her memory, and then stepped back.

"He said he'd hurt her. I couldn't risk not going with him."

Jason nodded. "Until we figure out who he is and what he wants, Sadie can't be left alone."

"Jason, she's eighteen months old. She can't be left alone anyway." She smiled to take the sting out of her words.

"Right." He grinned. "You shouldn't be alone either. It's obvious you were his main objective."

She sighed. "Jason, I've told you. We," she moved her finger between them, "aren't a thing. Don't try to use this as some way to slither your way back into my good graces."

He stiffened. Hurt and anger flashed in his eyes. She immediately regretted her words.

He turned and started walking away from her. "I need some air. Tell Sadie I'll be back in a little bit."

Emily reached out a hand. "I'm sorry," she said softly.

Turning, he glared at her. "Excuse me for still caring about you. But hey, you've proved just how independent you are. I get it. You don't trust me. You don't need me." He turned his back on her. "Do what you want. You've been doing that all along, anyway. Why stop now?" With that stinging barb, he stalked off.

Gina appeared behind her. "What's his problem?"

Shaking her head, she cast sad eyes on Gina. "I messed up."

"Care to elaborate?"

"Not right now." She looked back at Jason's retreating back and for a split second thought she should chase him down. But what would she say?

What hadn't been said a thousand times already?

Chapter Twenty-Eight

"Let's go, before they drink all the beer." Gina stood at the door, keys jangling in her hand.

"Like that'll ever happen." Emily laughed, grabbing her purse and joining Gina by the door.

"If it does, it'll be today—the day we need it most," Phoebe said, opening the screen door and walking out onto the porch.

They climbed into Gina's SUV and Emily immediately rolled the window down. The fresh air felt good on her face, and she couldn't remember the last time she breathed in clean air. It felt good to fill her lungs with air that didn't have car smoke and pollution tainting it.

"The service was nice," Phoebe said softly.

Emily nodded.

"Why isn't Hope joining us tonight?"

"Derek has to fly out tomorrow. Something happened with one of his clients and it's an emergency, I guess. So she went to Santa Fe with him."

"What's he do?"

Emily shook her head. "I have no idea. I thought he was in insurance, but Dad said it has something to do with finances. And Tyler said something about buying and selling companies." She blew out a breath. "I have no idea, but he's successful at whatever it is he does."

"Hm," Phoebe said.

"Sadie and Jason seem to be thick as thieves," Gina observed.

"That they are," Emily admitted.

Phoebe clapped her hands. "Yes!"

"And?" Gina asked.

Shaking her head, Emily sighed and looked out the window. "And what?"

"And are you moving home?"

"Nooo," Emily drawled. "Not going to happen, guys. You know that."

"Why not?" Gina and Phoebe demanded.

"Because," Emily said, splaying her hands in front of her, "we have a life in Boston. It's the only life Sadie knows. But mostly," covering her face with her hands, she dropped her head, chin tucked against her chest, "because I still love him," she whispered.

"What was that?" Gina asked.

"Did you say what I think you said?" Phoebe shrieked.

Emily nodded and looked up through the windshield. "I do. I knew it as soon as I laid eyes on him at the hospital and I confirmed it this afternoon when he pulled me in for a hug."

"What?" Gina squealed. "When did this happen?"

"What are you talking about?" Phoebe demanded. "We want all the deets. I can't believe you've waited this long to tell us!"

"There's nothing to tell. I was upset and he must have read the signals wrong."

"You know he loves you, too," Gina said.

"It takes more than love. It takes trust, too. And I'll never be able to trust him again."

"But —"

"How about we talk about something else?" Emily asked again. "For now, let's assume Jason and moving back here are off limits. We can talk about anything else."

"You really know how to dampen the mood," Gina said dryly. "But we shall abide by your wishes."

Phoebe patted Emily's shoulder. "Have you ever had Love Potion?"

Emily sighed. "Is this your way of abiding by my wishes?"

Phoebe laughed and shook her head. "It's a drink, silly. It's Malibu, Peach Schnapps, and cranberry juice."

"Sounds delicious." Emily smiled. "Do they have it at The Dustbowl?"

Phoebe nodded. "Ben keeps the ingredients on hand for me. It's my favorite."

"I can't wait to try it." She turned to Gina. "What does Ben keep for you?"

"Just beer," she answered, turning into the back parking lot.

They gathered their purses and stepped out of the SUV. Linking arms, they sauntered around the building to the front door. When they stepped into the bar, Emily released a sigh of contentment. The inside of the bar was dark, the music loud, and the chance for anonymity high. She wanted to disappear, drink away her blues, and be with her girls . . . and this place seemed to be the answer.

They chose a table in the back corner, away from the TVs and pool table. Even the restrooms were at the front of the bar, so they were well and truly isolated. Phoebe went up and bought the first round, leaving Gina and Emily at the table.

"Looks like we got here at the right time, this table is usually the first to go," Gina said.

"I'm glad. I plan to keep my back to the crowd tonight and get my drink on."

"This is Jason's table. Anytime I'm in here, he's at this one."

"Hm," she replied.

"Someone will recognize you at some point tonight."

"I know, but I'm going to try my best to stay hidden for as long as possible."

"No one has seen you in years, you can't expect them not to greet you home."

Emily nodded. "I know. But tonight I just want to disappear."

Phoebe returned with their drinks. They touched glasses before taking their first sips.

"Oh my!" Emily gushed. "This goes down extremely easy, Phoebs."

"Told ya!"

"This will be a good night!" Emily said with a broad grin. She upended her glass and swiftly drank the entire glass down. She set the glass on the table with a firm clunk and wiped the back of her hand across her lips. "It's on, girls. Keep up!"

Gina and Phoebe followed suit, and Gina took herself off to the bar for the second round.

"Ben wants you to come up and say hi to him before it gets too busy in here," Gina said on her return.

"I can do that," Emily agreed. "I'll buy the next round and say hi to him while I'm up there."

The next two hours followed the same routine with Gina and Phoebe running to the bar for rounds and talking above the music as best they could. They had years to catch up on and nothing loosened the tongue like drinks and absence.

"I have to use the restroom," Emily announced. "I'm going to brave the crowds."

"Better put on your hat and sunglasses," Gina giggled.

"Good call!" She dug her sunglasses out of her purse, putting them on her face before stepping away from the table. She wound her way through the crowd and was quite pleased with herself when she made it to the restroom without being accosted by a well-meaning neighbor. Finished emptying her bladder and washing her hands, she snuck out the front door to get some fresh air. She breathed deeply, again realizing how much she missed the clean, fresh air of the desert. If only she could bottle it and bring it with her back to Boston.

When she got to the end of the building, she paused, staring out at the last rays of the setting sun. The sky was mostly black, a faint glow of red and gold tinged the horizon.

"Excuse me?" a man asked close to her ear.

She barely suppressed a shriek, turning her head to find the voice in the dark. The big city had changed her. She knew everyone in this town, and her moment of fear was a casualty of her time in Boston. "Hello," she said with a smile.

"Are you Emily Camacho?"

Emily nodded, the smile dimming slightly. There was something familiar and faintly menacing about that voice.

"I thought so," he said, wrapping his arms around her torso and putting a hand against her mouth. He dragged her, kicking and squirming, around the building and threw her into the trunk of his waiting car.

Emily kicked and screamed against the trunk and frantically searched for the handle to pop the trunk. She felt her pockets for her phone and cursed when she realized it was sitting on the table with her purse. She briefly wondered how long it would take Gina and Phoebe to notice she was missing and then pushed the thought right out. She had to find a way out of this trunk. Where was the handle? Or was that a TV myth? Wasn't there an episode of CSI where they talked about cars manufactured after a certain date had to have the handles for situations such as this?

Why was she even wasting her time thinking about that? She needed to find a tool or something . . . some way out of this trunk. Where were they going? Why had he taken her?

Her thoughts swirled in her mind and she felt herself losing control. Panic was starting to take over and she knew she had to get herself under control if she was to find a way out of this. Breathing deeply, she relaxed and focused on making a plan.

After what felt like hours, the car came to a stop. Emily situated herself so she was ready when he opened the truck.

As soon as he had the trunk open, he reached down and Emily kicked him in the face. He fell out of sight, and she wasted no time in scrambling out of the trunk. She didn't check to see if he was knocked out; tunnel-vision had her running for her life. She wanted to put as much distance between herself and this man as possible.

She only made it about ten steps before he body-slammed her to the ground. She fell hard, the air forced from her lungs. He rolled her over and punched her in the face. The last thing she saw before her world went black was his rage-filled eyes and the cold smile on his lips.

*****

She'd been gone too long. Jason saw her use the restroom and had resisted the urge to follow her outside. He kicked himself now. He checked his watch. Ten minutes. Too long. He got up from his table and slipped outside. He walked the length of the building and turned the corner that led to the parking lot. He recognized Gina's SUV right away and walked over.

As he got closer, he knew she wasn't in there. His gut told him something was wrong. Emily wasn't overly fond of the dark, and he knew her well enough to know that she wouldn't just wander off without a good reason.

He checked the vehicle to make sure, even though he knew she wasn't in there. He called out her name, hoping she was just in a shadow and he'd missed her. She didn't respond so he hurried back inside, praying he'd somehow passed her and she was safe inside with her friends.

No such luck. He bumped into Gina as he entered the bar.

"Is Emily in here with you?"

"No," Gina replied, shaking her head. "I was just on my way outside to find her."

"She's not out there."

"Well, where is she?"

"Don't know, but I have a bad feeling." He went on to tell her about the mystery man from earlier in the day.

"She left her phone and purse on the table. She was just going to the restroom."

"I think she went outside for some air and I think that creep took her."

"I'll call Fred. He'll know what to do," she said and ran back to the table. She snatched up her phone and speed-dialed her husband.

"What's going on?" Phoebe asked, slow on the uptake thanks to two and a half pitchers of Love Potion. "Where's Emily? Oh, hi, Jason," she purred.

"Fred? Emily's missing. She went outside for some air and now she's gone. Jason thinks some creep stole her!" She went on with the details Jason had given her, turning her back when Phoebe's concern rose to epic levels.

Jason put his arm around her shoulders and shushed her. "We'll find her, Phoebs. Did she say anything to you about leaving?"

"No," she replied, scrunching up her face. "All she said was she had to pee. I guess it has been a while since she left. Wow, time sure does fly when you're drinking."

He rolled his eyes. He loved the girl dearly, but she was a ditz of the highest order when she'd been drinking. He checked his watch. Another fifteen minutes had passed and he was itching to be gone. He needed to be out looking, searching for Emily.

"Who else saw this Edward at the house today?" Gina asked Jason, holding the cell phone away from her face.

"I don't know," he replied.

"No, she wouldn't just disappear. That's not her style," Gina said angrily into the phone. "She didn't disappear, she left with her sister. She left a note for her parents. She sent me and Phoebe a text. And anyway, that was a totally different situation."

Jason snatched the phone out of Gina's grasp. "We don't have time for this," he barked into the phone. "I've been watching her at the bar, keeping an eye on her because the guy was a creep. I was worried for her. He now has a good half-hour lead and who knows where he's taking her."

"I understand what you're saying, Jason. But we're talking about a situation you want me to use manpower on.

We're not sure she's actually missing. No one knows who this mystery man is. She's disappeared in the past . . ."

"She didn't disappear," he said slowly. "Gina just told you that."

"Fine, she has a history of running. Perhaps her stepmother's death was more than she could handle right now and she needed to get away."

"She wouldn't leave Sadie behind. And she wouldn't leave without telling someone."

"You don't know that."

"Yes, I do."

"Jason, be reasonable. None of you have seen her in two years. She lives in the big city now. She's changed."

"Not that much. Are you going to do something or not?"

"I can send someone over to take statements and see if anyone saw anything. Other than that, my hands are tied until she's been missing for twenty-four hours."

"Are you serious? She could be dead by then!"

"It's policy . . ."

"I don't give a rat's ass about your policy," he interrupted. He tossed the phone in Gina's direction. "Way to marry a cop. What the hell good is he if he won't help his wife find her best friend?"

Jason stormed out of the bar and jumped into his truck. He needed to calm down and think. Who was this guy, where could he have taken Emily, and why had he taken her? Who had a grudge against Emily? The only person he could think of was Lila. But would she do something this crazy? What would she hope to gain by doing it?

So lost in his thoughts, he didn't realize Gina was outside his window until she tapped on it. Rolling window down, he raised his eyebrows in question.

"He's going to help us."

"How did you manage that?"

"I told him if he didn't get his head out of his ass, he'd be sleeping on the couch for a very long time." Gina grinned.

Jason let out a bark of laughter. "So, what's he gonna do?"

"He's sending someone down here to question people at the bar. Not that I think he'll get very far with that, everyone in there is drunk, except Ben."

"The guy never came in. I sat by the door the whole night. Only locals came in. It's a waste of time."

"I think Tyler may have seen this man. He mentioned some guy showing up to talk to Emily today during the reception."

"Good. I'll head out to the ranch right now to talk to him."

"Okay. I'm going to run Phoebe home. She's beyond drunk and won't be any good to us anyway. I'll meet you out there."

Jason nodded and rolled up his window. He started out of the parking lot, glad to have something to do.

Chapter Twenty-Nine

She couldn't move her arms.

It was the first thought that came to mind when she woke up. A second later, memories flooded her mind and she realized she wasn't passed out from a night of overindulgence. No, she was in trouble. Big trouble.

She struggled against her restraints, hoping the man hadn't tied them tightly, but no such luck. Did she dare scream on the off chance someone might hear her and come to the rescue? The last thing she wanted to do was to anger him any further. But she didn't want to hang out and wait for whatever cruel intentions he had for her, either.

He seemed familiar to her, like she'd seen him somewhere before. She wracked her brain, trying to remember. It was floating on the outer reaches of her mind and she couldn't quite get a good grip on it.

She was gathering her courage to scream for help when the door opened and a beam of light shone in the room. Outlined in the doorway was the last person she expected to see.

"Lila?" she croaked out.

"Hello, hello, Emily. So glad you were finally able to join me."

"What are you doing? Why am I here?"

"We'll get to all that shortly. I just had to see for myself that you were here and restrained." She laughed. "Oh, it's so good to be the one in charge now."

Lila turned and walked away, closing the door behind her.

Emily's mind raced. Thoughts, feelings, impressions rushed back and forth, but nothing would stick. Nothing popped to the surface and said "This is what's going on." All she had were questions. Why was Lila doing this? What could she possibly want with her?

It's not like Emily had any money. Neither Clint nor Grace had money. And even if Grace had money, she wouldn't have left it to Emily—it would go to Hope. Besides the fact, Grace had just been buried today. The reading of the will, if there was one, wouldn't be for at least another week.

Her heart was racing and her hands were clammy. Sweat beaded on her lip and forehead. She continued pulling on the ropes and twisting her wrists, hoping against hope that they would loosen enough for her to slip her hands free.

The last thing she wanted was to be at Lila's mercy. She had to be up and able to face her—eye to eye—by the time Lila came back. Her wrists were screaming in pain, but she continued to pull at the ropes.

The door opened again. This time, Lila and the man entered the room. And she finally remembered where she knew him from. He was the same man from earlier this afternoon, who'd threatened Sadie. Edward.

"Where's your phone?" Lila demanded.

"I don't know. I'm not sure I brought it with me," Emily replied.

Lila cursed under her breath and turned to Edward. "He won't know it's her. And if I give her my phone, he won't answer."

"She could text him, announcing herself and asking him to call."

"But it's still my number. He might not even check the message. And if he does, then he'll know where she is and send the cops." She kicked the floor. "Damn!"

"What about my phone? No one knows the number. It would be unrecognizable."

Lila smiled. "Yes, that would work."

Edward handed her the phone and moved over to the door, standing guard.

Lila sauntered over to the bed and sat down next to Emily's hip. "I bet you're wondering why you're here," she began.

"Hm. The thought has crossed my mind."

Lila's eyes flashed with annoyance. "I wouldn't be smart, if I were you. You aren't exactly in the best position right now." She played with the phone in her hands, rolling it over and over. She took a deep breath and set the phone on the bed then reached behind her back. She pulled out a gun and pointed it at Emily's face. She smiled at Emily's sharp inhalation. "Now you see I'm serious."

"About what?" she whispered.

"About getting what I want. About finally being the one who wins."

"Wins what?" she croaked. "What do you want?"

"What do I want?" Lila laughed. "I want to win. I want your life. I want you and Hope to have nothing. To be the dirt beneath my feet as I've been yours since I moved here. I want Jason. I want your life."

"Take it!" Emily said. "Take it all. I don't want it. I don't want him."

"I've tried," Lila screamed, spittle flying from her mouth. "I've tried since the day I moved here to have Jason. But he doesn't want me. All he wants is you—all he's *ever* wanted is YOU!" She stood and paced in front of the bed. Heavy steps. Hard steps.

"I can't do anything about that, Lila. I've tried. For two years, I've tried to give him the hint. I've been subtle. I've been obvious. He doesn't get it. I don't want him. Why would I? I walked in on the two of you the morning of our wedding. Why would I tie myself to a man like that?"

"Because he's the father of your child. She's the reason he won't give up on you. Don't you see that? She's the one thing that keeps him tethered to you, always willing to keep trying to win you back."

"But I don't want him back, Lila. Can't you see that? I'm here, in town, for one reason only. To bury Grace. Sadie and I are returning to Boston next week. I'm not staying."

"That's not good enough," Lila said. "He'll just follow you. He'll keep trying. You need to make it plain and clear to him that you're done. That you want him to move on and be happy with me."

The crazy was taking hold and Emily could see it enter Lila's eyes. She was waving the gun wildly in her hands, and Emily feared for her life. If she wasn't careful, she wouldn't make it out of here at all.

She had to think. Think! What could she say to Lila to end this? The words she'd been saying weren't doing anything to calm the situation or ease Lila's mind.

"What can I do?" Emily finally asked.

"You need to convince him," Lila said. "You aren't leaving here until you do." Lila walked over and came to within inches of Emily. Leaning down, her face a breath away, she grabbed Emily's chin. "I want him. I've always wanted him. And I will have him, if it's the last thing I do." She pushed Emily's face away. "Are we clear?"

Emily nodded.

Lila picked up the phone and held it tightly in her hand. "You will make him believe. You won't tell him where you are. You won't tell him who you're with. You will be plain and clear and convince him that you don't want to have anything else to do with him." She began to dial Jason's number. "If you don't, I will shoot you and then I will hunt down your brat and shoot her, too." Lila held the phone to Emily's ear and stood sentry over the conversation.

As the phone rang, Emily wracked her brain for a solution, but her mind went blank.

"Hello?" he barked into the phone.

"Jason, it's Emily."

"Emily? Where the hell are you?"

"It doesn't matter. What matters is what I have to tell you."

"Tell me what? Everyone is worried about you."

"Jason, I'm safe and I'm fine. Tell everyone I just needed some air."

"Was it the guy from earlier? Did he take you?"

"Jason, listen. I have to tell you something," her voice cracked. "Please, it's important."

She could do nothing but stare into Lila's eyes while she tried to do as she'd been told. Even in the few seconds she'd been on the phone, she could tell Lila's patience was thinning. She shrugged her shoulders to let her know it wasn't her fault, but Lila glared and motioned with her head toward the phone.

"Where are you? Did he take you against your will? Just tell me where you are and I'll come get you."

Emily sighed. "Jason!" she yelled into the phone.

"What?" he asked, confusion evident in his tone.

"Please, I need to tell you something. I hate to do this over the phone, but I think it's the easiest way."

"Do what?"

Emily took a deep breath. "I don't love you, Jason. And it's time for you to stop pining for me. You need to move on with your life, find that special someone to be happy with. You'll always be Sadie's father, but you'll never be my husband."

"Emily," Jason breathed, voice cracking with pain. "What are you saying?"

"You know what I'm saying, but let me be perfectly clear. I don't love you. I don't want to move back to Mosquero. I don't want to be with you. I don't want to marry you."

"If you'd just let me explain, Em, I know you'd see things differently."

"Jason, you think no one has given me other scenarios? Like I've never thought of different scenarios?" Emily laughed. "Everyone is on your side, Jason. Everyone. And they all tell me that it's not entirely your fault. Bully for them. But I was *there* that night. I know what I saw. And I cannot forget it, Jason. I can't. You messed up, and the consequence is losing me forever. It's over, well and truly over."

"You can't mean it, Em. You can't. I love you!"

"You *think* you love me, but how would you know? You've spent all this time chasing after me, even after I told you I didn't want to be chased. You haven't given any other woman a chance."

"I don't want any other woman."

"It doesn't matter because I don't want you."

"Em." Jason sighed.

"No. It's over. I don't want to hear from you again." Emily turned her face from the phone and Lila pressed the end button. "It's done. I think he gets it now," she said sadly.

"We'll see, won't we." Lila reached down and ran the barrel of the gun down the side of Em's face.

Emily eyed Lila warily. "What now?"

"Now, I'm going to make myself a drink, sit by the fire, and call my future husband."

"What?" Edward grunted. "I'm your future husband."

Lila smiled and slowly walked toward him. She stood in front of him and raised her face. "Just joking, darling," and pressed her lips to his. "Of course you are."

As they kissed, Lila raised the gun and shot him in the head.

Emily screamed and slammed her eyes shut. She'd seen his head explode and knew that image would never leave her.

Lila laughed. "You're probably wondering why I did that."

Emily moaned and nodded.

"Because I no longer needed him." Lila smiled. "He's been a thorn in my side since I was a teenager. Frankly, it's a relief to be done with him."

"You've known him since you were a teenager?" Emily asked, astonished.

"He's *technically* the reason I came to Mosquero to begin with."

"Your stalker," Emily breathed.

"Exactly. And the man who knocked me up, which was the final nail in the coffin and the reason I really had to leave Boston. If Mom and Dad had found out, I'd have been done for. Socially and within the family. They would have shipped me off to God knows where, forced me to give up the child, and then cut me off."

"They wouldn't," Emily began.

"The hell they wouldn't! Their place in society meant the world to them then. I'm sure it still does, though I barely speak to them."

"But you're their daughter."

"Doesn't matter. Hope was lucky, she got the good Daddy. Mine, not so much. Power, fame, money—those were important to my father and having a daughter knocked up at sixteen would have been an impossible pill for him to swallow."

"I can't even fathom having parents like that," Emily said sadly.

"That's because you hit the jackpot on parents," Lila said meanly. "You could murder Mother Theresa and they'd still love you. They might be a bit disappointed in you, but you've been blessed with unconditional love."

"That's not my fault."

"No, but it is your fault when you flaunt that all over town. Rubbing it in people's faces and excluding them because you're better than they are."

"I do not!"

"You never accepted me, not once."

"Because you were such a bitch!" Emily said, exasperated. "You were always getting us in trouble, always butting in, always just in the way. You expected us to treat you like we'd known you forever when we didn't know you from Adam. You were manipulative, tricky, mean. Where in any of that was there room for us to open our arms and let you in?"

"Don't you know the people who need love the most are the ones who ask for it in the least appropriate of ways?"

"Sure, I know that *now*. But who knows that when they're in high school?"

"And yet, even knowing that now, you still hold me at arm's length."

"I hold you back because I don't like you, Lila. I don't like your personality. I don't like you as a person. You don't make my life better, you make it worse. And beyond all that, I could never forgive what you did with Jason."

Lila giggled. "Oh darling, we didn't *do* anything beyond what you saw."

"What do you mean?" Emily snapped.

"Tsk, tsk," Lila murmured. She raised the gun slightly, pointing it directly between Emily's eyes. "You need to be nice."

Emily's eyes darted to the doorway, revulsion and panic rising steadily. Lila was definitely not in her right mind and Emily needed to keep that thought in the forefront of *her* mind.

"I'm sorry," she said earnestly.

Lila nodded and lowered the gun. Smiling slyly, she continued her taunting. "We kissed, he fondled me, and then he passed out. About two minutes after you fled back home." She walked over to the door. "You can stew about how everyone was right and you were so, so wrong. How you could have had him all this time. How your pride was your downfall." Lila laughed a deep throaty laugh. "Now he's going to be all mine. I'm going to let you think about that for a little while. I need to go call Jason." She turned and waggled her fingers in Emily's direction.

Emily watched her walk gingerly around the pool of blood on the floor and then step lightly over Edward's body. She half expected his arm to shoot up and grab hold of Lila's ankle.

Barely suppressing a shudder, she turned her head and began working at her restraints again. Her hands had fallen asleep, and as she began to move them, the pins and needles vied for first place in the pain department.

She wanted to cry. Lila was right. Her pride really would be her downfall. He'd been telling the truth all along and she'd just ignored it. Ignored him and everyone else who'd tried to tell her.

Was it too late? Could she fix it? Would he forgive her? After the words he'd spoken to her this afternoon, she wasn't sure. He'd sounded finished with her and the whole situation.

She cursed herself for wasting all this time. She could have had the family she wanted. She could have been happy. She could have been loved.

She could have had Jason.

Chapter Thirty

Jason pulled up in front of the Camancho Ranch and jumped out of the truck. He took the porch steps two at a time and didn't bother to knock on the door.

"Tyler!" he bellowed from the entrance.

Clint popped his head out of the living room and eyed Jason warily. "Something the matter, son?"

"Where's Tyler? I need to speak to him."

"He went home; Sophie thinks she's in labor."

Clint's sister, Elizabeth, came out of the living room to stand next to him. "I should go help. Her mother isn't expected to arrive until the day after tomorrow."

"Shit," Jason said, looking down at his feet. "Perfect timing."

"Tyler said he'd call if they need you. Just sit tight, Lizzy." He turned to Jason. "Something I can help you with?"

"No, sir. Sorry to disturb you." He turned to Elizabeth. "Ma'am, have a good night."

He turned and walked out. Climbing into his truck, he tried to center himself. It couldn't be helped. He had to speak with Tyler, baby or no baby.

He waited until he was out of their driveway before he hit the gas and sped to Tyler's house on the other side of the property.

All the lights were on in the house, and Tyler's three boys were running wild in the front yard. They pounced on Jason as soon as he stepped from the truck.

"Mommy's having a baby tonight," Noah, the youngest at four, informed him. "Mommy wants a girl, but we hope it's another boy. Right, guys?"

"Right," they both answered.

"Where's your mom and dad now?" Jason asked.

The oldest, Matt, was trying to knock Jason off his feet. "Can we wrestle you?"

"No, I need to speak with your dad."

Matt sighed. "He's busy with Mom. Sent us outside and told us if we come in before he's ready, we won't be able to go to the rodeo next weekend."

Jason grimaced. That was a serious threat. The rodeo was a big deal in these parts, and he knew most boys waited with bated breath to go. Their favorite was the bull riding. He remembered watching as a child and for the longest time that was what he wanted to be when he grew up.

"All right, boys. I really need to go inside and talk to your dad. I'll see you in a few minutes."

The middle child, Adam who was five and very precocious, let out a low whistle. "Good luck, man. Dad's in a mood."

Jason grinned. "You would be too if you had a baby on its way."

"I don't want kids," he informed Jason. "Just dogs. Lots of dogs."

Jason laughed. "We'll see if you're still saying that in twenty years."

He turned and headed up the stairs of the front porch. He knocked loudly on the door.

"Just go in. They're upstairs in the bedroom," Matt called to him.

Jason nodded his thanks and entered the house. He could hear anxious voices upstairs and walked up. "Hey, Ty!" he said loudly.

Tyler stuck his head out of the bedroom door. "Uh, what's up?"

"Sorry to barge in. I know you're up to your eyes in a situation right now. But I really need a minute."

"Babe, you okay? I'll be right back. Swear!"

He stepped out of the room and shut the door behind him.

"Is it really time?" Jason asked.

"Seems so. Waiting on Lizzy and Clint to get here. I should know what I'm doing, but I freeze up and panic every time. I'm useless." He chuckled nervously.

"Okay, listen. I'm sorry, but I need some info, and you can't panic and I don't want your dad to know."

"Whoa, man, you're freaking me out."

"I know, sorry. Listen. Em was out drinking with Gina and Phoebe tonight."

"Yeah, I know."

"Right, but what you don't know is Emily's missing."

"What?" he asked, eyes wide.

Jason nodded. "She went outside for some air and disappeared. The guy that showed up today. Do you know him? Do you remember what he looked like?"

"You think he had something to do with her disappearance?"

"I don't know, but it seems odd, doesn't it?"

"Yeah. Yeah. Look." He glanced at the door to the bedroom. Sophie was moaning inside, and Jason knew he only had a minute left with Tyler.

"Anything you can tell me would be helpful. We're going to find her and maybe she's just off getting herself centered. But no one has heard from her and she hasn't called my father once to check on Sadie."

Another loud moan drifted through the door.

"Tyler!" Sophie yelled through the door.

"He was about my height. Dark brown hair and light brown eyes. He was dressed nicely, richly. Big city, I'm thinking. Definitely not from around here. He sounded like Grace did when she first moved here. New England accent. He was driving a car that looked a lot like Lila's. That's all I got. I gotta go," he said, pointing toward the door.

"Yeah, man, thanks." He darted his eyes to the door. "Good luck."

Tyler sighed, clearly torn between his wife and his sister. "Keep me in the loop."

"I will."

"Better get out of here. Dad'll be here any minute."

"I'm out." Jason ran down the stairs and out to the truck.

"Ready to wrestle?" Matt asked.

"Can't, bud, but your Gramps will be here any minute."

"Oh, he'll wrestle!" Noah shouted. "Gramps is always up for a match."

Jason jumped in his truck, and speeding down the driveway, he called Gina.

"Jase? Did you talk to Ty?"

"Yeah, and his wife is having her baby tonight."

"What? Seriously?"

"Yeah, perfect timing, right?"

"Wow."

"He remembered the guy. Edward. Said he was dressed nicely, big city. Had an accent like Grace's. Drove a car like Lila's. Brown hair and brown eyes."

"I don't know if that's enough for Fred to do anything with. Where are you?"

"Just leaving Tyler's. Do you know where Lila's parents are staying?"

"Hope mentioned they were staying in town at the B and B. They said something about Lila having to work and already having company staying with her."

"Interesting," he said slowly. "Who could be staying with her? I'm going to see them."

"You do realize the time, right? They're on east coast time; they're probably sleeping."

"Your point? If Em's in trouble, I don't care who I wake up."

"Right. Okay, I'll head to the station and see if I can light a fire under Fred's butt. See if the deputies found out anything at the bar."

"Let me know." He hung up and tossed his phone on the seat next to him. *Edward.* That named sounded slightly familiar. It hung back, just on the edges of his memory. He could swear he'd heard Lila talk about an Edward before. But when? And why?

Just then, his phone rang and he snatched it up. He looked at the caller ID but didn't recognize the number. The area code was Boston; he knew because he had Hope and Emily's cell numbers programmed into his cell.

He pulled over to the side of the road and answered the call. "Hello?" he barked into the phone.

"Jason, it's Emily."

"Emily! Where are you?"

She wouldn't answer him. Instead she kept telling him that it was over. She didn't love him and she didn't want to see him again. She sounded scared. Her voice wobbled and cracked—and for someone who was bent on convincing him it was over, she did a poor job of it.

"Em," he sighed, trying one last time to get a location or a clue or something.

"No. It's over. I don't want to hear from you again." The phone went dead, and he had half a mind to throw his phone out the window in frustration.

Now more than ever, he knew something was wrong. Ninety minutes at the most had passed since she'd disappeared, and with as much as she'd had to drink, she sounded too sober for the situation. Instead of going to his father's to pick up Sadie, she was who knew where trying to convince him she didn't want to have anything to do with him.

Not to mention the fear. He knew fear when he heard it and Emily's words were drenched in it. Someone had her. And someone forced her to call him. And based on the phone number, it was a good bet it was this Edward person.

He put the truck in gear and broke the speed limits to get into town. He was having that conversation with Lila's parents; he didn't care what time it was.

Twenty minutes later, he pulled up outside the bed and breakfast, and just as he was getting out of the truck, his phone rang again.

This time he recognized the number.

"What do you want, Lila?"

"Now, is that anyway to talk to your future wife?" she slurred sweetly.

"I don't have time for this," he growled.

"Did you lose something?" she purred.

He paused on the porch steps. "Why would you ask me that?"

"Just curious," she said.

He could hear her drinking something before she came back on the line.

"Are you lonely? Because I'm lonely. I want you to come over. I have a present for you to unwrap."

"I can't right now. I have something to do."

"Please," she begged. "I miss you. I miss us."

"There is no us. There never was," he roared. "I have to go."

He hung up and continued up the steps. He pulled open the door and rang the front desk bell. He knew the owners; they were from California. They'd moved out here a few years ago wanting a simpler life. They were friendly and the perfect couple to own a bed and breakfast. They'd been all over the world in their previous lives, traveling had been a huge part of their careers. Their children were grown with families of their own. They truly liked people and loved hearing their guests' life stories.

"Jason! How lovely to see you," Betty greeted him. "Is everything okay? It's very late. Do you need a room?"

"No, ma'am. I actually need to speak to one of your guests."

"All of our guests have gone to bed."

"I realize that, ma'am, but it's important. Emily Camancho is missing and I think Mr. Hillcrest might know the man who took her."

"I don't know. They went to bed a long time ago. I'd hate to wake them if you aren't even sure if he knows this person."

"But if he does, Betty . . ." He let the sentence hang and watched her eyes soften. "Well, all right. I can see what you mean. I'll go up and try to wake them."

"Thank you, Betty."

"Just wait in the living room over there." She gestured toward an archway.

Jason walked over and entered the room. It was an inviting room, with several plush couches and a fireplace. There were a few bookshelves full of books, and he knew from experience that every genre of book found a home on those shelves. A flat-screen TV hung on one of the walls above a stand full of video game consoles and DVD players. Another bookshelf in the corner housed every board game imaginable.

It was definitely a room for living, and he knew why people came from all over to stay here. Not just for this room, he was sure you could get it at any half-decent B&B. No, it was the owners and their absolute joy in showing their guests a good time. They offered several tours of the desert via horseback or jeep. They had day-trips into Santa Fe and Albuquerque for shopping and sight-seeing.

He broke out of his reverie when Mr. Hillcrest, Lila's father, came charging into the room. "What in the Sam Hill is going on? Why are you here and why am I awake right now?"

Jason held up his hands. "I'm sorry, sir. I know it's late, but it was urgent I speak with you."

"What's so urgent it couldn't wait until a decent hour of the day?"

"Sir, Emily Camancho is missing."

"Grace's stepdaughter?"

"Yes, sir. She disappeared outside The Dustbowl tonight. Earlier today, she was threatened by a man and I think he's from Boston."

"Son, do you know how many people live in Boston?"

"I know, I'm sure it's a lot. But hear me out. He has brown hair and eyes, he dressed well. He drove a car similar to Lila's."

"What's his name?"

"Edward. That's all I know."

"Edward? You mean Edward Wellington?"

"I don't know, sir. I don't have a last name."

"Well, I know he's here visiting Lila. It's why we couldn't stay with her."

"How long has he been here?"

"I don't know. We don't communicate with Lila much anymore. But it surprised her mother and me when she told us he was visiting."

"Why?"

"Because he's the kid who was stalking her in high school. He's the reason she moved out here."

Jason's eyes bulged. *That's* where he'd heard the name Edward before. It had been a long time, but now he remembered Lila talking about the boy she'd run from and how she was scared he'd eventually find her.

"I see." He nodded. "I appreciate you taking the time to speak with me. I'm sorry to wake you. And I'm sorry for your loss, sir. Grace was one hell of a woman."

"That she was. She was a good match for my brother. It's too bad his life was cut short. But she found a good man in Clint. She was happy out here."

"I best be off. Good night."

"I hope you find the girl. I know Lila doesn't care for her, but she's always been nice to Catherine and me." Mr. Hillcrest walked out of the room with Jason. "Good luck."

"Thanks."

Jason paused outside on the porch, collecting his thoughts. Edward Wellington had to be their guy. He called Gina to give her the information he'd found out.

"I can't believe she's running around with him again! I remember when she first got here and would talk about her stalker all the time."

"I'm going to head over to Lila's place and see what's going on, if anything. Her father said he was staying with

Lila. Who knows what's going on over there. He might have them both under lock and key."

"Fred's on his way. He says to stay outside until he gets there."

"Then he better hope he gets there before me. If Emily's inside, I'm not waiting on Fred to rescue her."

"You might get yourself killed, and then what good would you be?"

"Gina, she's the love of my life," he yelled into the phone. "I'm not going to let her be harmed if I'm there to stop it."

"Jason!"

He swore under his breath and hung up. He jumped into his truck and peeled out of the parking lot. Lila's place was only five minutes away and he was there in less than two. Bonus to a town with little to no traffic and zero streetlights.

Chapter Thirty-One

"It's too bad for you," Lila announced as she entered the room. Casting a disgusted look down at Edward, she shook her head. "Someone needs to take out the trash."

Emily stared wide-eyed at Lila.

"I just got off the phone with Jason. It doesn't seem like your chat with him did the trick after all." She raised the gun and fired.

It took a moment for the pain to register. It started out as a slight burning and then her shoulder exploded in fire. She writhed in pain, trying her best to keep her head about her. She didn't want to give Lila the satisfaction of screaming. Blood oozed, warm and sticky, down her shirt and off her shoulder.

"Damn, I was aiming for your head," Lila said nonchalantly, looking down at the gun. "Oh well. This will do." She pulled her phone out of her pocket and turned it to face Emily. "You need to call him again, and this time get it right. I want him to call me, groveling, begging me to be his."

"I don't know what more I can say or do," Emily pleaded.

Lila stepped closer and put the muzzle of the gun right at Emily's temple. "You better figure it out. I won't miss a second time," she threatened.

The steel was warm against her skin, a potent reminder of what Lila was capable of. Despite her best efforts at not showing fear, she shuddered. She needed a solution that didn't involve another phone call to Jason. Nothing she said to him would change his mind.

With Lila listening in, she wouldn't even be able to give him hints about who had her or what she needed in order to be set free.

"I-I-I don't know if me calling him again so soon will accomplish your wishes," she stammered. Her hand felt cold, her whole body felt cold, actually. But what was really weird was she was sweating like she'd just run five miles.

Lights flashed on the wall, and Lila turned her attention to the window. She walked over and moved the curtain to the side ever so slightly. Peering through, her face lit up.

"Looks like I was wrong. He does want me after all."

She practically skipped to the door and pulled it closed behind her, leaving Emily in the dark with Edward's corpse.

Her shoulder throbbed, and she wondered how long she could lie here before she bled to death. Could she even bleed to death from a shoulder wound?

The room began to spin and Emily couldn't figure out why. It was like riding one of those carousel rides. They were fun and she really wanted to take Sadie on one. Maybe, if they were still here next week, she'd take her to the rodeo. Usually there was a carnival in the parking lot, which garnered just as much traffic as the rodeo itself.

Maybe Jason would want to join them. She was so tired of fighting. Lila had admitted she hadn't done anything with Jason that night, right? Why hadn't she listened? Why hadn't she given him a chance to explain? She'd wasted so much time. She should have had more faith in him. More faith in their relationship.

The room continued to spin and she felt tired. She wanted to close her eyes and let it all go.

"Don't go to sleep, Emily. Stay awake. Jason will be here soon."

"Mama G?" Emily tried to rub her eyes, sure she was seeing things, before she remembered they were tied down. "How are you here? I miss you so much."

"Don't go to sleep, Emily. Don't go to sleep. He'll be here soon."

"I should have listened to you. Why didn't you make me? What are we gonna do without you? I love him, Mama G. I always have. It just hurt so much."

"Stay awake, Emily!"

"I'm so cold, Mama G. Can't I just rest my eyes for a minute? Lila is crazy. I'm sorry. I think it's my fault she is."

"Stay awake, Emily. He'll be here soon."

"I'm so tired, Mama. So tired. Of fighting. Of living far away. Of being without all of you. If I hadn't been so prideful, we'd have had all this time with you. Sadie would have grown up with you. You can't really be gone. We need you too much."

"Stay awake, Emily."

"Why won't you say anything else to me?"

"Stay awake, he's coming."

"I can't do it, Mama. I'm so tired. I'm just gonna close my eyes for a minute."

"Emily! He's here. Wake up!"

"You're here!" Lila exclaimed, throwing open the front door and grinning widely.

"Where is she?"

"Who?"

"You know damn well," he shouted. "Where is Emily?"

"Haven't the foggiest." She waved a hand in dismissal. "Come inside, let's have a drink."

He took a menacing step closer. "Where is she?" he asked through clenched teeth.

Lila looped an arm through his and hugged him close. "I'm so glad you came to your senses. We're gonna be perfect together. I love you so much."

He looked down into her upturned face. Her eyes were glassy and her cheeks were flushed. He figured she'd already been at the booze, and if that was the case, he wasn't getting any straight answers out of her. He decided to humor her until Fred arrived. Which better be soon, he thought to himself, casting a surreptitious glance over his shoulder as he allowed her to take his hand and lead him into the house.

"Maybe a drink wouldn't be a bad idea," he said as they walked through the foyer and into the living room.

"I'll go get it," she said in a singsong voice.

"I'm just gonna use the restroom real quick," he improvised, thinking he'd check the bedrooms down the hall by the bathroom. Maybe he could find Emily before she got back with the drink. And where the hell was Edward?

"Oh! Don't go down there," she exclaimed, clamping onto his hand. "Use the powder room by the kitchen."

"Why?"

"I've been purging and there's a bunch of piles of trash down there. It's embarrassing. You know how I like everything to be neat and tidy. Please?" she asked, tugging on his hand.

He looked down into her eyes and noted a bit of fear hidden there. Why would that be? Unless she had something to hide. He would bet his life savings that Emily was down that hall somewhere. "Okay, whatever you say."

He stopped into the powder room to cover his lie. He flushed the toilet and washed his hands, knowing if he skipped it, Lila would know something was up. He found her in the kitchen, staring out the window into the inky blackness.

"I made you a Jack and Coke, okay?"

"Sure," he said, a bit taken aback that she knew he'd entered the kitchen. She was still gazing out the window, and it was rather unnerving.

He accepted the drink from her and took a small sip. He had to keep his head about him if was to be any good for Emily. "So, what do you want to do?"

"I don't care. I'm just so glad you're here." She turned and smiled at him. Then she picked up her drink and walked over to his side, snuggling in and taking his arm, wrapping it around her shoulders.

"What have you been doing tonight while you waited for me?"

"Oh, a little of this and a little of that."

"Saw your mom and dad tonight. They said you had company. I'm not interrupting anything, am I?" he asked, looking around the kitchen.

"Oh no." Lila giggled. "I already took care of it. That was the trash I was talking about earlier."

"Anything you need help with?"

"No, not right now, anyway. Let's just enjoy each other's company."

He let her lead him out of the kitchen and back into the living room. She had a blazing fire in the hearth despite the summer temps outside. She sat down on the loveseat, directly in front of the fireplace, and patted the seat next to her.

He sat down on the edge of the cushion, too much nervous energy to sit back and relax. He needed to be on his toes, had to be ready, in case Fred ever showed up. What was taking him so long? And where was Edward?

She pulled on his arm. "Snuggle with me. Doesn't the fire make you want to take a nap?"

"I've been sitting most of the day," he said, explaining his reluctance to sit back and relax with her. He stood and moved over to the mantle.

"It's been a long day, hasn't it?" she asked. "Emotionally and mentally exhausting."

"Yeah," he replied. "And it's not over yet," he muttered into his glass as he took another sip.

He watched her lean her head back against the cushion, her eyes fluttering shut. He stood rooted to his spot, holding his breath, hoping against hope that she really was falling asleep. When her drink tilted and spilled all over the carpet, he took his chance.

He ran out of the room and back down the hall toward the kitchen. Just before he got there, he turned right and headed to the back of the house. First up was the bathroom. He flipped the light on, looked behind the shower curtain, but found nothing. Turning the light off, he went to the next room. One of two guest rooms, she used this one mostly for crafting and as her office. He checked the closet and under the bed. Nada.

Next up was the second guest room. He tried to push open the door, but it only opened a small bit. Something on the floor was blocking the way, but he couldn't figure out what. He reached in and flipped on the light switch. He poked his head in and looked down, briefly closing his eyes at the horrific sight in front of him. He squeezed through the opening and stepped over the body. He didn't bother to check for a pulse, the whole right side of his face was destroyed. He now understood what Lila had meant about the trash and he figured he'd found Edward.

He glanced up and his eyes were immediately drawn to the bed. Emily lay there, still as death, blood covering her chest and beginning to drip down the side of the bed. He took a tentative step toward the bed, afraid of what he'd find.

He prayed. He begged. He bartered. Anything and everything, so long as the love of his life was still alive.

He reached out a shaking hand and touched his fingers to the side of her neck. Relief flooded through him when he found it. A pulse. Weak, but it was there. He hauled out his phone and dialed 911.

After giving the particulars, he hung up and quickly untied Em's wrists. Afraid to hurt her more than she already was, he sat down next to her and picked up her hand. It was freezing. He tore off his shirt and pressed it to the wound in her shoulder. He had no idea how much blood she'd lost, but it looked like a lot. A whole lot.

"I told you to stay away from this end of the house!" Lila screeched from the door.

Jason started and jumped from the bed. He turned to face her and found a gun pointed at him.

He held up his hands. "Lila, baby. Put down the gun."

"Why do you love her? Why?" she screamed. "I've wanted you from day one. I've loved you every day since I met you. I'm available. I want you. I love you. Why isn't that enough? Why has it never been enough?"

She was waving the gun around and Jason was afraid it was going to go off any minute. She wasn't paying attention to it, and based on what he'd seen of Emily's chest, not to mention Edward's fate, Lila had no qualms about using it.

"Lila, please," he begged. "Please, put the gun down."

"NO! No, I am so tired of being ignored. Of not being good enough. Of never being yours."

"Honey, please. Put the gun down and we'll talk. We'll be together, I promise. Let me just get some medical attention for Emily. And then you and me, we'll pack some bags and take a nice trip away. We can go to Paris or Hawaii or Italy. Somewhere, just the two of us. How does that sound?" He held his hands out, taking a couple steps toward her.

She lowered the gun. "That sounds lovely, Jason. Do you really mean it? Really?"

"I do, baby. I do. Just you and me." He got within a half step of her. He reached out. "Let me have the gun, honey."

A loud crash sounded from the front of the house, and it seemed to bring Lila out of the crazy trance Jason had just put her in. She raised the gun and pointed it straight at his head.

"Who is that? Who did you call?"

"Just the paramedics, Lila. For Emily. Don't panic, we'll still go away, together."

"No! I remember another time you were all sweet to me. Took me to lunch, my favorite restaurant, and then tricked me into going to the doctor and dropped me like a hot potato when we learned I'd miscarried our baby."

"I was a different person back then, Lila. Emily had just left and I was beside myself. But you're right. You've always been right. Why should I be with someone who doesn't want me? Especially when I have a wonderful woman, like you, waiting patiently for me?"

She shook her head. "No, I don't believe you. I don't. You don't love me. You never have. Never!"

With a shaking hand, she raised the gun again and pointed it straight at him. "I thought that the best revenge would be to kill Emily. But now I know that's not the case. The best revenge is killing you. And letting her live with that for the rest of her life."

"Lila, NO!"

He heard a shot.

He saw Lila crumple at his feet.

He saw Fred poke his head inside the door.

And then he turned back to Emily. He only had eyes for her.

Chapter Thirty-Two

Emily woke slowly. She could hear beeps and a humming noise. Even behind her closed lids, she could tell the lights were bright. Her throat was dry and she wanted to cough, but as she tensed to do so, a sharp pain shot out from her shoulder. She moaned, trying to figure out why her shoulder hurt so much.

"Emily?"

She cracked an eye open. "Where am I?"

"The hospital. Can I get you anything?"

"Water," she croaked.

Jason stood and brought the straw to her lips. She drank thirstily. "Whoa, just small sips. Doctor's orders," he said with a small smile.

"Sadie?"

"With your Dad. She's safe."

"Thank God." The short conversation had exhausted her, so she fell back to sleep, her mind at ease over Sadie. When she woke a little while later, some of the events came back to her. Grace, the funeral, Lila going crazy. The lights were dimmer in the room now, so she chanced opening both eyes this time.

"Is Sadie safe?"

"Yes, she's with your Dad."

"And Lila?"

"Dead. Fred shot her."

"Does Sadie know where I am?"

"Yes. She knows you got hurt and are spending some time in here. When you feel up to it, she wants to see you."

"How long have I been here?"

"Three days."

"What?" she asked in a panic, trying to sit up. The pain in her shoulder made tears spring to her eyes.

Jason gently pushed her back against the bed. "Lie down, Em. You need to rest. You lost a crapload of blood and your shoulder required surgery."

"But three days?"

"You obviously needed the rest. You've been through a lot, and did I mention you lost a lot of blood? You weren't conscious when I found you."

"My baby. She's never been away from me this long."

"She's doing fine, I promise. To her, it's all a big adventure. Plus, she has Hope."

Emily sighed. "Right. Okay." She took a deep breath. "How long do I have to stay in here?" she asked, yawning.

"I don't know. The doctor will be around first thing in the morning."

"Why am I so thirsty?" she asked, eyeing the pitcher of water again.

"Don't know? Blood loss? The fact you've been asleep for three days? Who knows. Another question for the doctor in the morning."

"And I'm so tired," she complained, fighting her eyes to stay open. "I have more questions."

"Sleep, Em, we can talk later."

She nodded and promptly fell back to sleep.

When she woke the third time, it was with a squeal of pain as she tried to roll over on her injured shoulder.

"Em?"

He was still here, oh God. What was she going to do? How could she face him? What could she say to him to make up for the horrible things she'd said and done?

She kept her eyes closed, praying he'd leave if he thought she was asleep.

"Emily? Are you in pain?" He took her hand in his and caressed the back of her hand.

"Why are you still here? What have I done to deserve it?" she whispered, keeping her eyes tightly closed. Afraid of what she'd see if she looked at him.

"Because I love you, Emily. Because when I found you, in that room, blood everywhere and you unconscious, I thought you were dead. My heart shattered. I prayed. I begged. I bartered my life for yours. You are and have always been my true love. You will always be my entire life."

She cracked an eye open, peering up into his eyes filled with love and concern.

Hers filled with tears. "I'm so sorry. Can you ever forgive me?"

He leaned closer, his fingers tightening on her hand. "What do you have to be sorry about?"

"So much, but mostly for running away without giving you a chance to explain. And for keeping Sadie away, you missed all her firsts."

"Well, yeah, I guess there's that," he said, smiling.

"With everything that's happened, I feel like an utter fool for letting it go on so long. All I can say was that I was hormonal, excited, nervous, scared, and I couldn't see past what was right in front of me."

"I didn't remember a thing. The only way I know nothing happened was because I woke that morning fully clothed."

Emily giggled. "Well, we know that's not normal behavior for you."

"See, and that's what I tried to tell you all along. I don't remember her being in my room. I don't remember kissing her. I can't imagine we got far. I woke up with a hangover you wouldn't believe. And my first thought was that you were gonna kill me for being late to pick up the cake and man flowers. Then I heard your dad downstairs putting up a ruckus. I raced downstairs and he clocked me," Jason said, rubbing his jaw like it had happened that morning.

"He didn't," she gasped.

"He did. Knocked me back against the railing. Would have done more, too, if Dad hadn't pulled him off me!"

She ran her hand down his face. "I'm sorry."

"It might have been worth it," he grinned, raising his eyebrows. "If this conversation is going in the direction I hope it is."

"And what direction is that?"

"In the direction of you plus me equals happily ever after." He lifted her hand to his lips and placed a delicate kiss on her palm.

"I have a life in Boston. It's going to take me some time to extricate myself from that."

"Understood. We can make it work, we can make everything work—so long as we believe and trust in each other," he said earnestly.

"You're right," she said, taking a long, deep breath. "We can and we will."

"When they let you out of here, I have something special to show you."

"Are you really going to do that to me?"

"What? Leave you in suspense?"

"Yeah." She nodded.

"Sure am. I figure I have a few freebies to use and this is one I can't pass up. It'll be totally worth it."

Emily grinned, inclining her head. "You do. And I guess I'll try to be patient."

"How long do you think it'll take for you to pack up your life in Boston?"

"I don't know. I have some projects to finish up. I won't leave Kendra in the lurch. Ideally I'll wait until she hires my replacement, but I can work from here. Well, once my shoulder is healed." Her eyes widened and she gasped. "Oh no." Her eyes darted around the room. "Where's my phone? Oh crap!"

"What?"

"The proposal and Maryanne," she groaned.

"Calm down. I spoke to some guy named Phil. He called your cell phone the other day, and I answered it after the fifth time he called."

"You did?"

He nodded and smile reassuringly. "I did. I told him what happened and he said to tell you to take your time, take it easy. He has the proposal well in hand. And he presented everything to Maryanne. She loved your design with the new window and wants to go with it. And she's willing to wait until you're all better to get started."

"Are you serious?"

"About what?"

"Maryanne."

"Yeah, that's what Phil told me. He also said to tell you: 'You're the Man.' Whatever that means."

Emily barked with laughter, which quickly turned to a moan when her shoulder resisted the sudden movement.

"Please be careful," Jason pleaded.

"We bet on Maryanne's designs," she explained. "I won. That's what he meant." She giggled, trying hard not to move her shoulder. "Anyway, as I was saying. Ideally, it would take about a month to get situated, but here's the thing." She paused to catch her breath and gather her thoughts and courage. She took a sip of water and looked him straight in the eye. "I love you, Jason. In fact, I never stopped. I dreamed of you almost every night. I wished for our life, the one we planned in our apartment in Santa Fe after we found out I was pregnant with Sadie. I longed for your arms around me, your strength, your sense of humor. I longed for a partner, someone to snuggle with in front of the TV, someone to cozy up to in bed. Every breath I took was yours. Every beat of my heart sang your name. I am *so* sorry for running away. I promise never to do that again." She finished strong. No tears and she was proud of that. She wanted him to know she meant what she said. No questions, no qualms, no worries.

"Ah, Em." He rested his forehead on the hand he was clutching in his. "Do you know how long I've waited to hear you say that?"

"Like two years?" she laughed.

"Yeah, like that." He bent over and placed a tentative kiss against her lips.

She wasn't having that. She reached up with her good hand and pulled him closer. She parted her lips, letting him know she was all in.

God, how she'd missed this. Missed him. She wanted more. So much more. She slanted her head, trying to get more. And he gave her more.

It didn't last nearly long enough. He pulled away.

"Em, we need to slow down. You are in *no* shape for this."

"But it's been so long," she cried in frustration.

"It has," he agreed. "But you still need to rest. And besides," he said, sitting back down in his chair. He reached into his shirt pocket. "I can't give this back to you if your lips are busy with mine." He held up her engagement ring. It sparkled in the fluorescent lights, and she gasped in delight.

"How did you?"

"Grace found it one day while she was cleaning. Gave it to me, just in case."

Emily reached for it.

"Uh-uh." He raised it just out of her reach.

"Hey!"

"Nope, you can't just have it back. It comes with conditions."

"Oh, really?" She raised a brow. "Like what?"

"Like, you have to promise to love me forever."

"Done. Promise."

"You have to promise to move back here and live happily ever after."

"Done. Promise."

He dropped to one knee. "You have to promise to marry me."

"Oh," her voice cracked, tears gathering in her eyes. "I promise."

A smile, bright as the summer sun, bloomed across his face. "All right then. I guess you can have this back."

She held out her hand and he slid the ring back on her proper finger. It still fit perfectly, and it felt so right to be wearing it again.

"I love you, babe," he said as he placed a gentle kiss on her forehead.

"I love you." She sighed, leaning her head back against the bed. "Will you be here when I wake up?"

"Wild horses couldn't drag me away. I'll have your Dad bring Sadie in the morning."

"Perfect. I miss her." Her eyes drifted closed. Just as she drifted off to sleep, she remembered the canceled hotel. "There's just one thing I can't figure out," she said sleepily.

"What's that?" he asked, stroking her hair.

"Who canceled our hotel room? Lila never mentioned it, and I would assume after everything she confessed, she wouldn't have forgotten that."

"Oh," Jason said, smiling brightly. "That was me."

"What?" Emily gasped.

"Yep. They were booked solid, so I canceled your rooms, knowing you'd have to get some elsewhere. It was my sneaky trick to spend more time with you while you were here."

Smiling to herself, Emily laid her head back against the pillows and closed her eyes. "Sneaky, indeed. But it worked. You started worming your way back into my heart."

Jason leaned forward and placed a kiss on her lips.

"Thank you Jason," she mumbled, quickly losing her battle with consciousness. "Thank you for not giving up on me."

"Anytime, babe," he whispered, brushing a lock of hair away from her eyes as she drifted into sleep. "You don't give up on the one you love. Ever."

Epilogue

Six weeks later

"Where are we going?" Emily asked, looking out the window of Jason's truck.

"It's a surprise," he replied, grinning.

"Are you finally going to show me what you promised me in the hospital?"

"I am."

"We have enough time?" she asked, glancing at the clock on the dash.

He nodded. "It's on the way, and it shouldn't take too long."

Emily smiled and reached for his hand. She tilted her face to catch the warm breeze blowing through the truck's window. In a few hours she'd be on a plane back to Boston to start packing up the apartment. Jason would be following next week with Sadie and they were going to drive the moving truck back to Mosquero.

Emily smiled to herself, thinking back on the couple of weeks after she'd gotten out of the hospital and was recuperating at home. She'd been half-afraid to call Kendra and offer her resignation, but she knew it was the right decision. She wanted to move back to New Mexico, to be with Jason and close to her family. If Grace's death and her own near-death experience had taught her anything, it was that family was important and you never knew when your time was up.

So, when she'd called to offer her resignation, Kendra refused to accept it. Instead, she'd given Emily her dream come true. She offered Emily a partnership in the company, an equal partnership, and suggested Emily open an office in New Mexico.

She was still pinching herself. She'd been calling around Mosquero, Logan, and Roy looking for office space, but so far she hadn't found anything she liked or that worked for her purposes. She didn't really want to go to Santa Fe, the commute and time away from her family wasn't something Emily was excited about.

Phil was planning to take over all of Emily's Boston projects, starting with Maryanne's remodel. When Emily got back to town, she and Phil were going to go over all the plans and Emily was going to help him start the remodel later in the week.

She lifted her arm to put her hand out the window, wincing a bit at the pain in her shoulder. The doctors told her she'd feel it for at least a few more weeks and encouraged her to continue with the physical therapy. She just wanted to be better, and the drive into Santa Fe twice a week was starting to wear on her.

Jason had been her constant companion. He'd surprised her several times with romantic dinners, picnic lunches, and hours of togetherness. She was enjoying getting to know him again and loved watching him with Sadie. He was a terrific father, and Sadie was blossoming under his love and attention.

The aftermath of Mama G's death was still hard to come to terms with. There was a huge empty hole in the family and Emily could feel it even in the house. Clint was throwing himself into work on the ranch and spending time with all his grandchildren. There wasn't a quiet moment in the house when Clint was away from the ranch work. Emily would catch glimpses of his grief deep in his eyes when he didn't think anyone was looking.

Hope was grieving in her own way. She'd flown Lila's body to Boston and attended the funeral. Lila's parents had kept her crimes a secret and no one could blame them. There was nothing to be done anyway; Lila had paid the ultimate price for her crimes. Death.

Hope was contemplating a move to New Mexico as well. Derek had kept himself close, working from the kitchen and being available for Hope. They'd chosen a date for the wedding, Grace's birthday, and were busy planning the big day.

Emily felt Mama G's presence often in the past weeks. A smile on Sadie's face for no reason, the scent of her perfume on the breeze, a bit of peace in the midst of grief. Yes, moving back was the right choice, and if she had but one regret, it was that she'd ever left in the first place.

"Here we are," Jason said quietly, pulling her from her thoughts.

Emily looked up and then turned to Jason.

"What is this?" she asked, confusion marring her face.

"Our home," he said simply. "At least, I hope it'll be our home."

"Our home?" Emily asked, pulling the handle on the door and jumping out.

Jason grinned and joined her in front of the truck. He took hold of her hand and started leading her to the front door. "Our home. This was supposed to be your wedding present. Of course, it wasn't finished then, basically just an idea on paper. But I'd gotten Dad to give me some land and started gathering bids for the job."

"Oh, Jason," she croaked, tears gathering in her eyes. She turned stricken eyes on him and leaned her forehead against his chest.

"I had hope that I'd win you back eventually, so I chose a company to build the house. And after you said you'd marry me, I called them and had them build an addition."

They'd reached the front door and Jason opened it. He bent down and scooped Emily into his arms, walking her across the threshold. "Welcome home, babe." He leaned down and brushed a gentle kiss across her lips.

"This is the sweetest, most amazing gift," she whispered.

"I hope you like it," he said, setting her on her feet.

They spent the next twenty minutes exploring the house. The huge kitchen with bay windows overlooking the backyard. The four bedrooms upstairs, one already decorated for Sadie. The master bedroom and bathroom adjacent to the kitchen. The great family room, complete with fireplace and large windows. Emily oohed and aahed over it all, finding no fault with anything she saw. Excitement bubbled up inside her when she thought of all the ways she could decorate.

"One last thing before we head to the airport," he said, taking her hand and leading her outside. They rounded the side of the house and Jason led her into what Emily assumed was the garage. But once she crossed the threshold, she realized what she was actually looking at.

The perfect office space.

"It's not attached to the house; you have to go outside to get to it. I can have them change that, but I thought it would be a better idea to have it separate. That way it really feels like an office and you don't have clients going through our house."

"It's wonderful," she said, eyes bright with more tears. "It's perfect."

"You like it?"

"I do, I really do." She turned and wrapped her arms around his waist. "Thank you."

He kissed the top of her head, wrapping his own arms around her. "I love you, Emily."

"My heart is overflowing, Jason," she said, squeezing him tightly. "I love you."

"Good surprise, then?"

Emily nodded and grinned up at him. "I notice there's four bedrooms upstairs. Is that a hint?"

His eyes crinkled with mirth. "Maybe."

"We'd better get started," she said, raising up on tiptoes and fixing her lips on his.

"You'll miss your plane," he warned, fisting his hands in her hair.

She pulled his shirt from his jeans. "I'll get the next one."

"I love you, Em. God, I love you." He scooped her up and took the stairs two at a time.

"I love you, too."

The End

Thank You!

Dear Reader,

Thank you for reading *Emily's Choice*! I sincerely hope you enjoyed it. As I mentioned above, this book has been in the works for over 20 years. You have no idea how thrilled I am that it is *finally* in your hands and that Emily and Jason's story has found a special place in your heart.

If you would take a moment to leave a review on retailer or review site, I would appreciate it greatly.

Are you interested in reading my other books? Find them on your favorite retailer: *To Love Twice* and *Back to December*.

For more information about me, my novels and what I'm working on next, please visit my website:

http://www.heathermccoubrey.com

You can find me on Facebook at:
Facebook.com/AuthorHeatherMcCoubrey

On Twitter & Instagram at:
@runmookiewrites

On Goodreads at:
Heather McCoubrey on Goodreads

On Pinterest at:
Heather McCoubrey on Pinterest